A Land Too Far

by

Kayla Danoli

COPYRIGHT

Cataloguing-in-publication data
Creator: Danoli, Kayla, author

Cataloguing-in-Publication details are available from the National Library of Australia www.trove.nla.gov.au

ISBN: 978-0-9953533-9-8 (paperback)
ISBN: 978-0-6483950-0-3 (eBook)

Contents

Chapter 1 The Storm

"Come quick, Mr Ballard. There be a body on the beach."

"Calm down, calm down; you'll be doing yourself no good running about like that. See here, Boy, one dead animal be no reason for getting all excited. If we've lost only one animal after last night's storm, it be a miracle."

"No, Mr Ballard, it's not one of our stock. It be a *real* body, Sir. … Like as not, a man's body."

"Good God, not one of ours I hope."

"I don't know. I didn't go so close as to see who it was, but it was a man, right enough, of that I'm sure."

Anxious to lead his boss back to the body, the boy took off at a trot. "No need to rush, Lad. If he's as dead as you reckon, he'll still be dead when we arrive." Mindful of the need to maintain a composure befitting his position of foreman, Syd Ballard, in measured steps, strode over the dunes and onto the beach following the lad. After pointing out the body between rocks, the boy opted to remain atop the headland rather than venture onto the beach again.

"Where have you gone…? Get down here you daft thing. Like you said, he's dead, so he won't be jumping up to grab you or nothing. Come down here and give me a hand to turn him over to see who he is."

"I don't like touching dead bodies."

"How would you know? Done a bit of it before have you? No… well, there's a first time for everything. Get down here and give me a hand."

With no other option other than defying his boss, young Toby took his time clambering down onto the beach.

1

"Right now, grab his legs and let's roll him over. Come on, look lively… grab his legs and let's get it over and be done with it."

Toby gingerly took hold of the legs. One leg wasn't so bad. Its stocking remained half on. Having lost its stocking completely, the other leg was naked. There was nothing for it but to grab the man's bare flesh. Cold and clammy, it felt 'pudgy'. Out of the corner of his eye, Syd Ballard noticed the young lad shudder at his first tentative touch of the legs. He offered encouragement.

"That's it; grab a firm hold. Now then, one mighty heave-ho and it will be all over."

That's more or less how it happened. The body, bloated from being in the water for some time, flopped about a bit alarming Toby. "Aargh, that's revolting. I think I'm going to be sick."

"Pull yourself together, Lad," Ballard managed to snarl after swallowing hard to control the bile rising in his own throat. "Not one of ours, I think. Do you recognise him?"

"Nay, ne'er seen 'im before… funny clothes for these parts though."

"Aye, not what we would wear for work."

Ballard went down onto his haunches for a closer look at the body. The face and hands were deeply tanned and leather-like, while other parts of the body showed no tan at all. One of the man's hands lay palm up on the sand beside him. It sported heavy callouses. "…Not a stranger to hard work by the look of that hand," Ballard observed.

There followed a brief silence as Syd Ballard visually assessed the body … and Toby inched himself away from it. Yelling coming from further along the beach interrupted the moment. With wildly waving arms and yelling at the top of his lungs, a tall lanky figure raced towards them.

"It's Lofty…! What's up wi' 'im?" Toby exclaimed.

"Lord protect us from anything else today. We have enough to deal with."

"Mr Ballard, Mr Ballard; Come quick. We've found…" At that point Lofty stumbled over something on the beach, his pending revelation left hanging until he regained his feet. As he picked his way around the rocks to where Syd Ballard and Toby waited, Lofty began his message again. "We found a … Oh, Lord! We found one of those."

"One of those what, Lofty…? Come on, Boy, what have you found?" Ballard demanded.

Lofty leant up against a rock and, pointing a shaky finger, stammered, "…Another one of those, Sir, another body on the beach down there by the point."

With Lofty leading and Toby bringing up the rear, the trio set off for the point. As they neared the spot where a 'lump' became visible on the beach up ahead, Lofty dropped back to join Toby a short distance behind Ballard. "That's 'im up there, Mr Ballard. That's 'im; that lump on the beach along there."

Now closer to the body, Syd Ballard noticed a short stocky man with bowed legs standing atop a prominent rock amid the tumble of rocks stretching down to the water at the point. "That will do, Syd. No need to come any further," John Oakes called from his vantage point before scrambling down and coming towards the trio. "…Nothing for the boys to see along here."

"They have to grow up some time, John. They have seen two bodies already," Syd said. A bit apprehensive about what might lie ahead, the two lads slowed their pace and dropped further back behind Syd.

When John Oakes caught up with Syd, he leant in close and dropped his voice to a murmur. "Two more bodies, Syd, an older woman and a young girl, by my guess. I don't think the young lads should see them."

"A body is a body, John. They have to learn to cope with such things."

"These women have lost some of their clothes... if you know what I mean. I don't think it good for young lads to see such things."

"Ah, right; I see what you're getting at." Syd strode back to where the boys waited. "Toby, go on back to the homestead and find Mr Grant. Tell him what's happened on the beach and that we need him to take charge of things here. Lofty, you go back along there and watch the body you found."

"Eh... what for? He's dead. He aint going nowhere. Can't I go back with Toby? I could help him find Mr Grant."

"No you can't go with Toby. Do as you're told, Boy. Stay with the body."

"If Toby goes to fetch Mr Grant, who's gonna be watching that the body Toby found doesn't run away?" The rebuke that earned Lofty sent him scurrying back to the 'lump' on the beach he'd found earlier.

With the two lads sorted out, Ballard nodded to John Oakes and they went to inspect the latest finds. "I hate to say this, John, but I can't help wondering how many more we might find washed up."

"Aye, all from another shipwreck, I reckon. Those waters through the Strait be treacherous enough in fine weather. A boat caught in there during last night's storm had not a chance."

"I agree, and that's why I think there could be more bodies yet to come ashore somewhere on the island."

*****

Although the threat of rain continued after the fierce tropical storm that persisted for most of the night, morning arrived grey but cool and dry. Ned Rixon and his manager, Alf Grant, ventured out to survey the storm damage.

"Looks like we've lost quite a few trees," Alf observed. From the front yard of the homestead, the men had a clear view of much of Ned's property. "I sent the foreman and most of the boys to check the fences. I'm sure there will be a few down. Stock will be all over the island by now. It will take them some time to round up the animals and sort ours out from everyone else's."

"It's unseasonal to get such a storm at this time of the year. Pity about the wind, but the rain was most welcome. No good standing here wondering about how much damage we received. Come on; let's ride out to see for ourselves."

"Right Boss, I'll fetch the horses. I imagine you'll want to go and check on the store sometime today as well."

"Yeah, the store… There's a strong chance that's going to present a bigger problem than the fences and the stock here. The store is running low on just about everything thanks to the next supply ship's late arrival. That includes the fencing material which property owners are going to need after last night."

Ned had a soft spot for his large general store, his first commercial venture established in the town almost at the start of settlement on the island. It helped finance the subsequent landholdings he acquired, and continued to line his pocket well. A good manager running the store allowed Ned to relocate from his cottage on his town block to the new homestead he built on his grazing property. Managing the two properties gave him a few headaches in recent times, not the least of which was the erratic arrival of supply ships out of Port Beauchamp.

"Damn and blast…!" Ned exclaimed as he slapped his battered hat against his thigh.

"What's up, Boss? What did you see…? What's happened?" Alf Grant stopped suddenly, alarmed by his boss' action. The horses he was leading barrelled into his back almost knocking him off his feet.

"Sorry, Alf… Nothing for you to worry about… Talking about the store and supply ships made me think about the store at Port Beauchamp. I guess the day is coming when I am going to have to think about what I'm to do to make it all work."

"I thought everything was going well for you. It seems to me you're doing all right up here on the island, and your store at Port Beauchamp always has been a good little earner – or so you've said in the past. From where I stand, it seems you've done well for yourself since you moved to the Albert River, and even better since you moved on to Sweers Island. I don't know what's bothering you but, if there's anything I can help you with…"

"Thanks, Alf. There's nothing you can do, but I'm going to have to work something out soon. My brother, Thomas, is supposed to be running the business at Port Beauchamp, but I'm getting some alarming comments about how that's working out."

"Hmm…," was Alf's noncommittal response. A few months ago, when in Port Beauchamp to oversee the loading onto a supply ship of a few new head of cattle for the island, he found Thomas Rixon passed out from drink in the back office of Ned's store, which he was supposed to be managing. From a chat with the ship's captain on the way back to Sweers Island, Alf discovered Thomas Rixon spent much of his time in an alcoholic daze. Not wanting to cause his friend concern, Alf didn't mention it to Ned.

Now the subject of the Port Beauchamp store had come up, should he tell his boss about what he learned at the Port? Caution won out again. Alf decided this might not be the best time to share his knowledge. They had been best friends since boyhood, but now Ned also was his boss. If blood is thicker than water, as the saying goes, making disparaging comment about Ned's brother was unlikely to go down well.

"Mr Grant, Sir! Mr Grant, wait up!" A breathless Toby managed to croak out as the two men were about to swing into the saddle. "Please, Sir, I have a message from Mr Ballard."

"Settle down, Lad. Get your breath back," Ned said. "There… that's better. Now what is so important to have you run all the way from Mr Ballard?"

"Mr Grant, Mr Ballard said for you to come quick. There are bodies on the beach along by the Point. Mr Ballard wants for you to take charge please, Mr Grant."

"Thank you, Toby. Mr Grant and I were about to ride out to inspect the place, but we will go directly to Mr Ballard. Drink some water and rest for a few minutes before you head back. Walk this time, don't run."

They rode to the Point in silence, each man lost in his own thoughts and his own personal dread of what awaited them. As they reined in their horses to allow them to pick their way safely down onto the beach, Ned looked across at Alf Grant and noted the firm set of the man's square jaw. "Someone will need to go for the Police. They'll need to go across to the mainland to report it. The local bloke is laid up with 'the fever'. Might as well send Mr Ballard I suppose. You're going to have to handle things here anyway, so he'll be free to go."

Ballard strode along the beach to meet them. "...Morning Sirs; nothing pretty to see here today. We've five so far. God knows how many more might turn up."

"Five...?"

"Yeah, five... Lofty, come and take the horses please, Lad."

"Okay, Mr Ballard, lead on," Ned said. "We better find out the worst. Come on, Alf, we'll look at what's here, before we ride further around the island to see if any others have washed up." By the time Ned finished speaking, the three men were off towards the first body.

A cursory look at each of the bodies as they walked past was all the men required to realise the situation confronting them had the potential to become much worse. "Alf, you will need to send a couple of men along the coast past the Point. The hope is there aren't any more, but instinct tells me there are more bodies washed up somewhere. I'll leave you to organise Mr Ballard before coming back to the Homestead to collect one of the wagons. The bodies need collecting. Put them in one of the unused buildings until the authorities collect them. Bring back some blankets to cover them after you load them into the wagon. The least we can do is provide them with some degree of dignity. Oh, and before you come back to collect the bodies, perhaps you should round up our carpenter. Get him up off his arse and tell him he is going to be busy making pine boxes for a while."

"Stir the carpenter into action…?" Alf replied in mock horror. "I get all the hard jobs, but I will try. He keeps a couple of coffins propped up in the corner of his workshop. As he likes to tell everyone, they are there 'just in case'…" Alf chuckled at the thought of his conversation with the carpenter.

"He be needing a few more than the two he has now by the time we finish rounding up what last night's storm delivered," Ballard commented dryly.

After giving Ballard instructions, Alf and Ned abandoned their intention to ride further around the island and returned to the homestead together. A thought occurred to Ned as they rode. "We should send the other wagon into town for fencing material. Do we know what fencing material we have here?"

After a moment's thought, Alf replied. "We've a bit of most things in stock I think. John Oakes is the man to ask. He keeps an eye on that and will be able to tell you off the top of his head what we've got and what we need. In spite of the likely amount of damage we received last night, I think we should have enough materials on hand."

"I still want to send a wagon into town to 'top up' what we have. A run on fencing material in the next few days is probable and I know there isn't much of anything in the town store until the next supply ship arrives. As they say, 'first in…', might apply to this situation."

"I take your point. I'll organise Toby to take a wagon into town today, after I talk to John Oakes about what we might need. I'll head off now, Boss. I have people and wagons to organise and a rather gruesome 'treasure hunt' to undertake." Alf dropped Ned a mock salute, turned his horse and rode off.

"I'll be riding into town myself this evening, Alf. It depends on what I find there how long I'll be away. With everything that's happened, you're going to have your hands full while I'm not here."

The sun was sliding towards the horizon as Ned rode into town. He went straight to the horse yard behind the store and turned his horse out as Toby loaded the last of the fencing supplies onto the wagon drawn up to the loading platform at the rear of the store. "Ah, Boss, I'm about to head back. Everything Mr Oakes told me to fetch is loaded, and a few other bits and pieces that might be handy as well."

"You can't be heading back now. The sun will be down in about half an hour. Better you spend the night in town and go back in the morning, rather than go tearing across the island in the dark. Leave the wagon and the horses in the yard here and hop across to the pub. See if you can organise yourself a cot for the night. Put it on my account. I've got things to do now, but I'll see you in the morning before you head back. Don't leave before I talk to you."

Inside, the store looked bare. The good townsfolk came shopping today. Goodness knows there was precious little on the shelves before; now many of the shelves were bare. Although the store lacked supplies, the premises sustained no damage from the storm. In fact, tucked away in the sheltered cove as it was, the town seemed to escaped unscathed. After a brief check on the situation at the store, Ned wandered onto the street with the intention of walking the short distance to his cottage to spend the night. At the corner of the street, he encountered Syd Ballard on his way to the horse yard behind the store. "Good evening, Mr Ballard. I thought you might be over on the mainland."

"No Sir, no need to go… The local copper is out of his sick-bed and up and about again. He sent one of his boys across to the mainland to fetch the coroner. I was on my way to get my horse to head home."

"Not such a good idea I think, Mr Ballard. See if you can organise a cot at the pub for the night. Keeping young Toby company there is much safer than riding back in the dark. Tie your horse on behind and ride back on the wagon with Toby in the morning."

*****

First thing, after seeing the two workers off on their way back to the property in the morning, Ned spent the rest of the day attending to business in town. His suburban allotments, on the outskirts of the township were a forlorn sight. They too escaped much of the storm's fury, but the heavy rain flattened most of the vegetable crop. Ned's head gardener assured him most of the plants would recover after some sunshine, but the lettuces looked battered. Still, if the locals wanted fresh vegetables, they would buy the stuff even if it looked the worse for it all.

At the close of his second day in town, Ned intended riding back to the homestead after another quick check on the store. The store manager rushed after Ned as he made to leave. "Mr Rixon, Sir, we've received word of a supply ship coming through the Strait. It is reported sailing towards the quarantine depot on the north-eastern side of the island."

"Is it too much to hope it is our much overdue supply ship finally arriving?" Ned asked his store manager.

"I doubt it's our ship, Sir. Ours is only coming from Port Beauchamp and would have no need to call at the quarantine depot. More likely it's a vessel that ran into trouble coming through the Strait and is calling in for repairs or the likes. The best we can hope for is that it has some news of our supply ship. Perhaps it's a godsend that our ship, and the one that is coming in now, weren't sailing through the Strait the other night when the storm struck."

He is right, Ned thought. If that be the case, we have a lot to be grateful for. With the prospect of a ship's arrival and the possibility of receiving news of their supply ship, Ned opted to spend another night in town.

Word that the ship in question had tied up at the quarantine depot reached town the next day. As it came through the Strait on its way to London, The *Cathay* picked up a few shipwreck survivors. Those survivors, with nothing more than the clothes they stood up in, were taken into quarantine. After only a brief interruption to deal with the survivors, the *Cathay* resumed its course for London – but it delivered good news. It reported observing the ship *Clara*, under Captain Till, making its way under full sail through Torres Strait and likely to make Sweers Island within the next couple of days.

With the supply ship *Clara* likely to tie up so soon, it seemed pointless to rush back to the homestead only to return days later to supervise the unloading of supplies. Ned convinced himself he could find something to do in town until the boat arrived.

Chapter 2 The Eriksens

Towards the end of the second day after word of her impending arrival was received, the *Clara* tied up. Amongst the first of the cargo unloaded were the shipwreck survivors previously deposited at the Quarantine Depot by the *Cathay*. The supply ship collected them on its way around Sweers Island to Carnarvon township.

"What a sad motley lot they are," a bystander commented to the local copper as they watched the survivors come down the gangplank.

"They don't be looking too bad," the cop replied. "Thanks to the townsfolks' donations, they be decently attired now. Poor wretches had only the clothes they stood up in, and scant enough left of some of the clothing at that."

"What's to become of them now?" Ned enquired.

"W-e-l-l, now there's the problem, you see. They can't be put up at the Quarantine Depot. Long term accommodation is not allowed there. Nor would it be safe to have people there if something unpleasant requiring quarantining had to be taken in." Constable Patrick Laverty stroked his chin as he pondered the question. "The local hotel said they were not a charitable organisation. They could take maybe three or four of the survivors but someone would have to pay for their lodgings and food. Now, it's a certain thing the survivors can nae be paying for anything themselves. They lost everything when their ship went down; lucky to be alive I'd say. And then there is the language problem. They don't speak English. One or two might have some English, but the others can't understand or speak it at all."

"Perhaps those who can speak a little might be utilised as interpreters or translators for the rest of the group."

At first, Laverty's reaction indicated he thought Ned's suggestion a radical idea, but he soon realised the value of such an approach. "Perhaps you might come with me, Mr Rixon, to see what we can find out on the matter." The two men strode towards the survivors standing close together in a nervous group.

The captain of the *Clara* stepped from the gangplank. Ned and Constable Laverty stopped abruptly to avoid colliding with him. "Thank you, and good day to you gentlemen. You look as though you are on a mission of some importance. I wouldn't want to get in your way," the captain assured them.

"On the contrary, Captain; perhaps you may be able to assist. We were on our way to determine whom, if any of the survivors, can speak English," Ned replied.

"Ah well, in that matter I can help you. See the man on the far side of the group...? The one with the lad and the young girl standing close by him..." Ned nodded. "That trio speak good English and proved useful in dealing with the rest of them while they were on board."

"What can you tell us about the group, Captain?" Laverty asked.

"Not much; every one of them lost one or more family members in the shipwreck. The man I pointed out lost his wife and three of his children."

"Where were they headed before their ship went down?" Ned asked.

"From what I could make out, they are Scandinavian and were on their way to Port Beauchamp to start new lives in the colony."

"Not what I'd call an auspicious beginning," Laverty murmured.

"Right," said Ned. "Let's have a word with that chap. Are you coming, Laverty?"

Laverty set off in double-time to follow Ned. "I believe he's a carpenter, " the captain called after them. That halted Ned.

"I could do with a decent carpenter right now," Ned murmured to no one in particular. "Constable, how soon could you find out what is to become of the survivors?"

"That's an easy one to answer, Mr Rixon. They are to remain on Sweers Island until a suitable vessel is available to take them on."

"Do we know how long it may take to arrange for such a vessel?"

"No, Mr Rixon, that's the part we don't know… and I think nobody knows. It's up to the government bureaucrats or the immigration agents – someone like that anyway – to organise for it to happen as soon as possible. That's all I know, Sir. That and the fact that nobody has made any arrangements to house the poor blighters until such time as a ship comes to take them away from here."

"I think I might be able to solve the matter for that trio we are going to speak to," Ned said and gave Laverty a smug look.

As Ned and the Constable approached, the man spread his arms and drew the two youngsters close to him. "Excuse us, Sir. We mean you no harm, but we ask a few moments of your time if we may." Ned spoke in a quiet measured way so the man he addressed might understand.

"It appears we are not going anywhere for the moment. These are my two children. The only two I have left now. How may we help you?" the man said as he cast a wary eye over Laverty's police uniform. "We have done nothing wrong; broken no law."

"Sir, I am Edward Rixon. I own several properties here in Carnarvon Township and a large pastoral property in the centre of this island. I believe you are a carpenter. It so happens I have need of a carpenter on my pastoral holding. I wonder whether you might be interested in some work until other arrangements are in place for you to continue your journey around the east coast."

"Thank you, Mr Rixon. That is most kind of you." The man exchanged a look with his daughter before continuing. "It would be necessary for my children to accompany me. After everything we have been through, I am not prepared for us to be separated."

"Of course they should accompany you. If your daughter is interested, she might help my aged housekeeper with the domestic chores."

Constable Laverty cleared his throat. "Ahem, I'm not sure anyone should be leaving town until things are sorted out, and that could take a few days."

"That's not good enough, Constable," Ned retorted. "These people are here through no fault of their own. I will leave for my property in the morning and this family will go with me if they so choose. They can spend the night in my cottage. I will find a bed at the hotel or somewhere in town. You have until morning to sort out whatever there is that needs sorting out, but we will be leaving for my homestead in the morning."

Laverty wanted to object but struggled to find his voice in his shock at being spoken to so authoritatively. By the time he had his vocals working again, Ned once more had the floor. "Now, Sir, if you will come with me. I'll take you to my cottage where you and your family may spend the night in relative comfort, regardless of whether you choose to come with me to my homestead tomorrow. By the way, I didn't catch your names."

"My name is Mads Eriksen, and this is my daughter Mathilde. Please call me Mads. The boy is my brother's son, Emil Eriksen. His father asked us to bring him to Australia with us so he might have a better life. He almost lost his life coming here. We all did."

*****

Ned eased himself off the hotel's hard, lumpy bed. After a few moments spent stretching to ease his back, he headed for the wharf. Unloading the *Clara* started early. The area was bustling with activity when Ned arrived. About half an hour later, his store manager arrived to take over supervising the unloading of the store's supplies. After a quick breakfast at the pub, Ned returned to his cottage.

All three guests met him at the door. With his wide smile matching the excitement evident on the youngsters' faces, Mads greeted him. "We are ready to go. Do you want us to leave with you now?"

"Er, no; not right now. It might be lunchtime before we head out. Please feel free to make use of the cottage until then. I'll be back for you as soon as my supplies are unloaded."

That wasn't quite the truth. On his way to the cottage earlier, it occurred to Ned that he had only his horse in town. How was he to transport the other three to the homestead without a wagon? He pondered the dilemma as he strode back to the wharf. So engrossed in his thoughts, Ned didn't see a man before he barrelled into him.

"Ouch, watch where you're going. You nearly knocked... Mr Rixon! Sorry, Sir. I didn't realise it was you who bumped into me." Syd Ballard spun around to face his assailant after almost being knocked off his feet by being ploughed into from behind, and was surprised to see it was his boss. "That's a bit of luck actually. I came down to the wharf looking for you."

"It's me who should be apologising. I wasn't paying attention. What brings you to town again today?"

"Ah well, that's why I was looking for you. Mr Grant sent me in with the wagon. I had to bring the carpenter and his wife to town ... with their belongings."

"With their belongings...? What happened?"

"It seems Mr Grant told the carpenter he had quite a few extra coffins to make, and sent him to the shed to measure up the various bodies. He took one look in the shed where the bodies were stored and told Mr Grant he would have to get someone else to deal with that lot. There was an exchange of ideas about that, if you get what I mean. It ended when the carpenter again refused to do the job and Mr Grant sacked him. So, now you don't have a housekeeper or a carpenter, because the carpenter's wife left with him. Well, I suppose she would wouldn't she? They took the cutter across to the mainland soon after we arrived in town. Some family member has a business over there on the Albert River and that's where they were headed."

"Well, I don't think either of them is much loss. Neither was too fond of work... And the situation might not be as dire as it seems. How soon before you leave for the homestead?"

"About an hour I think. I have to load some supplies. Now that I've told you what happened, I'll do that."

"Good; there will be three passengers for the wagon and I will ride back with you. You know where my cottage is?"

Ballard nodded. "When you're finished loading up, meet me there."

With unloading of the store's supplies almost completed, after a quick word to his store manager, Ned collected his horse from the yard behind the store and rode to his cottage to await Syd Ballard's arrival.

They set off for the homestead with Mads Eriksen sitting up beside Syd Ballard and the youngsters perched atop various boxes and bags in the back of the wagon. Ned rode along beside. As it was after one o'clock when they reached the property, the first task to deal with was lunch. Once Mathilde was introduced to the kitchen, she organised a meal for everyone, including Alf Grant who joined them.

By the end of the day, Mads had taken over the carpenter's workshop, Mathilde had dinner on the fire and Emil, having completed his duties as potato-peeler, was exploring the homestead's immediate surrounds with Alf Grant. Ned felt pleased with himself as he came back to the homestead after receiving reports on the storm damage. He was confident the Eriksens would settle in well. That thought brought to mind the fact that he and his new employees left town without first establishing what arrangements were being put in place for the shipwreck survivors. "Who cares?" he said aloud as he leaned on the top rail of the house horse yard. "The Eriksens are here. They seem happy enough, and I intend keeping them for as long as I can."

*****

Once the last of the storm's aftermath was cleared, Mads Eriksen embarked on a program of maintenance in and around the homestead. Mathilde kept the house spotless and proved to be an accomplished cook. Young Emil loved the outdoors and took to accompanying the men on musters and other jobs around the property. Time slipped by almost unnoticed. Everything seemed well with Ned Rixon's world… everything except for his store at Port Beauchamp.

Over the past few months, disturbing rumours regarding the Port Beauchamp store came to his attention. Although often second or third hand by the time he heard them, Ned knew their origin was the ships' captains who frequented the pub when docked at Sweers Island. "Idle gossip, I'm sure," he told Alf Grant over their evening rum toddy. "At least, that's what I've been telling myself. Now it's reached a point where I can no longer ignore the comments or dismiss them as embellished fabrications."

"I've heard some disturbing reports too. Like you, I dismissed them as rubbish; nothing more than the grog talking."

"The supply ship *Windsong* is due here tomorrow. I've a mind to return to Port Beauchamp on her when she sails again. Things are running well at the moment. The place won't be much of a challenge while I'm away. I might be gone for a while though. It depends on what I find at Beauchamp and how long it takes to sort out any mess there."

"A wise move on your part, I think. Don't worry about this place. I've managed it for you before and I can do it again. Better you sort out what's happening at Beauchamp than sitting here worrying about it."

Five days later, Ned was listening to the captain's none too encouraging comments regarding the management of the store's operations there as they sailed through the Torres Strait on their way to Port Beauchamp. Although he believed he was braced for whatever he might find, nothing prepared him for the situation he discovered.

It required only a cursory glance at the cattle awaiting shipment in the yards at the wharf to send Ned scurrying to his store. A chorus of 'good afternoon, Mr Rixon' greeted him as he strode through the store and into the small office in a rear corner of the building. The office appeared empty, but the paperwork haphazardly piled up and almost covering the desktop caught his attention. This was not paperwork stacked in neat piles. This was invoices, bank statements, bills of lading, letters; all manner of documents relating to the business flung onto the desk and abandoned where they fell.

Ned continued to the desk and stood hands on hips studying the mess. A fine coating of dust covering much of it indicating it hadn't been disturbed for some time. The sight shocked him. He stood, frozen for a few moments, before extending his hand to stir through what lay in front of him. As he bent to give the piles of paper a peremptory stir, he noticed a leg protruding from under the desk. It was the only bit of its owner visible. Another shock awaited Ned on the other side of the desk. His brother, Thomas, lying on the floor under the desk, appeared unconscious.

In the belief Thomas had been assaulted, Ned's first thought was to send for the police. When he dragged Thomas out from under the desk, no injuries were obvious. It was while Ned was hunched on his haunches next to Thomas that the store's senior clerk came into the office. The sight of Thomas sprawled on the floor didn't cause the clerk any alarm. "Out to it again, is he, Sir?" the clerk asked, and reached in for the empty rum bottle lying in the shadows towards the back of the space under the desk.

"What do you mean by 'again'?" Ned demanded. "Is this not the first time this has happened?" The clerk threw back his head and roared laughing for a moment before realising the inappropriateness of his action.

"Not exactly, Sir, but it is the first time I've seen him like this today."

"Please fetch a couple of the backroom workers to help take him back to his lodgings. I assume he still has a room at the hotel."

With Thomas safely back in his hotel room, Ned returned to the store and settled into the office. After about an hour spent sorting the paperwork into neat piles, he called the senior clerk. "Mr Kincaid, you have served in this store for some time and know the running of the place better than anyone. Would you have any objection to being appointed the new acting manager?"

"Acting manager...? No, Sir, I wouldn't object, but Mr Thomas Rixon might."

"Mr Thomas Rixon will no longer have any involvement with the operations of this establishment... as he will discover as soon as he is coherent enough to understand."

"Thank you, Mr Rixon, but may I be apprised of what my new position might entail and for how long the appointment might last?"

"You will take over all those duties formerly associated with the manager's role. I will become manager but might not be here every day. Therefore, you will have full responsibility for the continued running of this store and its associated operations. You report to me directly but, in running the business, you have responsibility and autonomy of a manager. I propose an annual salary increase of twenty-five percent to reflect your increased responsibility. In making this appointment, I see it continuing for some time into the future. I appreciate you may wish time to think on this matter, but I require your response by close of business tomorrow. Is that acceptable?"

"More than acceptable, but I need no time to consider the offer. I give you my answer now. Thank you, Sir. I accept the position on the terms you stipulated. Might I speak openly…?" Ned nodded and Kincaid continued. "Good; what you propose as the responsibilities attaching to the position of acting manager are no more than what I have been doing for some time now. If anything, it will be easier to carry out those duties under this arrangement."

The rest of the day Ned spent tackling the mountain of paperwork on the desk. With a stack of orders in one hand and a bundle of bills in the other, he went in search of Mr Kincaid. "I can find nothing to indicate whether any of these have been dealt with. Please have your clerks apply utmost urgency in dealing with them."

As he made his way back to the office, it occurred to Ned that the capacity of the clerks' ranks might be stretched by the elevation of the senior clerk to acting manager. "No need to rush on that," Ned murmured aloud as he pulled his chair up to the desk. "Let's see how they manage with one less before we give it more thought." Nevertheless, he made a note to ask Kincaid whether there was need to promote one of the clerks to the now vacant senior clerk's position.

After a late dinner in the hotel's dining room, Ned welcomed the solitude of his cottage. Alone with his pipe and a rum, he tried prioritising what he must do in the immediate future. He checked on his brother before leaving the hotel. Thomas remained on his bed where they left him earlier that day. The hotelier told him it usually took a couple of days for Thomas to venture out again after one of his heavier drinking bouts.

Ned started on his list of things to do. His first job was to advise his staff of the new management arrangement. He hoped Thomas would join the real world again sometime the next day so he too could be told. The list of urgent tasks grew longer over the next half hour before Ned drew a line under it. He puffed up his cheeks and let out a low whistle. "I don't know how long all this is going to take, but I am going to be bloody busy getting it done in a hurry," he told the empty cottage.

With the dank stillness of the humid night delaying the onset of sleep, Ned remembered something else to add to his list: relocate from Sweers Island to Port Beauchamp. That required considerable thought. Alf Grant could continue to manage everything on the island, but he wanted Mathilde at Port Beauchamp to keep house for him. To have Mathilde here means relocating all three Eriksens, he reminded himself. After what they experienced, they will refuse to be separated. And relocating the Eriksens would leave Alf without a carpenter/handyman on the property. There are worse things that could happen, Ned consoled himself.

As his eyelids drooped, Ned's last thoughts for the day were on how soon he could return to Sweers Island to put in place everything to ensure the swift and smooth relocation of him and the Eriksens. And none of that could happen until everything at Port Beauchamp returned to satisfactory operation.

Chapter 3 Sweers Island

Sorting things out at Port Beauchamp took longer than anticipated. It was a few days after Christmas 1868 when Ned departed for Sweers Island on the supply ship *Lilly*. Filthy weather caused delays. After spending several periods hove-to in sheltered reaches along the coast, it was ten days later before Sweers Island appeared on the horizon.

A quick check on his interests at Carnarvon township raised no concerns. Anxious to be on his way to the homestead, Ned rushed to the rear of the store, arriving at the loading platform as Syd Ballard tied up. "I couldn't believe my luck when I saw you bring the wagon into town. If you're returning to the property today, I'll ride along with you."

"Mr Rixon, Sir, we weren't expecting you. Yes, I'll be going back as soon as I load up. This was just a quick trip for extra fencing wire. Something spooked the cattle roaming wild around the island since that big storm. They damaged our fences. Nothing serious mind, but it involved a length of fence we weren't counting on having to repair again so soon. If you want to hang around, it won't take me more than a few minutes before we're on our way."

They rode in silence for a while after leaving the township. Ned constantly scanned the countryside. "It looks like you had decent rains. Everything is green and lush."

"Aye, there have been plenty of regular good showers. The property looks good. That's more than you can say about anything else on the island."

"It sounds like there's a story I need to know about behind that comment."

"...Been a few deaths lately."

"You better elaborate, Syd. 'A few deaths' doesn't tell me much, but it does suggest something abnormal happening."

"Sweers Island be not a good place to live at the moment, Sir. So far, about ten people have died of a terrible fever. People think it came in about two weeks ago on the ship *Margaret and Mary*. The captain's wife died of it before the ship made Sweers. By the end of that first week, all the crew were dead from it. Then the townsfolk started dying too. We've lost three of our boys to it so far. There will be more. It spreads everywhere, this Gulf Fever, and there is nothing anyone can do to stop it. Some settlers already left the island. Others say they will follow. Like as not, the island will be deserted – abandoned – before long."

"This is worrying news, Mr Ballard. Do you hold concerns for your own wellbeing?"

"Me...? Nah... well, mebbe. This Gulf Fever isn't selective. It takes all before it. No one is safe. So, yeah, if I allow myself to think on it, I do worry about surviving it."

"...And no doubt others on the property do too. Thank you for bringing it to my attention. I must discuss it with Mr Grant as soon as I arrive."

Mathilde met Ned at the homestead and rushed to put the kettle on. Ned followed her into the kitchen. "Mathilde, you look terrible. I don't mean to be rude, but what has happened to wear you out like this?"

"I am fine; just a bit tired."

"From what...? Is looking after the house and Mr Grant becoming too much for you?"

"No, no. That is fine. It is from looking after the men who have become sick. Sometimes I must sit up with them all night, sponging them down to try to break their fever."

"Are you well? No sign of coming down with the fever yourself?" Mathilde shook her head. "What about your father and Emil, are they okay?"

"Yes, all the Eriksens are well so far, but I do worry about Emil. He spent so much time with the men, I worried he would catch this fever. I do not let him go with the men anymore. Papa is well. He made a few more coffins last week. They were for our workers this time, not shipwrecked sailors."

Ned sat at the kitchen table drinking his tea. Mathilde was uncomfortable. It was not normal for the boss – Ned or Mr Grant – to even enter the kitchen let alone sit at the table there. Silence reigned for a few minutes before Mathilde spoke again in the hope of encouraging Ned to leave the kitchen. "Your room remains made-up and ready for you, Mr Rixon. If I knew you were coming, I would have opened the window to air the room. I'll do it now."

"Thank you Mathilde; I will open it. Do you know where I might find Mr Grant?"

"No, I don't know where they went today. He works all day with the men now that we have lost some of the workers. He doesn't come back to the homestead until the men come in from the paddocks at dusk."

So far, there was no good news from anyone. Mathilde's comments worried Ned. The last thing he wanted was for the Eriksens or Alf Grant to die while looking after his interests. He didn't want that for any of his men. Common sense told him that, as it had already happened to some, more of his workers were likely to fall victim to this deadly fever. In the first instance, everyone should be given the freedom to leave the island as soon as possible, and that included the Eriksens and Alf Grant.

By the time Alf came in that evening, Ned had drawn up a rough plan. Dinner provided an opportunity to discuss it with Alf. "So, I would rather abandon everything on Sweers than lose you, the Eriksens or any of the men – any more of the men – to this damned fever. I have in mind to take the Eriksens to Port Beauchamp with me when I return. I realise that will leave you without a housekeeper and a bloody good handyman. Do you think you might manage without them for a short while? My mind is made up. I am shutting down everything I own on Sweers."

"I agree the Eriksens should leave with you – and I hope that is soon. I am concerned for Mathilde. She insists on nursing the men when they become ill, and she could go the same way. If you close down this place, what will you do about all the stock? We have only a handful of sheep left, but our cattle numbers are strong."

"As soon as I return to Port Beauchamp, I shall try to arrange a ship to collect what stock we have and bring them to Beauchamp. You should travel with the animals."

Alf nodded and took another suck on his rum swizzle. "I ran into our neighbour, Jim Greenhill, while I was riding the boundary fence between our properties today. He tells me quite a number of residents are booked to depart on the ship *Margaret and Jane*, when she arrives in the next couple of days. Captain Till agreed to take them on board and deliver them to the Albert River settlement on the mainland. Old Jim tried to have him and his wife included in the contingent, but Till already filled his set quota of passengers. There are so few ships calling at Sweers since the outbreak of this fever epidemic, it is difficult to leave the Island, and almost impossible to secure a passage to any of the southern ports."

"I am having trouble understanding the magnitude of this fever that's wreaking havoc on the population. Syd Ballard said ten townsfolk had died."

"Jim said the latest count is fifteen, with another five not expected to last beyond a day or so. We have lost four workers, and Syd Ballard took another three into town in the wagon today. I doubt the medical care available there will make much difference, but we have to try. It is better to remove the sick ones from the other workers."

Before turning in that night, the two men agreed Ned would talk to Mads Eriksen in the morning, and that he and the Eriksens would leave for town that day to join the *Lilly* when she set sail for Port Beauchamp the following day. The workers would be told they could leave whenever they felt inclined. Alf Grant and any others who chose to stay would manage the stock until whatever ship Ned managed to arrange arrived to load the animals for shipment to Port Beauchamp. Alf, Syd Ballard and any others who remained at the property would travel with the stock to attend to its needs on the voyage.

*****

Although Ned watched the Eriksens constantly while on board the *Lilly,* he detected no sign of illness in any of them. In fact, the sea air appeared to return the bloom to Mathilde's complexion. The *Lilly* left Sweers with only two other passengers. After dropping them off at the Albert River settlement and taking on board a load of hides and tallow, the ship headed out of the Gulf and down the East Coast of Queensland to Townsville. Much of the cargo on board the Lilly was consigned by Robert Towns' Albert River operation to his main distribution warehouse at Townsville.

The ship overnighted there before pushing further south to Port Beauchamp. That night, in the dining room of one of the town's hotels, Ned heard further horrendous stories of the devastation caused by the Gulf Fever ravaging Sweers Island. It seems a large group from Sweers who managed to secure passage on a passing vessel opted to disembark at Townsville. In the days subsequent to their arrival, many died and most of the remainder were critically ill.

Preoccupied with keeping the Eriksens quarantined as much as possible, Ned insisted they eat on board that night and that they not venture into the town. The stories he heard in the dining room made him wonder whether those escaping the fever on Sweers brought the dreaded disease with them, thereby allowing it to become established in this place too. He applauded his foresight in confining his charges to the ship. "I will not rest easy until all of us are safe and settled at Port Beauchamp," Ned told the star-studded black sky as he made his way through town to Ross Creek where the *Lilly* lay at anchor.

A band of squalls swept along the coast forcing the *Lilly* to lose another night sheltering tucked in behind Cape Upstart. Still no sign of illness appeared in anyone on board. Ned heaved a sigh of relief as he followed the Eriksens down the gangplank after the *Lilly* tied up at his wharf complex at Port Beauchamp. Although all appeared in good health, it would be a few weeks before Ned relaxed and accepted everyone had escaped the Sweers Island fever.

While he worried about the Eriksens, chartering a ship was crucial to removing the rest of his people and the remaining stock from Sweers. It took some negotiating but, a couple of weeks later Ned met with success when Captain Till agreed to return to Sweers with the *Clara* to undertake the evacuation. Three days later, Ned was on his way once more to Sweers Island to take charge of the operation.

On their arrival, they found the township of Carnarvon a virtual ghost town. His store manager kept the store open, but only the occasional pastoralist ventured into town now. After borrowing a horse, Ned rode to the homestead. What he found there came as an even greater shock. Only Alf Grant, Syd Ballard, John Oakes and young Toby remained on the property. A few workers left of their own accord, while others, too ill to do so, died. The one uplifting thing Ned found was all those who remained appeared healthy and claimed to have no symptoms of the illness.

Over a salt beef and damper dinner washed down with sweet tea followed by several rums, Alf gave Ned a status report. "There were few sheep left. They escaped when one of the fences came down and we had no one checking fences. They now are wild in the bush or on Jim Greenhill's abandoned property and not worth worrying about. We mustered the remaining cattle and keep them in the home paddock so they will be easy to herd down to the port when required."

"I have charted the *Clara.* She brought up supplies for the Albert River settlement and has gone across to the mainland to deliver them. She returns to Sweers the day after tomorrow. We need to be in town and ready to load the moment she arrives." A cheer went up from his audience. This was the best news in months.

No problems occurred with moving the cattle from the property to yards in town ready for loading the next day. Ned noticed a degree of uncertainty about the men. "What's the problem? Something seems to be bothering you."

"Uhmm, we were debating whether to try breaking into the hotel to camp there for the night."

"Good Lord, no. The Alhambra Hotel is locked up tight. Even 'mine host' has abandoned the place in favour of the mainland. I wouldn't allow you to sleep there anyway, not after it served as a makeshift hospital for many of those with the fever. I doubt it's a healthy place after that. You will stay at my cottage with me."

Although not a large house, they spent a comfortable night together, and were up early the next morning to meet the *Clara* when she returned to load the cattle. As the crew made fast the lines, Captain Till called Ned on board.

"I have a message from the Towns Company store on the Albert River. The Manager there says he is prepared to take all existing stock in your store here on Sweers if you are closing it. He would like an answer soon please, Mr Rixon."

"Well now, I hadn't thought about that but, now the offer is made, I see some advantage in closing the store and accepting his offer." As Ned went to walk away, he noticed Captain Till shuffling from foot to foot. "You appear anxious, Captain. Is there something else you need to discuss with me?"

"Aye, there is something else. You see, the warehouse over on the Albert River is crammed with hides, wool and tallow awaiting shipment to east coast ports. There be good money involved were I to take the load with me on my return journey."

"There are five of us – maybe six – and the cattle and horses. Will there be room on board for much else?"

"Ah well, you see, that's the problem. I might not be able to take the cattle this trip. The Albert River cargo needs to be brought to market with some expediency. So, I need to give that priority. After all, you and your operation here on Sweers, along with just about everything else on Sweers, is finished. I will get no future work from here, but there will continue to be plenty of business from the Albert River settlement."

Ned was not impressed with Till's breach of contract. Although heated words were exchanged, Ned understood the Captain's situation. "Am I to assume then that you intend to return to the Albert River forthwith?"

"Aye, Mr Rixon. That is my intention. I will sail there on tomorrow evening's tide … with or without the stock from your store for the Town's Company store over there."

"Very well, I will sell our stocks to Towns' store. We will spend the day packing the stock for shipment ready for loading tomorrow. I will consider the rest of what you have told me and will speak to you again later today." With that, Ned turned on his heel and strode off the ship.

Before doing anything else, he needed to tell his store manager, Tom Croxley, the store was closing, and he should prepare all remaining stock for shipment to Albert River. Alf and the others were feeding and watering the cattle in the yards by the dock when Ned left the ship. One look at Ned and it was clear to Alf something was amiss. He raced after Ned and caught him by the arm.

"What went down between you and the Captain up there on the deck? By the look of your face, it was all bad news."

Although impatient to go to the store, Ned realised the men needed to know their situation had changed. He explained to Alf. Alf took a moment to consider Ned's information.. "That might not be so bad. As I see it, it's only a short sail across to the Albert River settlement. We could stand being jammed up tight on board for that short trip. Then, instead of the cattle being shipped to the east coast, we could do a cattle drive from the Albert River across to Townsville. It might take a while if we do it in easy stages, but the cattle won't be knocked about or lose condition that way."

"You're right. Thanks, Alf. I was so angry with Till, I couldn't see any way around it. Right, take Syd Ballard and John Oakes with you. Ride back to the homestead and load one of the wagons with all the camp gear. Be back here by tomorrow morning at the latest, or tonight if possible. Toby can help Tom

Croxley clear out the store. When I talk to Croxley, I'll tell him he can travel across to the east coast with you and the cattle. He can drive the wagon, set up camp each night, cook, and take care of those odd jobs associated with a long cattle drive. Okay, round up Syd and John and be on your way"

News of the store's closure didn't cause Tom Croxley any heartache. He had wondered how he could extricate himself from the store and be off Sweers without upsetting his boss, Ned Rixon. Today's news was more than he dared hope for. Of course, he would be happy to accompany the cattle drive. Anything was better than being marooned on Sweers Island, and he had done similar work on cattle drives in the past. Yes thanks, he would be delighted to leave the store and drive the wagon.

Tom got to work as soon as Ned left the store to go in search of Toby. About ten minutes later, Ned and Toby returned. "The first thing for you to do, Toby, is to bring the store's wagon around to the loading area out back. As we pack things we'll load them into the wagon ready to take to the wharf in the morning. Once the wagon is full, we will stack everything else on the loading platform ready for the next load," Tom instructed Toby.

Ned hung around until he was no longer required. He was on his way out of the store when he heard Tom shout. "No, don't touch that lot. Don't touch anything in that corner over there." Thinking his departure premature, Ned hurried back. Toby looked terrified. He wasn't used to being yelled at. Well, not when he was working as fast as he could... and he hadn't been given any instructions regarding the stuff starting to accumulate in said corner of the store.

"What seems to be the problem here?" Ned demanded.

"No problem, Mr Rixon." Tom looked sheepish. "Sorry Lad; I shouldn't have yelled like that. Don't take any of the stuff I put over there. It will be our supplies for when we are on the cattle drive. We'll load it onto Alf's wagon when it gets here." With peace re-established, Ned again felt it safe to leave the store. He did want to return to the wharf. There was a delicate, and no doubt complicated, conversation to have with Captain Till.

As expected, negotiating the new arrangement with Till was testing. By lunchtime, Ned breathed a sigh of relief. Alf's alternate plan was in place. Then it was time to pack the few things he would take with him on the *Clara*. He doubted there was any likelihood of his returning to Sweers Island ever again.

At dusk, the men returned from the property with one of the wagons. "We chose the largest German wagon to be sure there was enough room for everything, and its high sides allow canvas to be tied over the top in the event of rain," Alf said.

"Good thinking. Take it over to the loading dock at the store. See if you can make enough room to fit in whatever supplies Tom Croxley is putting aside for you."

Ned's cottage housed a melancholy group that night. While every one of them wished to be gone from Sweers and the threat of the fatal fever, leaving brought an end to an otherwise happy era in their lives. None, with the exception of Ned perhaps, knew what the future held for them, but they knew leaving Sweers while still healthy offered a reasonable life expectancy. After an evening of mixed feelings, plenty of reminiscing and too much rum, they all were late to bed and not particularly bright next morning.

Chapter 4 Port Beauchamp

Somehow, everything managed to fit on board the *Clara,* although the passengers were forced to find whatever space they could. Sleep was not an option on the trip to the mainland, not unless you could sleep standing up or while perched on a crate. A cool night with a light steady breeze made for a smooth, fast crossing.

The cattle were unloaded immediately the ship tied up at the Albert River wharf, and the men returned to spend the remaining few hours of the night stretched out on the ship's deck. At first light the next morning, the Robert Towns Company's wagon arrived to collect the stock from the Sweers Island store. Croxley accompanied the wagon to Towns' warehouse to oversee checking the inventory. By that afternoon, the stock ex-Sweers Island was paid for and everything was in place for the cattle drive to get underway next morning.

With a view to having an early night, over a rum or two after a quick evening meal, the men reviewed their plans with Ned. "When we leave here, we'll head south to the western end of that new Cobb & Co coach route and follow that towards the coast. Then we'll pick up the route heading south before cutting across to the coast at Port Beauchamp," Alf explained. "It won't be a quick trip. What do you reckon, six weeks or more?" The others were nodding when John Oakes spoke.

"Might take a bit more than six weeks by my calculations; could be more like eight weeks."

"How long it takes isn't an issue. I have Letters of Authority for you, Alf. If you need anything along the way, use one of them to secure credit against me. After assuring the men their safety was more important to him than the cattle, Ned bade them goodnight and all five turned in.

*****

Once the men left on their long cattle drive, Ned went in search of Captain Till who was overseeing the loading of cargo from Towns' warehouse. "Just about all loaded," Till said as Ned came on board. One last lot of hides and we're done. We'll set sail on the late-morning tide. I take it you still intend to join us for the voyage to Port Beauchamp."

Surprised they would be sailing a day earlier than anticipated, Ned took care of a few matters before settling on board the *Clara*. On the half tide soon after eleven o'clock, they set sail. They experienced pleasant sailing conditions as they rounded Sweers Island and headed out of the Gulf and into Torres Strait.

Conditions through the Strait were the worst Ned had encountered. The crew spent much time aloft reefing sails as the ship pounded through waves that crashed over the bow and washed across the deck. In spite of telling himself Captain and crew seemed unperturbed by the conditions, Ned couldn't persuade himself to relax. After spending much of the time through the Strait huddled below decks to keep dry, it was a relief when they rounded Cape York and entered the calm water behind the Great Barrier Reef along the east coast.

They spent the better part of two days moored in Townsville's Ross Creek while the hides, wool and tallow from Albert River were unloaded. The pleasant conditions when they departed Townsville for Port Beauchamp soon changed. He again found himself huddled below decks as the *Clara* sailed headlong into a tropical storm. Once again, their arrival at Beauchamp was delayed by time spent hove-to in the lee of Cape Upstart.

Apart from the strong south-easterlies swirling in gusts across the top of the hill to pound the ship, conditions were pleasant in the bay compared to those around the front of the Cape in the open sea. Still, Ned struggled to cope with the frustration of being delayed when so close to his destination. After two days, the south-easterly bullets ceased. Two of the crew took a row

33

boat around the tip of Cape Upstart to gauge the conditions out to sea. Their report was favourable. The decks became a flurry of activity as sails were hoisted and the *Clara* headed for open water.

With the short remaining leg of the voyage incident free, the *Clara* docked at Port Beauchamp under a searing sun and with little breeze to cool its decks. As the crew made fast the lines and attended to the myriad of things that seem necessary for the ship to remain fast to the wharf, Ned, leaning on the upper deck railing, surveyed the township stretched out before him. Port Beauchamp, now much larger than when he first arrived a decade ago, had slowed its growth to almost nothing discernible over the last year.

Had Port Beauchamp run its race, he asked himself. Was this a lull before the death knell sounded and it began to plunge to its death? He grimaced at the thought. Maybe not 'death', but 'stagnation' might be a more accurate prediction for the town's future. Any further dark thoughts were interrupted by his name being called by someone on the dock. He peeled his eyes from the townscape to search the dock area.

Mathilde ran towards where the ship was tying up. She seemed frantic and kept calling his name. Ned waved and descended to the lower deck where the gang plank would be extended. Realisation that Mathilde was frantic about something finally registered with him. "Captain Till, I need to go ashore immediately. Something is amiss there. Please have the gangplank lowered," Ned commanded.

Ned stepped onto the dock at the same moment as Mathilde reached the ship. Out of breath and with her face flushed from running in the heat, Mathilde gasped out her message.

"Come quick please, Mr Rixon. Mr Thomas Rixon is seriously ill in hospital. The doctor fears he will not last much longer. You should go to the hospital at once to be with him at his end."

It took a moment for Mathilde's message to register with Ned. When it did, he found himself torn. Did he want to be with his brother? His disgust at his brother's drunkenness and mismanagement of the store was such that he cut Thomas out of his life. Despite that, the pull of family was strong. "Thank you, Mathilde. I will go to the hospital to be with my brother. Please ask Captain Till to unload my belongings onto the dock. I will collect them later."

What passed for a hospital was a roughly constructed timber building with, for the most part, a dirt floor. Inside, the heat was oppressive. Nothing moved the heavy humid air around. Ned was taken to a cot in a far corner of what served as a ward. A doctor in a once white coat fussed about the patient.

"Excuse me, Doctor. Mr Rixon's brother, Mr Ned Rixon, is here." The nurse's announcement of Ned's arrival interrupted the doctor's ministering to his patient.

After being bent over the bed for so long, the doctor eased himself upright and stretched his back before speaking. "He is very near the end," he said and added a jerk of his head towards Thomas ... as if Ned might be confused about whom he was speaking. "I shouldn't think more than an hour or two; surprising he's lasted this long. It might be he tried to hang on until your return. There is nothing more I can do. Sit with him in peace for as long as you like. Call out if you need me for anything."

With the doctor off attending to other patients, Ned was alone with Thomas. Feeling awkward and unsure what to do, Ned slowly reached over to take Thomas' hand. In not much more than a whisper, he poured out his sadness and guilt. "This is a sad thing to come home to. I spent the last weeks amidst death and tragedy. I don't know if you can hear me, but I wish you to know. I blame myself for the situation we are in. I should have spent more time with you; paid more attention to you and your needs. These past few weeks saw connections severed. Connections severed with people I knew and our workers who died... and with Sweers Island. I doubt I shall return there. Now, it appears I am about to sever my connection with you, at least in this mortal life. I will miss you, Little Brother. We are the last of our line. Soon it seems there will be only me. I will mourn your loss and the grief will ease with time, but the guilt I feel about losing you will remain until the next life."

"Doctor, Doctor...!" Ned shouted. A nursed rushed to his side.

"What is it, Mr Rixon?"

"He squeezed my hand. Thomas squeezed my hand, only softly, but he did squeeze my hand. I wasn't sure he could hear me, but he must have."

The nurse checked Thomas' for a pulse. Without returning her eyes to Ned, she asked, "Are you sure, Sir? I think it unlikely he heard you or could respond." She hurried over to the doctor. Ned watched the nurse and doctor turn to face him. In long measured steps, the doctor came to stand beside Thomas' bed. A quick check for vital signs before the doctor cleared his throat.

No words were necessary when the doctor turned to face Ned. His face and voice said it all. "I'm sorry, Mr Rixon. Your brother is gone. If you would leave us now, we will take care of him and arrange for the undertaker to collect his body. Uhmm... a word of advice if I may before you go... The nurse tells me you think your brother squeezed your hand in his last moments. If you dwell on it, that can be an unsettling thought to carry with you. I assure you any such action on your brother's part at that time is highly unlikely, if not impossible. Instead of letting such thoughts torture you, take comfort in the knowledge he suffered no pain or stress as he slipped away."

Blinding sunlight brought him to his senses. Ned had no recollection of anything after the doctor spoke to him until he emerged into the sunlight. After the shady interior of the hospital, this world outside was too bright and too hot for his current mood. Unaware of his surroundings, he strode through town to his cottage. Ned was vaguely aware of his belongings stacked outside the front door as he pushed open the door and went in.

"Here's sweet tea, Mr Rixon. I'm told that is what is needed at such times," Mathilde said as she handed Ned a steaming mug of tea. "I asked Mr Kincaid from the store to send someone to collect your belongings from the ship. They can stay outside until you are inclined to deal with them."

Ned took the tea and a measure of rum through to his room. It was after dark when he emerged looking weary and wrung out. "It's very quiet, Mathilde. Where is everyone? They should not stay away on my account."

"No, Sir. They are unaware of today's tragedy. They are at Mr Fisher's property along the river a way where they have been working for the past three days. Papa expected they would return tomorrow if the work went well."

*****

At the risk of making a nuisance of himself, after Thomas' funeral, Ned threw himself into his work, visiting every section of his operations at Port Beauchamp at least once every day. He would no longer be an absentee boss. It was too late to help Thomas, but he would look after the rest of his staff. Mathilde became concerned at the increasing frenzy of Ned's activities. He was gaunt and looked much older. She felt a ripple of relief surge through her when Ned announced at dinner one night that he would be leaving at first light to spend a few days at Marathon. Whatever he has to do there, she thought, it probably involves less rushing about than he has been doing here.

"Mads, if you have no work here requiring immediate attention, perhaps you would accompany me to Marathon." Mads confirmed he was free to go. "Good, I would welcome your thoughts on some work I propose for my block of land in that township. Emil will not be required on this trip. He should report to Mr Kincaid to work at the store in our absence."

Emil gave a half-hearted nod, but his face said he wasn't happy about being left behind. It was no secret he did not enjoy working at the store. The dining area cleared quickly that night as the men disappeared to their rooms to pack for tomorrow's trip, and Emil retired to his room to sulk. After finishing in the kitchen, Mathilde welcomed the chance of an early night. On her way to her room, she stopped by Emil's room to offer a few words to ease his disappointment. Then a quick goodnight to her father and she was on her way to bed. She was a few paces further along from Ned's door when she stopped, turned and retraced her steps to knock softly on his door.

"Mathilde…? Has something happened?"

"No, Sir. I just wondered whether there was anything you need me to do for your trip. I have put together some rations to take with you, but I wasn't sure whether anything else was required."

"Thank you, Mathilde, but there is nothing else. I hadn't given thought to food for the trip, so you were way ahead of me in your thinking. We will leave early in the morning. It would be appreciated if you could manage breakfast for us before we leave."

"Of course, you shall have breakfast before you leave."

Ned reached down and took her hand. "Thank you, Mathilde. You are indeed a treasure. Although they were tragic circumstances that brought us together, I have benefitted handsomely from them."

She felt the heat rise up into her cheeks. Her face remained bright red when she checked it in her mirror. Ned Rixon isn't the only one to benefit from that shipwreck in Torres Strait, she told her mirror as she undid her hair and let it fall loose over her shoulders. In life, one doesn't often find such kindness and consideration as we – as I – have found here. A strange light-heartedness made falling asleep difficult for Mathilde that night.

The usual flurry of activity associated with a trip dominated the morning as the spring cart was loaded. Breakfast was a hurried affair before the two left in the cart and Emil went to report for duty at the store. After the morning's chaos, the cottage seemed deathly quiet. With her chores out of the way, Mathilde took advantage of the solitude. She took a mug of tea and her needlework into the garden. Seated in the shade of a big old tree, she revelled in the joy of having time to herself.

As she worked her needle to create fine precise stitches, she reflected on how her workload seemed halved now the men were away. While there remained all the cleaning and laundry to do, and she and Emil had to eat, everything seemed to take half the time, leaving some time spare for whatever she chose to do with it. Emil even took to helping her with the garden in the evening after he finished work, not that there was much garden to worry about. In the heat, few vegetables survived and blooms of any sort were restricted to the big old flowering trees dotted around the area.

While she enjoyed her new leisurely lifestyle, she missed having the others around. If I'm honest, she told herself, I miss having Ned Rixon coming home every evening. "My God…! What is this?" she exclaimed, and then looked around to see if anyone was within earshot. What she had admitted to herself shocked her so much, she pricked her finger. A red streak smeared the pristine white petticoat she held. "Damn, now look what I've done. It serves me right for my impure thoughts." After a quick sponge to remove the blood, the half completed petticoat was draped over a chair to dry, and Mathilde was off for a long walk around town to clear her head of any further such nonsense lurking there.

Days flowed into weeks and still nothing was heard from Marathon. Just on dusk one evening, Emil stomped into the kitchen and announced, "It is not worth worrying about the vegetables anymore. Those still alive are either wilted or flowering in readiness to die. It is too hot for vegetables; too hot for everything, including us."

"At least on Sweers Island there always was a breeze. Here, as the humidity increases, the breeze disappears. I saw dark clouds rolling over the hills this morning, but they disappeared again this afternoon. Mrs Porter from along the road said the clouds will come for many days to tease us before delivering their promised rain. If she is right, it will be hot for days yet before the rain comes to cool the place down. It will not be pleasant for the drovers bringing the Sweers Island cattle to Port Beauchamp if the summer storms come while they are on the track. I hope Papa and Mr Rixon return from Marathon soon – and before the rains come."

"What's so important about this Marathon place that they have been away so long? What's that place like anyway?" When Mathilde turned to answer Emil, she noticed the deep frown creasing his forehead and saw concern in his eyes.

"When we left to come to Australia, we planned to make a new life at Marathon. Papa heard stories of vast areas of fertile land available for agricultural or pastoral ventures. Although Papa is a carpenter, and a skilled one, he always wanted to be on the land. However, your father, as the eldest son, went onto the family's land and Papa had to do something else. He became a tradesman. Papa was enticed by the stories of so much land available to buy so cheaply, and of the area's healthy climate that would suit his younger children who had health problems. He told your father of his plans. Uncle Ole, your father, asked Papa to take you with us to give you a chance at making a better life for yourself. The family farm is small and crops have not been good. Many of the farmers in Denmark struggle to survive on their farms."

"O-o-h, I thought …. Never mind what I thought. I'm pleased you told me that. But I still don't know what this Marathon place is like. Would I like living there? Is it just another small settlement the same as Port Beauchamp? Do you know anything about it?"

"I read a bit about it in the brochures Papa collected before we sailed for Australia, and since then I have heard others speak of it. I will tell you all that I know, but it is from memory not from any real knowledge of the place, so don't ask too many questions."

"Anything will be more than I know now. Do you think Uncle Mads still intends to settle in Marathon, or will he stay here in Port Beauchamp with Mr Rixon?"

"That, I cannot answer. Perhaps now that Papa has spent a little time there, he will make a decision about that. Now about Marathon…. It is some distance south of Port Beauchamp. I hear it takes about a month to go by wagon from Port Beauchamp to Marathon. While it is a newer settlement than this one, it is growing faster. Some people say it might become the main port for the region. Townsville and Marathon would become the major ports of entry at the cost of Port Beauchamp."

"That won't be good for Mr Rixon's business, especially since he has closed down his Sweers Island operations."

"I suspect he is looking to the future. The early land sales for Marathon were held here because there was no courthouse or other facilities at the proposed Marathon township. I think Mr Rixon bought land at Marathon at those sales. Perhaps, as part of his plan for the future, he and Papa have gone there now to look at that land and plan what to do with it."

With Emil's questions about Marathon exhausted, he retired to his room. Mathilde was relieved she satisfied his curiosity. She hadn't been sure whether she was dealing with his concerns about the future, or her own, as she tried to provide the information Emil sought.

Around midday on the third day after Emil's questions regarding Marathon, Ned and Mads returned to Port Beauchamp. As soon as they unloaded the wagon, both men disappeared into town to attend to whatever tasks demanded their immediate attention. Her impatience mounted as Mathilde counted down the hours until they would all sit down to dinner together. She knew Emil would share her hope that over dinner the men would share news of their trip to Marathon.

Disappointment visited both Mathilde and Emil that evening. Ned and Mads both claimed they were tired after the trip. After a hastily dispatched dinner, the men retired to their rooms. Their only comments about the trip to Marathon were that it went well, and it achieved their expected outcome. Frustration and disappointment kept Mathilde awake a long time that night.

Chapter 5 New Ventures

Two weeks after the men returned from Marathon, Alf Grant and the others arrived with the cattle from Sweers Island. Ned surveyed his cattle in one of the yards at the port. "They're in such good condition. I expected them to look poor by the time they arrived. Instead, they look better now than when we took them off Sweers," he told Alf. "I made tentative arrangements with James Fisher to keep the herd in one of his paddocks until we sort out something more permanent. They will benefit from staying in the one place for a few days before we move them out to Fisher's property."

"Are there any thoughts on their long-term future? Will they be sold, or are you planning on establishing a herd somewhere?"

"A few weeks ago, I would have admitted to not having any firm plans. Then, while in Marathon recently, an interesting possibility opened up. I expected someone to arrive today or tomorrow to finalise a deal we negotiated."

That visitor arrived at the cottage later that afternoon. Richard Meadows came by boat and expected to depart again within a day or two on the next southbound vessel calling at Marathon. "My time is tight at the moment," Meadows told Ned, "I would appreciate finalising our arrangement as soon as possible." Ned told Mathilde there would be one extra for dinner before ushering Meadows through to the back veranda.

By the time Mathilde called everyone to dinner an hour later, Ned and Richard Meadows had a partnership agreement in place. Once dinner was over, Ned hitched the buggy and drove Meadows to his hotel. Then Ned went to the other hotel where Alf Grant was in the dining room chatting with two other hotel guests. Alf excused himself and joined Ned at a table in a back corner of the room. "Apologies for interrupting your evening, Old Chap," Ned began. I'd like a meeting at ten o'clock tomorrow here at this hotel. There's someone I want you to meet, and by then I should be able to tell you what we are going to do with the Sweers Island cattle."

*****

Ned left the cottage early after telling Mathilde he would not be back for lunch, and asking Mads and Emil to come home a little earlier today if possible as he wanted to discuss something with all of them before dinner that night. When Ned returned that afternoon, Alf Grant accompanied him. A look of disgust crossed Emil's face when Alf walked into the cottage.

"What's the matter with you?" Mathilde hissed at him. "Why did you look at Mr Grant like that?"

"I thought Mr Rixon wanted a meeting with us to tell us something important – important just to us. Now Mr Grant is here too, so it won't be about just us. I thought maybe we were special and Mr Rixon was going to share some big secret with us because we are special to him."

"That's silly. Mr Grant and Mr Rixon have been friends since they were children and Mr Grant is important to Mr Rixon's businesses. Maybe the meeting will be about all our futures."

They sat around the dining table with Ned in his usual position at head of the table. "I know it's unusual for us to have such group meetings, but what I want to discuss today is of interest to all of you. It's easier this way instead of speaking to each individual." Ned had everyone's attention. After a quick glance around the table to confirm that was the case, he continued.

"Two things are about to happen. They are important to all of us. The first involves the recent trip Mads and I made to Marathon. On the land in that town's centre that I purchased at early land sales, a new Rixon and Co. store will be erected. With Sweers Island closed down, I wanted a suitable location for a new store. I believe Marathon will become a major port servicing its vast surrounding area. Development of the settlement has been rapid. Now I have confirmation the necessary lumber has arrived, construction will start soon."

No one cheered or clapped at the news about the new store.

Nothing but silence ensued for a few moments as his listeners considered the information. First to find his voice, Mads cleared his throat before posing his question. "Will I be returning to Marathon soon to oversee construction?"

"That is correct, but I will speak with you separately about the timing."

"Are we all going to live at this Marathon place?" Emil asked, a hint of a challenge in his voice.

"No, Emil. I have no intention of moving my household to Marathon now, but I can't say what the future might bring."

After a few moments of murmured discussion amongst those at the table, Ned moved to the second matter he wished to discuss. "The next news I am to share is of particular importance to you Alf... to you and the men who came with you from Sweers Island, except for Tom Croxley. Be aware I have not spoken to Tom yet. I will do so in the morning. Please don't mention this to him before I do. Tom Croxley will accompany Mads to Marathon and be involved in building the new store. He will manage the store when it opens... assuming he accepts the position, of course."

"I don't think there is any doubt about that," Alf said with a chuckle. "While he is not a bad camp cook, Tom will be more than happy to return to what he does best."

"Right; the other piece of news I have was finalised only today. This morning I entered into a partnership arrangement with Mr Richard Meadows to take over one of the forfeited pastoral runs in the valley behind Marathon. Alf, although Meadows thinks that at some stage he will take up residence on the property, you will manage the place. The cattle and the men you brought from Sweers Island will move to that property. You and I will go in the next few days to look over the set-up there before anything or anyone moves on to it."

Alf did not look up when Ned finished speaking. Instead, he seemed engrossed in his hands steepled on the table in front of him. After waiting a couple of moments for a response, Ned sought an answer. "Alf…? I expected some comment from you. Have you nothing to say? Nothing to ask me about this new venture?"

"Yeah, I do. How confident are you about your partner in this 'venture' as you call it?"

"I think I'm a cautious man, and would not have entered into this partnership if I held any doubts" The mild rebuke was clear.

Alf retaliated. "I am a little surprised by your choice of partners. Mr Meadows has a dubious reputation in some parts as a result of some of his past business dealings. With you as an 'absentee partner' so to speak, I feel some degree of concern for your best interest in this arrangement."

"I have heard nothing against the man. Perhaps we should talk privately later." Ned and Alf exchanged a look and a nod. Peace appeared restored.

Despite the warning looks and the slight shake of her head Mathilde directed at Emil, he blurted out his question. "What about me? Where do all these arrangements and plans leave me? Am I to remain an errand boy at the Beauchamp store forever, or do you have something better planned for me?" The venom in Emil's questions was not lost on those around the table.

"Emil, mind your manners," Mads growled. "Remember your place."

"No, Mads, let the boy be. After all he has been through, I understand his concern about what and where his future might lie. All I will say here, Emil, is that you are a part of those plans. I will discuss your part in all this with you and your Uncle Mads at a separate meeting."

Although not intended to chastise, to Emil, Ned's response felt like a slap in the face. Without lifting his eyes from the tabletop to check how the others responded to the rebuke, Emil felt all eyes boring into him as he whispered, "Thank you, Sir. I would appreciate that."

The atmosphere at dinner that night might best be described as uncertain as everyone tried weighing up Ned's news in terms of his or her own future. Emil was relieved to learn he would go with Alf and once again be working with stock. Mathilde noted Mads seemed subdued. She wondered why when he already knew about the new store at Marathon – and probably of his involvement in building it. However, she knew that, when he is like that, it is as if a volcano is building within him… and then it erupts! If that is what happens this time, Mathilde didn't dare think about the possible consequences for all of them.

Foremost in Mathilde's mind, was how these new ventures might impact on her. Ned indicated he would remain at Port Beauchamp for some time to come, but would she continue as his housekeeper when Mads and Emil went to Marathon. Mathilde felt the heat rise to her cheeks as she found herself silently beseeching the gods to let her stay with Ned.

Straight after the meal, Mads and Emil went to Mads' room. Ned and Alf retired to the back veranda with a cask of rum. Mathilde heard Ned and Alf talking, but couldn't hear what was said. She detected no raised voices, no arguments. Alone in the kitchen, the loudest sound she heard was the banging of pots and pans as she cleaned up after dinner. Nevertheless, her unexplained foreboding persisted. Her stomach remained a tight knot. She tossed and turned for a long while before falling asleep that night.

Emil arrived first for breakfast next morning. His excitement almost palpable; food did little to interrupt his questions about the future. Mads arrived at the table a few moments later, and not in the same frame of mind as his nephew. His face grew darker by the second. "Enough, Emil! Finish your breakfast in silence please. No one here can answer your questions. We do not know anything about the new property or where you will be living."

Mathilde's intended questions about her future evaporated. This was not the right time. She did not want a similar rebuke. Silence blanketed the cottage for some time after Mads and Emil left for work. Ned and Alf appeared late for breakfast. Unaware that Alf spent the night on the day bed on the veranda, his presence surprised Matilde. She rushed to set another place at the table. Neither man had much interest in food. Both looked dreadful… probably due to the rum consumed on the veranda last night.

That evening, the volcano building inside Mads erupted. Raised voices raging through the cottage reached Mathilde in the kitchen. Then they sounded as though they were moving away. She realised Mads and Ned had taken their argument, or whatever it was, out into the yard. Although some distance from the kitchen, the faint sound of the heated discussion drifted through to Mathilde. Instinct told her the discussion was serious. That the men took the confrontation outside indicated they did not want her to hear. Her father's voice predominated. The way he spoke to Ned shocked her. Part of her wanted to know what caused the ruckus, while a part of her feared finding out. Somehow, she knew it involved her and she guessed it might have something to do with her future. "Please God, as much as I love my father, don't let him take me away from here," she whispered as she peeled the potatoes.

*****

Preparations and planning occupied everyone for a couple of weeks. Mads and Emil left first for Marathon. Emil would assist with the building project until Alf and the others moved the cattle to the new property called *Rangelands.*

Before he left, Mads enlightened Mathilde about the words he and Ned had earlier. At first, Ned thought to rent a cottage in Marathon for Mads and Emil to live in while constructing the new store. Ned would stay there as well when he visited Marathon. When nothing suitable was available, the plan changed. Mads and his nephew would stay at one of the hotels. Had Ned rented a cottage, Mathilde would go with her family to Marathon to keep house for them there. Now, she would remain at Port Beauchamp.

Mads' concern was for his family's separation and the prospect of Mathilde spending much time alone at Beauchamp. Ned reassured him she would not be alone. Alf Grant, Syd Ballard, John Oakes and young Toby would stay in the cottage, as would Ned, when they were in town. Alf Grant would be away setting up Rangelands much of the time. The others would take turns staying at Fisher's place to look after the cattle. At all times, it was likely Mathilde would have to do for at least two other people. Although reassured by Ned's explanation, Mads sought Mathilde's reassurance she was happy with the arrangement before consenting to it.

Life settled down to a steady routine. People came and went according to some roster that only they appeared to understand. It kept Mathilde busy managing the house for however many happened to be there at any given time. The weeks slipped by with remarkable speed, except for the fortnight when the rains finally came. Then, green furry mould sprouted on everything, adding to her workload. Laundering the men's clothes proved a challenge. The heavy work clothes took ages to dry at the best of times. With no break in the heavy rain for days, even drying the clothes in front of the fire proved almost impossible.

When the rains cleared, everything was fresher and brighter; the days and nights a bit cooler... but only for a couple of days before the humidity was back to suck the life out of everyone. The same rains deluged Marathon, delaying work on the new store and adding to mounting frustrations. The final shipment of lumber for the new store hadn't arrived when construction began, but was due within the first week. Some of it arrived after four weeks. The balance of the order remained outstanding.

The rain delay provided some leeway for delivery of the requisite material. Once work began again, those materials were needed within a week. Aware of the problem before the rains came, Ned boarded a coastal vessel for the south. His meeting with the southern supplier was fiery. He made it clear he would not be leaving until the remainder of the materials were on a ship and heading for Marathon.

The supplier insisted they had been shipped. In an effort to resolve the situation – and remove Ned from his office – the supplier resorted to calling in his ship's captain to help explain to Ned. With tempers frayed all round, it took a while for discussions to achieve anything. The clincher came when the captain produced the relevant shipping documents for the material in question. They clearly showed Ned's supplies, along with other building materials destined for that port, were unloaded at the port prior to Marathon.

As the supplier's ship was loaded and due to sail on the evening tide, Ned sailed with it to oversee the reloading of his materials when they reached that port. Then he stayed with his precious cargo until its safe unloading at Marathon and transfer to the construction site. By the time he arrived with the materials, construction had resumed two days earlier. Mads was frantic at the prospect of yet another delay. That evening, a few rums at their hotel helped restore both Mads' and Ned's good humour. The store would be ready for stocking in three to four weeks' time.

With one disaster averted, Ned turned his attention to progress on developing Rangelands. Next morning, he rode out to the property, arriving after lunch. He expected Alf Grant would be around close to the bunkhouse, but there was no sign of him. If Alf were working in one of the paddocks, he wouldn't return to the bunkhouse until around dusk. To fill in time until then, Ned rode out to look over the property.

Quite a bit of scrub was cleared and new fences erected, but a large area of trees remained at one end of the property. Ned's tour of inspection took him down to that area. After a quick ride through some of the area awaiting clearing, he returned to the bunkhouse to wait for Alf. It was just on dusk when he heard a commotion coming towards the bunkhouse. He heard cattle, and quickly mounted and rode out to investigate.

Single-handed, Alf Grant drove a herd of about ten cattle. The recent rains produced good green cover, and the cattle were more interested in stopping to graze than continuing to the home yard. He was having a hard time keeping the animals together and moving. With Ned's help, they soon had the small herd yarded. As they took their rum swizzles out to a couple of bush chairs in front of the bunkhouse Ned said, "Nice looking mob you brought in. Where did you get this lot?"

"I was talking to a bloke in town last week, a grazier from over the range. He's selling up and getting out of the game. He brought a mob of his poorer stock into the boiling down works, and planned bringing the better quality animals into the meat works this week. I arranged to meet up with him at the bottom of the range to look them over. Yesterday, I met him and picked out this lot to bring back today. That Letter of Authority you gave me when we left Sweers paid for them. You'll be surprised at how cheap they were."

"Where did the ones down in the scrub come from?"

"Eh…? What mob down in the scrub? We don't have any there. I intend going to Port Beauchamp next week to organise the boys to bring some of the herd back here. Those in the yard are the only ones I've brought onto the place. Maybe the ones you saw are scrubbers that went bush when the last owner was forced off the property."

"Maybe, but that doesn't fit somehow. They don't look like scrubbers, and there is a rough timber yard set up in that scrub. I take it that yard isn't your handiwork and you don't know anything about it."

"No, I don't. My plan is to clear from the bunkhouse out towards the boundaries. I clear the scrub as I come to it, and haven't wasted my time riding around in there to see what's still ahead of me."

"Interesting…; I suppose the yard could be a relic from the past owner as well. The trouble with that is, it didn't look old. Not to worry, I'm sure all will become clear in time. Until then, it will have to remain one of life's mysteries. When you go to Port Beauchamp, take Emil with you. I think the store is far enough advanced to spare him. He can assist with moving the cattle, and then stay on to help out around here. He's been good on the construction site, but I know he'll be a lot happier out here."

"Okay, will do. It will be handy having Emil here. Are you planning on staying long?"

"No. I'll just overnight before heading back tomorrow. Cattle are unloading at Port Beauchamp next week. I thought to look them over. If they are any good, I might have a few more to add to our herd. It would be best to leave them at Fisher's place for a while until they recover from their boat ride before moving them on again."

It wasn't a late night as both men wanted an early start the next day. All the way back to Port Beauchamp, those cattle and the rough yard in the scrub at Rangelands occupied Ned's thinking. The longer he rode, the more convinced he became that something was not right. He had no cause to worry. He knew Alf would not leave it alone until he discovered all there was to know about that situation.

Chapter 6 Delays

Even the best laid plans sometimes go awry. That was true for the new Rixon & Co store at Marathon, and it left the Port Beauchamp store in danger of exploding. Stock purchased in advance of the imminent opening of the Marathon store and stored in the interim at the Port Beauchamp store filled that store to capacity and then some. While it constituted a significant volume of stock, it offered a limited range of goods.

Further lines of agricultural supplies were required in order to provide the new landholders in Marathon's surrounding area with everything they might need to establish their various rural enterprises. An 'old hand' who fully understood the needs of such customers, Tom Croxley sent orders south in plenty of time for supplies to arrive a little in advance of the planned opening. At the end of the week prior to the opening, those supplies coming by ship from the south had not arrived. Their late delivery proved only a part of the problems delaying the opening.

Reassured by those who should know that the ship would arrive in a bout ten days' time, Tom Croxley headed back to Port Beauchamp. Mr Kincaid, so delighted to see him, even helped load Tom's wagon. After a quick turnaround, the start of his third day back at Port Beauchamp saw Tom on the road again with his big German wagon loaded to capacity. Perhaps even loaded a little more than is prudent.

A patch of rough track on the outskirts of the township was the wagon's undoing. It all happened in quick succession. One wheel hit a rock cracking the wheel before it dropped into a hole next to the rock. The load shifted as the wheel collapsed, placing excessive strain on one end of the axle causing it to snap. There was nothing for it but to unload the wagon and return the goods to the Port Beauchamp store while the wagon was repaired. Tom could unhitch the horses and ride one back to town for help, but leaving his precious cargo unattended was not an option. Not until after lunchtime did he manage to stop the first rider to come by.

As requested, the rider informed Mr Kincaid of Tom's plight. After dispatching four of his staff with the store's two wagons to retrieve the goods, Mr Kincaid found himself having to help out with customers for the remainder of the day. It was just on dark when the store's wagons returned, and sometime later before the supplies were once more safely stored. With the wagon emptied, Tom managed to rig a temporary repair using bush timber cut from the side of the track. He and his crippled wagon limped back in the dark to arrive at Ned's cottage at about ten o'clock.

*****

Tom Croxley wasn't the only member of Ned's staff heading back to Port Beauchamp. A few days after Ned's visit, Alf Grant sought out Emil at Marathon. At dawn the next morning, they were on their way to Port Beauchamp to start moving to Rangelands some of the stock held at Fisher's property.

Alf's first priority at Port Beauchamp was to check on the stock at Fisher's place. He expected to find only one man looking after the stock, and was surprised to find all three men there. In the interest of wasting as little time as possible before setting off of the return journey to Rangelands, after a few words to the men, and leaving Emil with them, Alf rode into town.

Mathilde met him at the door and her appearance shocked him. He had not seen her look so haggard since the Gulf Fever episode on Sweers Island. "Mathilde, what has happened? Are you ill? You look terrible."

"No. I am well; a little tired perhaps. It is Mr Rixon who is ill. He has some strange fever that makes him quite delirious. I have sent the other men away and forbidden them to stay here while Mr Rixon is ill for fear they too come down with the fever. Can it be we brought the Gulf Fever with us and it is now beginning again? The doctor came twice to see Mr Rixon, but nothing he does seems to make any difference."

As his own concern for his long-time friend escalated, there was little Alf could do to alleviate her concerns. Brushing aside her plea for Alf to leave the cottage and stay with the men at Fisher's property, Alf insisted on staying at the cottage and assisting to care for Ned. In a bid to find out all he could about Ned's condition, first thing the next morning, Alf sought out the doctor who visited Ned. "Although it is sometime since we left Sweers Island, is it possible Ned is suffering a visitation of the Gulf Fever that caused the death of so many on Sweers Island?"

"I think it highly unlikely. In my opinion, Mr Rixon has contracted a form of influenza currently wreaking havoc in this area and in the north as well. None of the usual remedies has any effect. The only course of action open to us is to allow the fever to run its course. In Mr Rixon's case, if the fever follows the same pattern as I have observed in others, we should see some improvement in the next couple of days. Once the fever breaks, he will remain weak for a few days. That may not be much comfort to you, but it is the best advice I can give at this time."

For Alf, there was no question about what to do. He would remain at Ned's cottage until Ned was on his feet again – and before thinking about moving the cattle to Rangelands. It took a few days but, as the doctor predicted, once the fever broke, Ned's recovery was swift. Although weakened by so many days of high fever and little food, Ned was able to leave his bed for short periods of time to sit in the garden or on the veranda. In spite of Mathilde's care and attention, it was a week later before Ned was well enough for Alf to turn his attention once again to moving the stock.

Alf spent the next few days at Fisher's property organising the long cattle drive to Rangelands. With the help of Toby, Syd Ballard, John Oakes and Emil, half of the herd was drafted into a small paddock. The day before their anticipated departure, Alf took a wagon into town to stock up on supplies and other equipment for their trip. While in town, he came across Tom Croxley also in the process of making ready to return to Marathon.

Marooned in Port Beauchamp while his wagon was repaired, Tom was anxious to be on his way again with his wagon load of goods. It was late in the third day after the accident before the wagon was ready for the road. After another day spent loading it, he contemplated leaving Port Beauchamp first thing next morning. A chance meeting with Alf changed that agenda. Tom decided to delay his departure to travel south with Alf and the others moving the herd. The arrangement suited Alf as it meant they would have an experienced camp cook accompanying them on what would be at least a two-week trip.

It was early morning of the fifth day after the incident with the wagon when Ned saw Tom off again with his loaded wagon. His parting advice to Tom was to delay the opening of the new Marathon store for at least another two weeks. With all his men away with the cattle, Ned took over looking after the remainder of the herd at Fisher's property. The now empty cottage allowed Mathilde time to herself. Time to rest and recuperate after the wearying days of nursing Ned back to health.

*****

No further incidents occurred along the way. The trip from Port Beauchamp, although uneventful, was slow to accommodate the pace of the heavily loaded wagon and to maintain the cattle in peak condition. On the second day into their trip, when the cattle settled down to the rhythm of the daily plod towards their new home, Alf sent John Oakes back to Port Beauchamp. His concern about Ned being left to look after the cattle so soon after his illness outweighed his need for John Oakes' help to move their small herd.

The group's last camp together was beside a waterhole in a clearing ringed by paperbarks and eucalypts. Although only a short distance prior to the approaches to Marathon, and they arrived at the campsite early in the afternoon, it was agreed to overnight there before parting ways the next morning. They kept the fire going until late that night. The late departure of the wet season meant autumn was lost in a continuation of the rain and humid weather. On the heels of an abrupt departure of the wet season, the chill in the night air heralded the imminent onset of winter.

After an early breakfast next morning, the group split up. Alf's mob turned off the main track onto a rough side track winding its way through the bush up the valley to Rangelands. Tom Croxley, after nursing his wagon and its precious cargo along for the past two weeks, heaved a sigh of relief as he drove his wagon into Marathon township.

"What a sight...," Tom whispered as he crossed the river. The new Rixon & Co store dominated Marathon. Much had happened in the township in the handful of years since the first settlers arrived. At its heart was a motley collection of rough shanties posing as the commercial centre of Marathon. Most were nothing more than a dirt floor with hessian and a few sheets of iron to keep out the weather. While little progress was evident on the construction of a couple of other timber buildings, Rixon's store stood out like a beacon towering over the surrounding ramshackle commercial premises.

When Tom Croxley left for Port Beauchamp to collect stock, Mads Eriksen worked alone to complete the finishing touches to the new store. There remained only minor interior work to complete and the installation of shelving and bins to hold smaller stock items. It was now over a month since Tom Croxley left. With all interior works completed and still no word from Port Beauchamp, Mads felt a growing concern in the pit of his stomach.

"Should I return to Port Beauchamp to see what is happening?" he wondered aloud. Still unsure what to do, the next morning Mads went to the store as usual – and spent the day there twiddling his thumbs. "Keeping busy is a better thing to do than this," he told the empty store as he locked the door for the night. "With nothing else to do inside, tomorrow I will start work on building the horse yard."

A horse yard in the cleared area behind the store was a necessity. It provided somewhere safe for pastoralists from the surrounding area to leave their horses and wagons while in town to collect supplies and attend to other business. Next morning, as Mads resolutely moved tools and materials to the area for the horse yard, Tom Croxley drove his wagon up to the loading dock at the rear of the store. Work was abandoned while Mads caught up on all the Port Beauchamp news over a pannikin of tea with Tom.

"I see you're about to make a start on the horse yard, Mads. Does that mean everything inside is complete?"

"Yes. It is ready to receive stock. This load you brought will occupy only a small part of the space in here."

"There is another load of stock still to bring from Port Beauchamp ... and Mr Kincaid will be pleased to see the last of it, I can tell you. As soon as we unload the wagon, I will check on the ship bringing the stock ordered from southern suppliers."

It was the next day before Tom Croxley approached the harbour master for information on the likely arrival of the stock. As Tom had few details to assist the harbour master identify the information Tom wanted, the meeting became a protracted affair. After much shuffling of paper, the harbour master suggested a ship due to arrive at Marathon in two or three days' time might be the one Tom inquired about. That was all Tom gained from his meeting. It was now a waiting game until that ship arrived. A part of him secretly questioned the veracity of the information provided by the harbour master. Perhaps it was no more than a ruse to get Tom to leave his office.

Two days after his meeting with the harbour master a ship did arrive. Its manifest did not include the much awaited supplies for the new store. When Tom met Mads at the store on the morning of the third day, he was almost convinced today's ship – if there was one – also would be a disappointment. He shared his thoughts with Mads. "If a ship arrives in port today, the question is whether it is any more likely to have our supplies on board than yesterday's vessel. If nothing arrives today, I will start contacting suppliers tomorrow."

"Perhaps, while you wait to see the harbour master, we might unpack some of the stock and set it on the shelves. Then, after we have our mid-morning tea break, it might be time to go to the harbour," Mads suggested.

Tom offered no argument, and the two men set about stocking shelves from the meagre range of supplies Tom brought from Port Beauchamp. By ten o'clock, they completed their task. "It's a bit early to take a break but, as we've finished stocking the shelves, perhaps we might indulge in a pannikin of tea before I go to talk to the harbour master," Tom suggested.

Mads looked over his steaming mug of tea at Tom. "You will be staying in Marathon now?" Tom nodded. "Where will you stay? Have you arranged accommodation?"

"I found a cot at a hotel last night, but I don't want to make that a permanent arrangement. I suppose I should give my future living arrangements some thought. What about you, Mads? Will you go back to Port Beauchamp when your work on the store finishes? By now, you must be tired of living in the poor conditions offered by that hotel."

"Yes, I grow tired of it. To stay there for a few nights is okay but, for me, it has been too long. I do not think Mr Rixon intends me to go back to Port Beauchamp. There is work to do on the new grazing property. That is where he will send me after work finishes here."

"Ah well, mebbe I better make a move if I'm to talk to that harbour master today," Tom said as he stood and stretched his back. Further conversation was interrupted by the sound of a wagon pulling up to the loading dock.

"Christ, John Oakes, what are you and that wagon doing here?" Tom asked as he strode out onto the loading area. "Last I saw of you, Alf sent you back to Fisher's place to look after the cattle still there."

"Aye, Alf sent me back, but the boss had other ideas. Mr Rixon sent me to the Beauchamp store with a message for Mr Kincaid. The boss said Kincaid was to make one of the store's wagons available and to load the rest of the Marathon supplies on it for me to bring here. The toffee-nosed bloke wasn't too keen to let me have one of his wagons. I said that was okay. I'd send Mr Rixon in *to give him the instruction personally.* That did the trick, and here I be with a wagon load of stuff for your store. Gimme a hand to unload, and then I'll be on me way back to Beauchamp."

"Mr Oakes, if you are here, Mr Grant and the other men are moving the cattle, and Mr Rixon is looking after the cattle at Fisher's place, who is staying at the cottage?" Mads demanded.

"No one I don't think. Well, that is, no one but Mathilde I suppose," John replied.

"That is not good. She is a young girl and should not be there alone. I am her father. I should be with her to keep her safe. I wanted her to come to Marathon to be with me, but Mr Rixon said she was needed at the cottage." Mads' dark scowl concerned Tom. He hurried to calm the man.

"Come on, Mads. You know the boss tried to find a suitable cottage here in Marathon. There is nothing available. And she couldn't stay at the hotel with you. Mebbe when those new ones are built it might be different but, what passes for hotels in the township now are not safe places for a young lass. She is safer in the cottage at Beauchamp, even if she is alone for a few days." Tom's attempt to diffuse Mads' concern brought only an angry snarl in response. He tried changing the subject.

"John, will you not stay the night here before returning to Port Beauchamp?"

"Nah, I prefer the bush. As soon as we unload, I'll be off. With an empty wagon, by tonight, I should be a good way along the track. Besides, Alf was worried about the boss since he was so ill recently. He didn't want the boss doing too much until he fully recovered."

With the three men applying themselves to the task, they finished unloading the wagon by lunchtime, and the three adjourned to the pub for lunch. John Oakes wasted little time over the meal before hitching the wagon and heading out of town. Tom and Mads chose to linger a little longer over lunch.

As they made ready to leave their table, Mads appeared deep in thought.

"What's bothering you, Mads? You seem concerned about something,"

"I thought about the amount of lumber we have left. I know there is still a small stable to build in the horse yard, and a privy way down the back past the yard, but I think there is enough to do something else as well. While you go to talk to the harbour master, I will allocate lumber to each of those jobs to see how much extra there is."

"I admit to knowing nothing about construction and such matters. I'll leave it to you to work it out. Now the time has come for me to have stern words with the harbour master. Only one ship arrived yesterday and it had nothing for us. I am not aware of any arriving today. I wonder what yarn the good harbour master will spin me today." With that, Tom got up and strode out of the hotel.

A few minutes later, Mads followed him out onto the street. Instead of going directly to the rear of the store, Mads stood on the street out front and studied the building. He felt more than a little pride. It was a fine building, and he applauded Ned's foresight in having the building raised a little in case the river should flood. Ned secured a large block for his new store. The four steps leading to the front door elevated the main part of the store above any likely flood level. The block, sloping steeply back away from the street provided an extra bonus for the building. By virtue of the sloping block, a large area under the main store provided a warehouse type facility for storage of extra stock. A large platform stretching out from the back door provided a loading area where goods could be stacked while awaiting loading onto wagons. A low earth ramp built adjacent to the loading area served a dual purpose. While it allowed wagons driven up the ramp to be at a comfortable height for loading, the ramp also prevented the ingress of rain and floodwaters into the lower level of the building.

Mads strode to the piles of lumber stacked at the rear of the store and set about creating neat piles for each of the projects: the stables, the privy, and an extra pile for leftover lumber. Yes, there is enough extra timber for what I want to do, he told himself... and promptly set to work.

While Mads was busy at the store, Tom was forced to wait for the harbour master to be finished with other business before he could ask about his ship. As Tom had run out of patience by the time the harbour master came to speak with him, the conversation did not start well. "You said to expect our ship to arrive yesterday or today. So far today, it appears no ships arrived. What have you to say now about all this?"

"As I said at the time, without details of the ship supposedly bringing your material, I can only guess at when it will arrive. Yesterday's boat could not be bringing your materials as it came from the north. Your stock is coming from the south. The arrival expected today is delayed. Squalls and mountainous seas along the coast forced the ship to take shelter in a southern port. It will remain there until conditions are safe for it to continue up the coast. We have no new expected date of arrival."

Disgruntled and at a loss as to what to do next, Tom stormed out of the harbourmaster's office and headed for the store. As his journey took him past two new buildings under construction, he decided to spend some time checking them out. This led to a number of conversations with various people and resulted in his not returning to the store until late in the afternoon. Anger at the non-arrival of the supplies still burned within him and he needed someone to vent to. He went in search of Mads and found him working in the warehouse area under the building.

"I thought you were finished with the building, Mads. What's this bit you're doing now?"

"Ah yes, my guess was correct. We have quite a bit more lumber than we need for the two remaining projects. I am putting it to good use. These walls I am building will enclose your accommodation. You will have a bedroom and another room to use however you wish. If you intend making other accommodation arrangements, these rooms could be used as office space. Does this meet with your approval?"

"I certainly do approve. That's brilliant thinking, Mads. My living on site will provide some degree of safety for the store and its stock. Once the privy is completed, I will move in."

"In that case, as soon as I finish these walls, I will construct the privy. Everything should be ready for you to move in within a week."

*****

It was three days after Tom's last conversation with the harbour master before the ship with their supplies from the south arrived. After hiring a couple of men and a wagon, everything was moved to the store and Tom set about finishing stocking the shelves. Once the two men Tom hired unloaded the supplies, Tom sent them to help Mads with the privy. After five days of solid work by Mads, Tom's new quarters were ready for him to move into. He hitched up the German wagon again and set out for Port Beauchamp, his intention being to finalise with Ned the opening of the new store, and to bring back to Marathon his few possessions and anything else the boss saw fit to send.

Chapter 7 Marathon

Leaving only Emil at Rangelands to look after the cattle, on the evening before Tom Croxley planned setting off for Port Beauchamp, Alf Grant, Toby and Syd Ballard rode into Marathon, their intention to check for messages or anything else Tom had for them to take back to Port Beauchamp before spending the night at a hotel. When they found Tom also preparing to hit the track the next day, they agreed to travel together. Alf told the others later, "At least this way we will have a half decent camp cook along for the trip."

At first light next morning, the three men on horseback and Tom with his wagon set off for Beauchamp. Hampered a bit by the wagon, the party still made good time, and rode onto Fisher's property five days later. John Oakes, having taken great care to nurse Mr Kincaid's wagon back to its owner, arrived at Fisher's place only four days ahead of Alf's group.

Leaving the others to look after the cattle, Ned tied his horse on behind the wagon and rode into town with Tom. Mathilde was delighted when the two men arrived. Alf's group spent the night at Fisher's before Alf joined Ned and Tom at the cottage. Over dinner that night Alf explained his unexpected early return to Beauchamp.

"There is so much work to do at Rangelands and, with only me and Emil to do it, things are moving at snail's pace. My thinking is to move the remainder of the herd to the property now. That will give me all my men at Rangelands to help with the workload."

Ned nodded thoughtfully before replying. "Yes, I agree. How soon will you set off?"

"I'll ride out to Fisher's tomorrow. If I get everything organised in time, we will move out the following day."

"There is one thing that might impact on your plans. I purchased ten head from a property a couple of days north of here. They will deliver them overland sometime in the next week. I know John Oakes does not much care for being in town, but he would survive a week or so here. Leave him behind to look after the cattle when they arrive. He can keep them in the yards at my wharf until I arrange to ship them to Marathon. He might need someone to help him move them from Marathon to Rangelands." Alf endorsed Ned's suggestion over a few rums before retiring for the night.

Next morning, as he prepared to ride back to Fisher's, Alf checked on Ned's plans for the immediate future. "I am half inclined to ride out to Fisher's this afternoon to spend the night with the men before travelling with you and the herd to Marathon. I'll have Tom load the German wagon with provision and a few other items I want him to take to Marathon. He can travel with us as well. The other thing I must organise today is for Mr Kincaid to arrange a ship to load those ten head of cattle when they arrive. John Oakes will travel on board with them. He and the cattle could arrive at Marathon before us and he will need to tend the animals until we move them up the valley."

Mathilde's elation at having Ned home again disappeared the instant he apprised her of his plans. "Mr Oakes will stay here until he sails with the cattle. Once the animals are here, I doubt you'll see much of him during the day. He should not create much extra work for you. Once he and the cattle sail, you will have this place to yourself again. I anticipate being away about a month or so, if other matters besides the opening of the new store arise. It is unfortunate a lack of suitable accommodation prevents your attending the opening."

Be natural, smile, nod your understanding, Mathilde told herself. Don't let him see your disappointment. She was relieved when, after a quick goodbye, he was on his horse and off to Fisher's to join the other men. John Oakes, taciturn and withdrawn by nature, would not create much work for her, but he wasn't much company either. The one thing dominating her thinking the rest of the day was that Ned 'would be away for about a month or so'. A month is a long time, especially when it follows so closely on his previous absence of two weeks.

*****

By taking a more direct – and less travelled – overland route, Two weeks after leaving Port Beauchamp the cattle were in Rangelands' home paddock. The men spent what was left of the day settling into the bunkhouse. While primitive, the building had plenty of rough timber bunks. Tom was the only one spending the night in more comfortable conditions. He left the main group a day and a half earlier to head into Marathon. Before they parted company, Tom and Ned finalised plans for their new store's 'grand opening'. They allowed little enough time for Tom to organise everything, and afforded no more than a day for Ned to check on progress at Rangelands before riding into town to assist with the opening.

While the others set about preparing an evening meal, Ned and Alf sat outside warming themselves beside a fire. "I will need to ride into town tomorrow afternoon," Ned said. "Perhaps we could look around the place before I leave. By the way, is everything all right with Emil?"

"Emil…? I think he is okay. He was delighted to be away from the town. Why do you ask?"

"I thought he seemed unsettled, almost a bit agitated about something. Keep an eye on him. The young bloke's been through a bit since they set sail for this country. He might be suffering a bit of a delayed reaction to it all."

"I hadn't noticed anything, but I'll watch him. It might be that the kid is feeling a bit homesick for his old country and missing his parents. Mads takes good care of him, but he is only the boy's uncle."

Early next morning, Ned and Alf rode out to inspect the progress so far. In the rush to accomplish everything before leaving for Marathon, Ned remained unaware of Emil's attempts to steal a few moments alone with him. Although a less favourable alternative, Emil resorted to an indirect approach. While Ned and Alf rode around the property, Ned's jacket hung on a nail in the bunkhouse. Emil slipped a hasty scribbled note into one of its pockets as he offered up a silent prayer that Ned would find it soon.

*****

The day prior to the opening sped past in a blur of activity. Tom had tacked up posters advertising the opening everywhere around town. His meeting with the newly appointed first magistrate for the town resulted in the magistrate's agreeing to say a few words and cut the tape to officially open the store. During conversation at the hotel the night before, Ned learned religion had arrived in Marathon. A Catholic priest arrived in town the previous week. Ned's task next day was to approach the priest about becoming involved in the opening. Although not in a position to veto it, Tom told Mads he did not support the move.

"I don't see the need for it meself. What good does a bloke in a dog collar do for the store? But Ned says a priest blessing the place will help bring the 'God botherers' to our door."

Mads nodded sagely and said, "Some of those people are established customers of another store in town. Anything that persuades them to change to this store is a good thing. Having the priest involved might suggest to the townsfolk this is an honourable establishment that will treat them fairly. You might not agree with the idea and would prefer it didn't happen, but it's only a minute or two of suffering for you."

Late in the afternoon, after learning John Oakes and the cattle arrived earlier, Ned went to the yards to speak to Oakes about moving the cattle to Rangelands. Almost convinced everything was ready for the opening, Ned called at the store to check again on his way back to his hotel.

Tom agreed they were almost ready. There was one last thing to do: organising the 'mystery free gifts' advertised on the posters all over town. These were Tom's initiative and a surprise to Ned. "Your posters say the first twenty customers will receive a free mystery gift. What are these gifts you plan to give away, and can I see them beforehand?"

Tom chuckled. "Better than that, you can help make them. They need putting together tonight in the hope that at least twenty people will purchase something from us tomorrow." With that, Tom pulled a bundle of flour bags out of a box and slapped them on the counter. "These have to be filled tonight."

Weighing, bagging and counting, occupied Tom, Mads and Ned until after midnight when they packed the filled flour bags into a box ready for the next day. Each bag contained small packets of tea, sugar, flour, salt, a packet containing four hardtack biscuits, and another with six horseshoe nails. As an afterthought, they also added two potatoes to each bag before tying each bag with twine. After a couple of pre-opening rums, Tom fell into bed in his quarters under the store as Ned and Mads made their way back to their hotel.

Determined none of the men should miss the opening, after completing essential chores, Alf rounded up his men and they rode into town. To avoid the expense and the hassle of finding beds at one of the two hotels in town, Alf's mob camped the night under the stars on the outskirts of Marathon, and rode into town the next morning. The official opening was set for ten o'clock.

Tom argued stores opened much earlier than that. "...And this one will in future," Ned assured him. "Today it will open later to give outlying farmers and graziers time to arrive in town before we open. An early opening might seem we intended none of them would have an opportunity to be among the first customers and not able to receive one of our free gifts."

People swarmed into the store as soon as the official ceremony ended and the doors opened. For the first hour or so, Tom felt his concern mounting. People packed the place, but so far there were only two sales. By lunchtime, he was more relaxed. After checking out everything on offer – and the prices – customers queued up to pay for purchases. Mads was overwhelmed by the wagons arriving at the loading dock to collect bags of supplies, fencing materials, and other agricultural bits and pieces. With a string of wagons starting to develop, Ned sent Toby to help. The twenty free gifts disappeared in record time, and seemed well received by the recipients.

Alf organised with the hotel to send food for his men to the store at lunchtime. While checking on the arrival of the food, Ned took Alf aside to discuss the cattle at the wharves. They agreed Emil would return to the property straight after lunch. That was in accordance with Alf's plan except, when Alf and his men left for the property the following day, they would take the cattle and the German wagon with them.

Ned stood on the loading dock watching Toby and Mads loading wagons. Ned slipped his hands into his jacket pockets … and found an unexpected piece of paper. He had scanned the note when Mads strode up and demanded an explanation. Unaware John Oakes was at Marathon, Mads believed he remained at the Beauchamp cottage with Mathilde. When he heard Ned and Alf discussing Oakes taking the wagon to Rangelands, he realised his daughter was alone in the cottage at Beauchamp.

An angry Mads confronted Ned about the situation. After a lengthy and heated discussion, Mads returned to loading customers' wagons. A temporary truce was in place, but Ned knew the matter was far from resolved. In a quiet moment later that day, Ned revisited his discussion with Mads. During his brief time at the cottage before leaving for Marathon, Ned noticed Mathilde looked tired. There was no cause for concern he assured himself. The lass wasn't ill. She even had gained a bit a weight. Nevertheless, she did look tired. Maybe being alone for a while would allow her time to relax and rest before they became busy with relocating his household to Rangelands. After giving the matter some thought, Ned convinced himself not mentioning any of this to the girl's father was the best strategy. He doubted Mads would see it in the same light as he did.

The confrontation with Mads was not the only worrying incident that day. There also was the matter of the note Ned found in his jacket pocket.

In response to that note, Ned went in search of Emil and found him at the far end of the horse yard hitching up the German wagon. The note indicated Emil needed to speak to Ned urgently, but he wanted their meeting to be away from prying eyes. After sauntering up to Emil in his best nonchalant manner, Ned explained to Emil why he and John Oakes would take the wagon to the property. Then, after scanning the yard for any 'ears' lurking nearby, Ned turned to the matter of Emil's note.

"We appear alone in the yard so let's talk. I found your note and thought we should discuss it before you left town. What is so urgent, and why the need for secrecy?"

"Sir, I don't think it is safe for me to be seen talking to you."

"Nonsense boy, you work for me. What can be wrong with a boss speaking with his employee?"

"It is what I wish to talk to you about that makes it dangerous." Ned's eyebrows shot up his forehead, but he nodded and gestured for Emil to continue. "Mr Rixon, funny things are happening at Rangelands. No, not funny, more like 'peculiar', I think is the word. Mr Meadows and another man – sometimes two men – come to the property. The first time Mr Meadows came, I don't think he knew I was there. When he saw me, he rushed over to introduce himself. He said he made a quick visit to check on the place."

"Mr Meadows isn't living on the property yet?"

"No, Sir."

"So, why do you think his visit 'peculiar'? He is part owner of the property. It is natural he is interested in what happens there."

"Yes, I understand that, but it was not his first visit. I saw him there twice before that. He didn't see me. That is why he didn't realise I was there. When I went to check the cattle after each of those visits, there were extra animals in the paddock. At first, I thought I was mistaken but, when it happened again after the second time I saw Mr Meadows and his men, I knew I was right. Even a few more cattle were in the paddock. That second visit was two days after Mr Grant left for Port Beauchamp. Two days after that was when Mr Meadows discovered I was there. Later that night, I heard our cattle. They were restless *for* a few hours. I wanted to check on them, but Mr Grant said, when I was there alone, I must stay in the bunkhouse at night. Our cattle remained restless the next morning, so I rode out to investigate. I heard other cattle somewhere not too far away and followed their sound. Some distance into the scrub ...”

“...And you found a set of bush timber stockyard holding cattle that were not Rangelands’ ... am I right?”

“Yes Sir; how did you know? Is that scrub part of Rangelands, or did I go onto someone else’s property and find someone else’s cattle? Did I do something wrong?”

“No, Emil, you did nothing wrong, but you must not go near those yards in the bush again. Mr Oakes will be with you on the property until Mr Grant and the others return. In the meantime, you must heed Mr Grant’s instruction not the leave the bunkhouse at night. I will give Mr Oakes the same instruction before you head back to the property. Should Mr Meadows visit again before Mr Grant returns, you must remain civil to him and say nothing about those things you mentioned to me. Do not mention this matter to anyone, unless it is Mr Grant who asks you about it.”

Their meeting over, as they parted company, Ned made a show of loudly instructing Emil to wait for Mr Oakes to arrive before moving the wagon to the loading dock for Toby to load it. John Oakes, who arrived at the store as Ned marched in through the backdoor, experienced a feeling of foreboding. The set of Ned’s jaw told him all was not well. Contrary to that tell-tale sign, Ned seemed his usual self when he gave John directions to where Emil and the wagon awaited him.

With the wagon organised, Ned went in search of Alf, Mads and Tom to organise a meeting for after they closed the doors for the day. Later, when they gathered with drinks in hand in Tom’s quarters, Ned informed them of his plans.

“Tom, you and I will look over applicants for the clerk and storeman positions tomorrow as planned. Alf, I assume you and your men will return to Rangelands tomorrow with the cattle from the yards at the wharf. Mads, you will ride with Alf and the others and will stay on the property after that. As soon as I am finished here, I will return to Beauchamp to prepare for my relocation to Rangelands. Mads, there will be work for you to do before I relocate. There is a small shed on the property. I think it was a dairy at some time in the past. It needs work to make it into a temporary residence for myself, Mathilde and Emil unless the lad prefers to sleep with the men in the bunkhouse."

"Will you not move into the homestead that is already there?" Alf asked.

"It has an earthen floor, thatched roof, and looks in danger of collapsing at any moment. I would be happy to stay with the others in the bunkhouse, and may end up doing that, but Mathilde deserves somewhere decent to live. It is small but it should provide at least two small bedrooms, and might need other modifications. Besides, if Mr Meadows decides to move onto the property, he will expect to inhabit the old homestead. In which case, any work to the building he considers necessary will be his responsibility. No, one of the sheds tarted up a bit will do us for now."

Mads' dark scowl as Ned spoke was evidence of continued dissatisfaction with all matters regarding his daughter. As he refrained from voicing his concerns yet again, the atmosphere remained strained but cordial. A bit over an hour later, the meeting ended. Last thing before they went their separate ways, they drank a toast to a successful opening. Tom reported the day's sales exceeded expectations.

*****

In the following days everything went much according to plan. Alf and the men moved the cattle from the wharf yards to Rangelands. Mads accompanied them. The day after the opening proved chaotic for Ned and Tom. Interviewing aspiring clerks and storemen had to slot in between dealing with customers. By the end of the day, both men were exhausted but suitable staff would commence work in the store the next day.

After another night at the hotel and a brief time with Tom before he left, Ned rode out for Port Beauchamp. As it was not much before lunchtime when he started out, Ned rode until darkness obscured the track before making camp for the night. The night had a chill to it and dew would soon blanket everything. Ned set his swag close to the fire and crawled in. It was a clear starry night. Of its own volition, in that short time before he fell asleep, his mind returned to Mathilde. Her flawless alabaster complexion showed off her gentle blue eyes and shiny golden hair coiled tightly at the nape of her neck. She was an attractive young woman and more than a competent housekeeper. As he drifted off to sleep, his last thought was about how much he missed her company in recent times.

It would take another four days of hard riding before his return to the Port Beauchamp cottage. His arrival was accompanied by a howling westerly wind that dropped the temperature several degrees lower than when he left. People on the streets were rugged up in coats and scarves against the cold. In spite of the warmth from the kitchen fire, Mathilde also sported a bulky over-coat that, over the next few days, he never saw her remove.

Over dinner on his first night back, he shared with Mathilde his plans to relocate to Rangelands. He felt a twinge of alarm when she appeared indifferent to the news.

Chapter 8 *Rangelands*

Following the store's opening, life at erupted into a flurry of activity. The extra cattle now on the property required more paddocks, and more paddocks required more land cleared of scrub. While the other men focused on clearing scrub and erecting fences around the newly cleared areas, Emil found himself left in charge of the cattle and spending his days away from where the others worked. He was relieved to see the area Alf chose to clear next was away from that patch of scrub concealing the bush stockyard. Ned hadn't said not to tell Alf about what was hidden in the scrub, but something told Emil it was best to say nothing and leave it to Ned to tell those who needed to know.

On the second morning after their return from Marathon, while the others went off to begin work for the day, Alf and Mads hung back at the bunkhouse. They inspected the various buildings on the property to enable Mads to determine the work required to create a suitable residence for when Ned relocated his household from Port Beauchamp. Ned suggested the former dairy might be a suitable building. It didn't take Alf and Mads long to dismiss that suggestion.

"You're the carpenter Mads, but I don't think any amount of remodelling will turn this into a suitable place to live. I can see it was a dairy sometime in the past, but it hasn't been used in a long time."

"Rough built of poor timber, and time has not been kind to it. It is easier to construct a new building than to make this into a sound home for my daughter. Perhaps one of the other buildings might be more suitable."

After inspecting two other small sheds, a larger building caught their eye. "That one over there by the well looks more promising, Mads. What do you think?"

"It is of more sturdy construction and is larger. The location is good. We need to see how much work is required before it is liveable."

Inspection of the building showed it was soundly constructed of quality timber, with no obvious ravages of time or neglect to contend with. Its deceptively spacious interior made the building an ideal choice. "The smell of leather is strong in here although the building is empty," Mads said.

"I suspect the area at the far end, beyond that rough partition, was a tack room. The smell of leather and leather dressing permeating the building probably comes from there."

"In that case, what was this big area of the building used for?"

"Those ruts in the floor suggest this part of the building housed wagons and carriages undercover. What are your thoughts about the floor? Should we leave it as an earthen floor, or would you do something else?"

"I am not used to buildings with earthen floors as I have seen in this country. If this building were to become a permanent residence, I would install proper flooring. Ned hinted at building a proper homestead sometime in the future, so I think it wise not to waste time and money on creating a different floor if it is to be temporary."

Alf looked distracted but nodded his agreement. "I'm thinking that old dairy might serve as a store for our supplies if it were improved a little. On the other hand, it might be decided that the building continue as a dairy after some minor renovations. I feel we should focus our attention on turning this larger building into a residence and wait until Ned arrives to determine what else he wants done. I've changed my mind. I think this needs a proper floor."

While Alf went off to spend the rest of the day working with the other men clearing scrub, Mads spent the rest of the day detailing the necessary work and estimating the materials required. He was waiting when Alf returned at the end of the day. "I have planned the work and made a list of the materials required. There are a couple of buildings I think might become unnecessary in the future. It would not take too much work to use some of the materials from at least one of those buildings as part of the renovations to this building. Is it possible to do that without first checking with Ned for permission?"

With Alf in tow, Mads strode across to the first of the buildings he identified as surplus to requirements. After a cursory inspection, Alf agreed the building was unlikely to be required in the future. He risked authorising its demolition and the reuse of whatever material possible. "That is good. My planning included using materials from that building, leaving less for us to transport from town. If you have no objection, I will take the wagon into Marathon tomorrow to collect the necessary materials to make a start on renovations."

"It will be good to get started as soon as possible. Although Ned didn't say how urgent he considered his relocation to this property, from what I know of Ned, once he decides to do something, he wants to do it now. Take Toby with you on the wagon tomorrow. He can give you a hand loading materials."

Toby remained with Mads for a couple of days to help demolish the surplus building after they returned from Marathon with the requisite materials. By the end of a week, renovations were well advanced. The building was now referred to as 'the cottage'. At the end of that week, over dinner one night, Alf checked on progress. "I had little chance to talk over the last week or so, Mads, but I see work on the cottage is well advanced. You don't appear to have any problems, but how are things going?"

"No problems so far, thanks Alf, and everything is going according to plan. I estimate work on the residence will be completed by the end of next week. What happens then? Do you know when Ned is likely to move here?"

"Ned's last instruction to me was to send the wagon to fetch him and his belongings when a suitable residence was ready.

We will look at the situation again at the end of next week before making any plans about fetching Ned from Beauchamp. Another week's time will suit me. By then, that current area of scrub will be cleared and I will be able to spare someone to go with you to help with loading the wagon. After giving some thought to that old dairy building, I am convinced nothing should be done there until after Ned relocates and he can make a decisions about it." The thought that, at the end of the week, he would be off to Port Beauchamp and would see his daughter, kept Mads' spirits buoyed over the ensuing days.

*****

After keeping a constant eye out for strange cattle or people coming onto the property, Emil recorded a small herd of about six head arrived towards the end of the first week of work on the cottage. He believed one distinctive beast was among those he observed earlier in the bush stockyard. With part of Rangelands' herd in the back paddock, as part of his duties, Emil checked the boundary fence close to the patch of scrub containing the bush stockyard.

Wracked by indecision for most of the day, Emil found himself torn between obeying Ned's instruction not to go near the yard in the bush, or giving in to his curiosity and desire to take another look. Curiosity won out. At a point where the fence was closest to the scrub, in the most casual manner he could manage, he sauntered into the scrub. His point of entry was some way along from his former track to the yard. It required him to navigate by sound and instinct to find the yard again.

No one was at the yard, but it now held ten or twelve head of cattle. Far too small to hold so many animals, the confines of the yard stressed the cattle. Emil noted how agitated they were, and how little water remained for them in the small trough in the yard. "There is nothing I am able to do for those poor beasts," he whispered aloud. "I must return to checking the boundary fence before someone notices my absence." So upset by the plight of the cattle in the bush yard, Emil hoped tomorrow would show ten or twelve extra head added to Rangelands' herd overnight.

He made a mental note to check stock number in the paddocks tomorrow.

Before the others finished breakfast the next morning, Emil tended the stock. Careful to follow his usual routine, he checked the numbers in each paddock. It was in the last paddock, the one from which he entered the scrub the previous day, that Emil found the number of head increased. He guessed the increase was about right for it to be the animals from the bush stockyard and was elated when he recognised one with an unusual coat as a heifer he saw in the yard yesterday. He knew they should not be there, but justified the situation by the thought that at least the animals would have good feed and water in the paddock.

Following his discussion with Ned, and with the intention of handing it to Ned when next they met, Emil kept a log of anything he considered unusual happening on the property. When drafting out a few head to move to another paddock, Emil noticed something peculiar about the brands on some beasts. The brands looked recent. Close inspection suggested they were branded over older existing brands to produce something far removed from the original configuration. The resultant effort looked close to, but not quite the same, as those on Ned's cattle brought from Sweers Island.

In spite of his surveillance of activities on the property, Emil felt frustrated. His record of events lacked anything significant or definite about what was happening. Everything he had to pass on to Ned simply echoed information already provided. Emil hoped to solve the mystery of the strange incidents on the property, and to be able to lay it all out for Ned the next time they met. The dream appeared lost by the end of the second week of work on upgrading the cottage. The big break in Emil's sleuthing came on the night before he, Mads and Toby were to leave for Port Beauchamp.

Sleep eluded Emil for some time after everyone turned in for the night. He felt he let Ned down by not getting to the bottom of what was happening. After tossing and turning for ages and worrying about being too tired to be much use to anyone tomorrow, Emil crawled out of his bunk and slipped outside to attend to a call of nature. One small ember glowed red among the remains of the fire they sat around to keep warm earlier that night. It was a black moonless night. As he stepped around the fireplace on his way to the bunkhouse door, something stopped him in his tracks: cattle bellowing.

The sounds of disturbed cattle floated in on the heavy, dew-laden night air. Emil shivered as he moved away from the bunkhouse and out into the open to see around the stand of eucalypt trees blocking his view. In only thin night attire and with no boots, he wasn't dressed to be out and about. The cold seeped into his bones as he scanned the paddocks to determine where the noise came from. Then he saw it. The cold forgotten, he set off on foot for the bottom paddock, the one closest to the scrub.

Lanterns moving about in the distance pinpointed the location of the problem. Without giving thought to the matter, he moved through the paddocks towards the lanterns. Familiar with every inch of the ground from his weeks of working with the cattle, he unerringly made his way towards the lanterns. When half-way across the paddock before where the lanterns still danced about, the reality of his situation dawn on Emil. This is foolish, he chided himself. I might not be around to tell Ned anything if I go charging in like this. A hasty detour seemed prudent.

Instead on bowling straight on into the last paddock where the cattle now created quite a ruckus, Emil took a diagonal line across to the adjacent block. The herd's familiarity with him allowed Emil to move through the paddock without drawing attention to his presence as he used the herd as a screen. This longer route had him at the fence line prior to the scrub some distance downwind from the paddock where the lanterns continued moving about. He stood unmoving against a corner strainer post. The slight lad blended perfectly with the shadow of the post. No one came to investigate his presence. After waiting a few minutes, he judged it safe for the next, and possibly most dangerous, few yards of his journey.

Choosing the 'right' moment to make a move was almost impossible. It was dark everywhere, so there was nothing for it but to pluck up courage and go for it. A couple of deep breaths and he scrambled through the wires to lie flat on the ground on the other side of the fence. Still no one appeared to show any interest. He hesitated for a moment after climbing to his feet. Then, after one quick look at the lanterns, he dashed across the short distance and entered the scrub. Again he waited. No one came to investigate.

Where he entered the scrub was an unfamiliar area. He strained his ears for sounds to help orientate him before moving to the edge of the scrub and peering out. The last of the lanterns disappeared into the scrub as he watched. "Which direction to the bush stockyard?" he whispered as he peered through the trees. If at all possible, it seemed even darker in the scrub. Then he saw it: the faint glow of a lantern in the distance and off to his right.

If only a straight course were possible. As he picked his way slowly and quietly through the undergrowth and around trees, Emil was desperate not to lose sight of that lantern in the distance. It became brighter as he moved closer. Then he saw the other lanterns not too far ahead. That must be where the bush stock-yard is, Emil told himself. As he paused to gauge how close he was to the lanterns, Emil saw the lantern he followed become indistinguishable as it mingled with the others. Convinced he was close, he lifted and placed each foot with increased care as he eased forward.

Emil's stealthy hike through the scrub came to an abrupt halt when he heard voices. After inching forward another couple of metres, he flattened himself against the trunk of a large tree. Just ahead was the stockyard. In the light from the lanterns, he made out four men, but there were five lanterns. Where is the fifth man? Emil peered about wildly in the dark. His chest tightened with fear as he searched for that missing man. It might be safer to be further away.

Before moving away from the tree, Emil took one last look at the scene around the stockyard. The feeling of relief almost made him weak at the knees. Beside the stockyard rails on the side opposite him, a lantern hung from the low branch of a tree. It still might mean there is a fifth man, a man who hung his lantern in a tree to free his hands to do something, but somehow Emil didn't think that the case. Feeling safer, Emil focused on what the four men were doing.

There appeared to be a dispute happening. Voices became louder. "Keep it down before we attract company," someone growled. "All we need tonight is to wake those up there in the bunkhouse." Someone turned a lantern towards the speaker. Emil gasped. It was Meadows, the man he met recently and the man who is a partner in the property. Why is Meadows sneaking around in the bush on his own property, Emil wondered, and why is he so concerned with not waking 'those up there in the bunkhouse'?

For a brief period, they spoke so softly, Emil couldn't hear what was being said, but he made out quite a bit of swearing. The volume of their conversation soon rose again. Several times over the subsequent few minutes, Meadows told the others to keep their voices down. Dissention grew within the group until one man's voice cut across the argument. "...Nothing we can do about it. Tonight is a bust and we almost got caught. I say we turn the half dozen head here in the yard out into the paddock and call it a night. Maybe better luck next time, hey?"

Another angry voice asked when they were going to start having some money to show for their efforts. Meadows, who seemed to be the boss, responded. "There is nothing for it but to wait another month or so before selling cattle if we want to avoid suspicion. It's a delicate situation. We will have to be patient until the right moment presents, a time when I, as the part-owner, can initiate selling a few head."

A few moments of silence followed until another voice reignited matter. "I agree. We need to lie low for a while after nearly being caught tonight." Not all of the others agreed and a brief argument broke out.

Meadows brought it to an end. "That's enough. It will be about another month until the next likely moonless night. None of us are stupid enough to try anything more before then." The murmurs that followed appeared to be the others signifying their agreement. A few minutes later Emil watched them ride off. Six head of cattle remained in the bush stockyard. What would happen to those six head, and how long would they be left there?

It was nearly an hour later when Emil felt it safe to move. He was stiff all over and wet through from the heavy dew, but he knew what he must do before returning to the bunkhouse. Easing himself away from the tree, he crept to the stockyard. From his earlier visit, he knew where the slip rails were. Within no time, the rails were down, and Emil was on his way through the paddocks back to the bunkhouse.

Shivering and wet through, he climbed into his bunk. While it was still dark outside, he knew there could not be much of the night left. The men always rose early. Tomorrow – or is that today – will see an even earlier start to the day. Before they turned in last night, it was agreed the trio heading back to Port Beauchamp would be on the road at first light. Emil groaned inwardly at that thought as he felt his eyes growing heavy.

*****

How long had he slept? Emil felt he no sooner closed his eyes than someone was shaking him awake. "Come on, get up. We need to be gone early," Mads growled at him as Emil's eyelashes slowly untangled themselves. "You're wet. What have you been up to?" As he hauled himself out of bed, Emil explained he went out earlier to attend to a call of nature and found the dew heavier than usual. It wasn't a lie, just wasn't the whole truth, he told his conscience to placate it.

Toby had the big German wagon hitched, loaded and ready to go. By the time they finished breakfast, the others in the bunkhouse were up and came out to see them off. Emil knew that, for the next four or five days, there would be long, bone-jarring hours followed by cold, damp nights in a swag under the stars. Compensation for all that would come at the end when he joined Ned and Mathilde again.

The thought of meeting Ned again caused a frisson of excitement. He felt well satisfied with his report for Ned on happenings at Rangelands, and his previous night's efforts were its highlight. It was with these thoughts running through his mind he nodded off. With a grin at Toby, Mads shoved Emil against the side of wagon to prevent him toppling over.

Chapter 9 Relocation

His Marathon affairs dealt with, Ned, eager to implement his next plan, rode hard from Rangelands to Port Beauchamp. He had plenty to occupy his mind until he made camp at last light each day. Rangelands predominated his thinking for much of the journey. The conditions applying to the pastoral lease had to be met within a twelve months' timeframe.

As new leaseholders, Rixon and Meadows were granted an extra twelve months in which to meet the conditions. Before he went broke, the original lessee failed to meet the relevant conditions. Those conditions related to the area cleared and fenced within the first year, and there were residential requirements. By that first end of year inspection, the landholder had to prove residency on the property for at least six months, and to have constructed an acceptable residence. Those conditions were in addition to payment of the requisite annual fee.

At the end of the previous lessee's first year, the lessee had defaulted on the clearing and fencing requirements, and the inspector deemed the principal residence constructed for the landholder and his family as substandard. Undercapitalised, the lessee then defaulted on payments of fees at the end of the first year. As was the practice of the day, he was allowed another twelve months in which to make up the arrears as well as pay the second year's fees. Failure to do so resulted in forfeiture of the land, and the loss of any investment already made. With the prospect of losing everything looming large, the lessee opted to sell his lease to escape with a few shillings in his pocket.

There was no doubting Rixon and Meadows acquired the property cheaply. They paid the arrears and the next annual fee to secure the lease, and paid the original lessee a small sum for his improvements. It was an excellent property with good alluvial soil and abundant water supply. The bunkhouse, dairy and store were substantial enough buildings for the present time, but the homestead was little more than a ruined shack.

Ned felt confident Alf and his men had cleared scrub in excess of the required acreage to meet the lease conditions. Although the herd remained small, Ned believed that, by the end of the year, stock numbers would be sufficient. After relocating within the next couple of months, the residency condition applicable to the lessee would be met. From the outset, he understood Meadows intended residing on the property, and was surprised when this had not yet occurred. Nevertheless, one of the partners in permanent residence on the property should suffice. That only left the matter of the constructing a durable homestead over the next few months.

Thoughts of Rangelands and his partner, Richard Meadows, took him back to his recent time in Marathon. While in the township, he had hoped to discuss the property with Meadows and to ascertain Meadows' future involvement. His inquiries around town drew a blank. Consensus was that nobody had seen Meadows for some time. He was thought to be out of town. Frustrating though it was, Ned accepted that, like himself, Meadows had other business interests to keep him out of town for periods of time. While he accepted the situation, Ned reminded himself that, as soon as the household relocated, there must be concerted effort to locate Meadows.

Long days of hard riding saw Ned make camp his last night under the stars a few miles out of Beauchamp. Sometime during the day, the weather developed a bite. Heavy dew coated everything by the time he stopped to make camp. After setting a substantial fire and an evening meal of dry bread and cheese, he was grateful for the warmth of his swag. Sleep would not take long to arrive tonight, he thought as he listened to the wind sighing through the surrounding bush. He looked forward to being back at the cottage tomorrow, and felt a tingle of anticipation at the thought of seeing Mathilde again.

As he drifted off to sleep, Mathilde's image floated before his mind's eye: flawless pale complexion, shining golden hair, and those enthralling blue eyes that swallowed you up at every glance. How did someone so young get to be so capable, so mature ... and so attractive? Ned sighed heavily and pulled the thin blanket higher over his shoulders.

Morning dawned cold and thin through the trees. Ned wasted no time rolling his swag and climbing back into the saddle. He would be in Port Beauchamp before lunch, and he had plenty to do once he was back in town.

*****

While Ned made camp that night, Alf inspected Mads' modifications to the former stores building. "Just a bit of tidying up left to do; should finish it tomorrow." Mads told him. "What do you think? Will it meet with Ned's approval?"

"You've done an amazing job, Mads. Ned will be hard pressed to recognise the building. I notice the smell of mould and leather dressing is all but gone. If we leave the place open until it's time to move stuff into it, all trace of the smell should disappear."

The old building now boasted a semi-detached kitchen complete with fireplace, a combined dining/sitting room area, and two small bedrooms. Mads beamed with pride when Alf declared it 'very nice'. Leaving Mads to work on in peace, Alf wandered off to think about what would need doing once construction was complete. Without saying anything specific, Ned seemed in a hurry to relocate to Rangelands. That only involved moving Mathilde, some furniture, and a few other bits and pieces from the Port Beauchamp cottage to the new property. Still, it would leave Alf shorthanded for a few weeks, and the old German wagon needed to be checked to make sure it was up to the job ahead of it.

It took Mads a little longer than anticipated to finish the renovations at around lunchtime on the second day after Alf's inspection. Over lunch, it was agreed Mads, Emil and Toby would leave with the German wagon the next day. "Should we also take the other old wagon I repaired?" Mads asked. "It might come in handy if there are many belongings to bring back."

"Good thinking, Mads. You and Emil take the German wagon and Toby can take the other one. Spend the rest of the afternoon preparing for a start at first light tomorrow."

The two wagons headed out as the sun made its way over the distant hills. Alf watched them for some way along the track before wandering aimlessly back into the camp. His mind wrestled with a thought that continued to trouble him. After exploring it for a few days, he was no closer to finding an answer.

*****

There was a distinct chill in the air as Ned Rixon rode into Port Beauchamp. Even for the height of winter in this part of the country, this was exceptionally cold. A strong dry westerly wind arrived a few days earlier and seemed in no hurry to leave. It gained strength overnight to tumble anything loose before it as it howled through the town. Decked out in overcoats and scarves, only those needing to be out braved the streets that day. Wasting no time on his way through town, Ned rode directly to his cottage and the warmth provided by the kitchen fireplace.

His unexpected arrival had Mathilde bustling about making tea, preparing his room, and fussing over him. After lunch, he rugged up and ventured into town to visit his store. Mr Kincaid, clad in overcoat, scarf and mittens, ushered him through to the back office. Even with the front door partially closed, the wind blew in, bringing a generous helping of dust with it. It was freezing inside the store and Ned wondered how staff managed to work under all their bulky winter clothing. After devoting a few moments thought to how to improve conditions in the store and deciding there was little he could do to alleviate the situation, Ned pulled his coat tighter around him, turned up its collar and took his place behind the huge wooden desk. He had a list to prepare. A bit of cold weather would not delay his plans.

By the end of the day, Mr Kincaid had a list of equipment and supplies to put together, as well as instructions to source the purchase of a suitable dray or wagon. The first stage of his relocation plan completed, Ned hurried back to the cottage.

Although heat from the kitchen warmed the cottage, Ned strode straight through to stand beside the kitchen fireplace. As he stood warming his hands, he stole a few glances at Mathilde as she went about preparing dinner.

Why is she wearing her coat, he wondered? It's quite warm in the kitchen, and must be hot standing there stirring the pots on the hob. Her face has a sheen to it and glows red. Is that from the heat of the fire, or because she is hot from the bulky coat she never seems to remove? It might be a 'woman thing' he decided, and opted not to ask about it. That decision probably was influenced in part by the fact that Mathilde seemed distant, a change in her Ned noticed shortly after he arrived.

At first, he thought it was because he had arrived unexpectedly and she was upset about not being prepared for him. If that were the case, things should have returned to normal by now. They hadn't and he became increasingly aware of the distance between them. He wracked his brain for some clue as to what he did to offend her, but found nothing. Nothing for it but to let it run its course, he told himself.

Over the next two or three days, the weather gradually warmed again as the normal south-easterly trade winds replaced the westerlies. The store kept Ned busy. Mr Kincaid had a list of issues for Ned's attention, accounts to pay and discussions to have with the bank manager. By the end of his first week back in Port Beauchamp, Ned believed everything was in readiness for their relocation. All that remained was to wait for the others to arrive with the wagons. Each evening over dinner, he discussed the relocation with Mathilde and updated her on progress. It left Ned mystified. Mathilde seemed interested but unenthusiastic. In desperation, he asked if she would prefer to remain at Port Beauchamp. She assured him she would not, and was looking forward to their new home on the property.

Then the wagons arrived and, for a couple of days, life became hectic. There was packing to do and wagons to load, and a suitable team to be purchased for the new dray. At one stage, Ned found himself wondering if it might not have been prudent to load it all onto the next boat heading for Marathon instead of messing about with wagons. That was until he realised he would still require wagons to move everything from the port at Marathon to the property. Emil was anxious to engineer some time alone with Ned, but the opportunity never arose. Everyone was too busy. He had to accept that his best opportunity might come on their way back to the property.

The night before they were due to leave Port Beauchamp, Ned organised a farewell dinner at a local hotel. Mr Kincaid, the bank manager, and a couple of other long-time business associates joined them. It was a strange night; a mixture of anticipation and sadness. Both Mads and Ned noticed Mathilde seemed a little withdrawn and showing no sign of looking forward to the journey ahead.

Ned dismissed it as sadness at leaving somewhere she had become settled. Mathilde spent a large slab of the day visiting neighbours. The two women living on either side of the cottage had become Mathilde's close friends. It wasn't too difficult to understand her sadness at leaving them behind, and the prospect of having to make a new start in a new location with no other females close by. Both he and Mads tried reassuring her but with little success.

It was an early start the next day as the convoy headed out of town. Mads and Mathilde travelled on the German wagon, while Toby and Emil rode on Rangelands' repaired wagon. Ned took the new dray, and tied his horse on behind. At a designated clearing on the outskirts of town, they waited for the others to arrive. There would be a significant number of wagons on this trip.

Soon after Ned's return to Port Beauchamp, Mr Kincaid apprised him of a recent spate of inquiries regarding travelling overland to Marathon. Some inquiries were from new arrivals in the community. Others were from people who lived in town for some time. A few Scandinavian new arrivals thought to load their few belongings into handcarts and walk to Marathon. There was a good chance they all would become lost. The track to Marathon was not well defined, and not for the inexperienced traveller. At Ned's urging, Kincaid became something of a trip co-ordinator. He managed to persuade the 'handcart brigade' to abandon their original plans and acquire three wagons to use between them. A large contingent of Irish immigrants straight off the boat at Port Beauchamp was a late addition to the cavalcade.

In spite of their early start, it was about nine o'clock, after much messing about sorting out people and wagons, before the convoy headed south with Toby and Emil's wagon in the lead. The German wagon followed by Ned's dray were on to the tail end. Wagons heavily laden with passengers and goods make slow progress over rough bush tracks. It would take at least four weeks of camping under the stars before they reached their destinations.

*****

Late on the seventh day out from Port Beauchamp, Mathilde became ill. She gathered firewood with Emil for their evening camp when the first pain came. After struggling back to the wagon, she sent Emil to fetch Mrs Tomlins from one of the wagons. "Tell her I am ill and I am not sure what I should do. Ask her, if she can spare the time, to come to me in my wagon." As she waited for Mrs Tomlins, Mathilde thought of the kind, elderly English woman with whom she had developed a friendship while travelling.

Although their camp for the night was in a large clearing, it wasn't big enough for all the wagons. Off one end of the main clearing were two smaller areas, each just large enough for one wagon. As the last two wagons to arrive, Mads and Ned parked in those small clearings. By the time Mrs Tomlins reached Mathilde in the German wagon, she was out of breath. "I ran all the way as fast as me legs would take me when the young lad told me you was so ill," she gasped at Mathilde. "What is 'appening here? Quickly, tell me."

"You told me you were sort of midwife back in your old country. I think I need your help now," Mathilde managed to say before the next pains stopped her.

It took Mrs Tomlins no time to assess the situation. "Is the father around? Do 'e know what's 'appening?"

"There is no father. Please send Emil away so he does not know what is happening."

After sending Emil back to his own wagon, Mrs Tomlins came back to Mathilde. "We need to get a few things together. This 'ere baby of yours is about to arrive and we be needing to be ready for it."

Mathilde pointed to a bag she had dragged close by. "I put together a ... a kit ... of what I think is needed."

Over the next hour, Mathilde tells Mrs Tomlins the story of her pregnancy. "I know nothing of this, or of giving birth, but a couple of women neighbours at Port Beauchamp helped me understand and prepare for the birth. But, from what they told me, it is too soon for this baby to arrive. I don't think the birth should be for another five weeks or more."

"Now, don't you be worrying your pretty head about that. Babies come when they decide. We are all set up for it. Do anyone else ... your father ... know about your condition?"

Mathilde shakes her head and bites her hand to stifle a scream before answering. "Papa and Mr Rixon are off in the bush somewhere collecting firewood. I don't want them here until this is over."

"Okay, I'll keep a sharp eye out for them coming back. Uh-oh, it sounds like the Irish mob are about to kick off their usual night's entertainment."

There was little chance of conversation after that. The Irish contingent had their fiddles and accordions out and singing around the camp's bonfire had begun. Soon the dancing would begin, and the volume of the music and singing would rise to deafening levels. Mrs Tomlins was thankful she was so far removed from it tonight. As she sponged Mathilde's face, Mrs Tomlins thought she heard men's voices approaching. She dashed out of the wagon in time to intercept Mads and Ned while still some distance away.

She did not mince her words when telling Mads his daughter was ill and wished to be left alone. "I must be with my daughter to look after her," Mads replied, and attempted to step around Mrs Tomlins. He hadn't counted on this feisty English woman.

"No you don't," Mrs Tomlins said as she slammed both beefy hands into his chest. "I am looking after her. She does not want you 'ere right now, so bugger off and find something to do elsewhere. I'll be letting you know when and if she wants to see you." Mads' attempts to bulldoze past the woman met with increased resistance.

Ned felt compelled to intervene. Clapping a hand hard on Mads' shoulder, he said, "Er, I think this might be women's business. Maybe we should make ourselves scarce for a while. Come back to the dray with me. We'll set a fire and have a tot or two of rum while we wait." While Mrs Tomlins spoke, a thought about what might be wrong with Mathilde started developing in the back of his mind. It was beyond belief – impossible – and he fought to prevent the rogue idea developing further.

As he shook off Ned's hand, Mads demanded of Mrs Tomlins, "What is wrong with my daughter? She was all right when we made camp. How can she become so ill so quickly? I am her father. I must go to her. Stand out of my way."

"Don't be stupid. Your daughter is about to give birth. That wagon is no place for you or any other man right now. As the man 'ere says," Mrs Tomlins said as she pointed to Ned, "This is women's work that's to be done. You can go find something else to keep you busy while we get on with it. Now, I need to be with my patient."

Ned again placed a hand on Mads' shoulder and said quietly, "Come, Mads. For Mathilde's sake, let the woman get back to what she must do."

"Take your hand off me," Mads growled as he spun around to face Ned. "You did this. What happened to my daughter is your fault. You must pay for what you have done. I will not let you get away with what you did to Mathilde." Mads lashed out at Ned, who parried the blow and stepped back a couple of paces.

"What are you accusing me of? I have done nothing to harm Mathilde. Are you saying you think the child is mine?" Mads tried again to make contact with Ned's jaw. Ned ducked the punch. "I have nothing but respect for Mathilde, and have always looked out for her. How can you accuse me of such behaviour? Of course the child is not mine."

"Maybe it is not yours, but it is your fault it has happened. I left my daughter in your care when I went away to work for you. You did not take proper care of her. If you looked after her properly, this would not happen. My daughter would not be going through what she is now in that wagon. I trusted you to look after her. You broke that trust." Mads tried to land another punch. It had as much success as his previous attempt.

"Stop that! You stupid man; trying to flog the daylights out of your mate 'ere won't change anything. What's been done is done. Now, we all need to think about what's best for the girl. As for you friend here being responsible, that's a laugh. If anyone is responsible, it's you, her father, who is responsible." Mrs Tomlins thumped Mads' chest in case there was any mistake about whom she blamed.

Mads looked shocked. He tried to speak but could only splutter. Then his shock turned to anger. Ned, seeing the change come over Mads, stepped between Mads and Mrs Tomlins. "Perhaps Mrs Tomlins should explain her accusation."

Mrs Tomlins did not require a second invitation. "It was you, her father, who did not protect her properly. Your daughter was raped on board ship earlier on the night you were shipwrecked. Down in the hold, everyone was seasick. She too began to feel ill from the smell. The need for fresh air made her go up on deck. A short while after she went up, a crewman grabbed her and raped her. When it was over, she rushed back down to you, but you and the rest of her family were so sick, she couldn't tell you about it. Then the ship went down, taking most of the family with it. By the time the three of you were safe again and things had settled down, it didn't seem so important anymore. Mathilde decided it would remain her secret. She hoped that, with time, she might put it out of her mind. It wasn't until sometime after you arrived at Port Beauchamp she realised what happened on board that night left more than a memory. Mathilde kept her condition secret; wore her coat all the time to hide her bump as it got bigger. A couple of women neighbours she befriended helped her understand what was happening and told her what to expect. Now, you 'ave wasted enough of my time. I 'ave work to do." With that, Mrs Tomlins turned on her heel and strode off. With the men dealt with, Mrs Tomlins' concern was for her patient.

Still in a state of shock and realising the woman was not going to let him see his daughter, Mads trudged after Ned to the dray.

"Oh Lordy; just made it the nick o' time," Mrs Tomlins announced as she checked Mathilde. "Your little one is coming out. It's lucky the camp's party is in full swing. Nobody can hear what's going on in here above that racket."

Then, after what felt like an eternity, Mathilde lay back gasping and exhausted.

"It's a boy," Mrs Tomlin announced with a noticeable absence of enthusiasm. "There's more for you to do yet. In the meantime, I'll do what I 'ave to with the little fellow."

No point in worrying her yet, Mrs Tomlins thought. Let her finish the job first and then see where we're at. It seemed to be a long time after he was born before Mathilde heard his weak little cry. She also saw the worried look on Mrs Tomlins' face, and noticed the woman was busy doing something where Mathilde couldn't see. Exhausted and confident her friend knew what she was doing, Mathilde lie back to wait for the moment when the little bundle wrapped in a piece torn from a bedsheet was placed in her arms.

He was tiny, barely moved and appeared to be asleep. Mathilde gave Mrs Tomlins a worried look that sought the woman's reassurance everything was okay. She had expected more. This seemed an anti-climax. Mrs Tomlins patted her hand and told her, "You just lie there and get acquainted with your little chap. I'll just nip out to let your father know it's all over and he now has a grandson." Before Mathilde could stop her, Mrs Tomlins was out of the wagon and on her way to talk to Mads and Ned who waited under the trees a little way off.

"It's all over. Your daughter is fine. You 'ave a little grandson." Mads made to stride past her to go to the wagon. "No, no, Sir. Hold up for a moment. There's more you need to know before you go blundering in there. The little fellow came early, is tiny, and was blue all over when 'e were born. I 'ad to rub and rub and rub before 'e would take a breath. Then, such a pitiful little cry... I've seen many like him in the past in the poorer parts of London. I fear 'e will not last long. They ne'er do. You should prepare yourself for that. I must get back to the mother. I'll fetch you when it's okay for you to see her."

Both at a loss for words, Mads and Ned wandered back to the dray to sit by the fire with their pannikins of rum. Each alone with his own thoughts; neither wanted conversation. A little over an hour later, Mrs Tomlins emerged again from the wagon. She didn't hurry to the two men who came to meet her. The look on her face said it all long before she delivered her message.

"The baby died a few minutes ago. I am so sorry. It was obvious from the moment 'e came out, 'e wasn't going to make it. Might be a blessing 'e went so quick like, and didn't hang around lingering. I think Mathilde realised what the outcome would be from the moment she first 'eld 'im. Your daughter is upset but she is sleeping now. I'll stay with 'er until morning. We'll see 'ow she is then." After Mads thanked Mrs Tomlins, he and Ned spent a few moments shuffling their feet and wondering what to do or say.

Mads felt the emotion building in his throat and, rather than let the others see, he turned to walk away. Mrs Tomlins quietly called him back.

"The law in this state is the same as everywhere else. All births and deaths need to be registered with the authorities. That same law applies to Mathilde's little chap. It seems like a lot of trouble to go to for someone who was 'ere for no more than a blink in time. That aside, there still is a tiny body that needs burying. We can't take 'im with us all the way to Marathon. Perhaps the sooner it's done the better … if you see what I mean. I'll leave you to think about the burial and the registration paperwork, but no one besides the four of us knows what went on here tonight. Mebbe it would be kinder for Mathilde if there were no record for anyone else to find out about it. In time, we all might forget about tonight. Like I said, I'll leave you to decide, gentlemen."

"No time needed, Mrs Tomlins. This quiet patch of scrub is a nice place to lay a child to rest," Ned said. "Mads and I will discuss the paperwork, but I don't think either of us is too fond of red tape. Unless you have some objection, we will keep the body with us before taking care of it at first light tomorrow." While Mads went back to the dray, Ned accompanied Mrs Tomlins to the wagon to collect the body.

With the body tucked out of sight on the dray, Ned and Mads sat in silence beside the fire – until Toby and Emil intruded. "Emil said Mathilde is ill; real sick," Toby said. "We didn't want to come and disturb her if she were resting, but we want to know how she is."

While Mads struggled to come up with a response, Ned stepped in. "Mathilde is much improved and is sleeping now. We'll see how she is tomorrow but we think she might benefit from a couple of days' rest. Toby, tomorrow you and Emil should lead the wagons out of the camp. Mads and I will remain behind. Everything should remain as normal for you and the rest of the travellers. Continue on your way until you reach the place where the track to Rangelands branches off the main track. Point the other wagons to Marathon and send them on their way. They can't get into trouble. The only track beyond that point leads straight on into the township. Once the others are on their way, you and Emil wait for us to join you at the start of the Rangelands track. We should arrive at the property together."

Toby said, "Yes, Sir, Mr Rixon. We can do that." Emil was not so keen. He looked pleadingly at Mads in the hope his uncle would allow him to stay and ride the rest of the way on the German wagon with Mads and Mathilde. It didn't work.

"No, Emil. You will go with Toby to help him and the rest of the wagons. I want no argument." Emil nodded his agreement, but disappointment masked his face. Now I won't be able to give Mr Rixon my report, he thought.

As planned, at first light, Ned and Mads made their way into the bush. Both men carried shovels and Ned also carried another small bundle wrapped tightly in an old oilskin. At a quiet spot some way into the bush, they dug a grave and buried Mathilde's baby. In response to Ned's concern animals might disturb the grave, they collected a few small boulders and placed them on top. For a brief moment, they discussed the fact that the child hadn't been named before agreeing that it didn't matter. Then, after Mads said a few words in Danish over the grave, the deed was done and the men were on their way back to the campsite.

Mrs Tomlins finished checking on her patient as the men reached the wagon. She confirmed that Mathilde was doing well and had taken a little nourishment. The men's intention to rest there for a couple of days met with Mrs Tomlins approval. Mrs Tomlins said goodbye and rushed off to join her husband on their wagon.

The planned rest days went by without further drama. By the time they were ready to move off on the third day, Mathilde insisted she was well enough to ride up front with her father … and they needed time alone together. They had much to discuss.

Although Ned did not anticipate seeing the travellers and their wagons again, he was surprised when, at the end of the last day before they reached the turnoff to Rangelands, they caught up with the others. After a surreptitious check on her patient, Mrs Tomlins pronounced Mathilde fit and well. Midwife and patient shared a long hug before the group split up, and Mrs Tomlins and the others headed for Marathon.

After watching the wagons for a short distance along the main track, Ned called his team together. "Right, if we get moving now, barring any mishaps, we should be home before dusk. Let's get these wagons moving." As she sat up beside her father, Mathilde couldn't decide whether she felt excitement or trepidation at what awaited her in this next phase of her life in this new land.

Chapter 10 The New Cottage

The sun was low to the distant hills as the convoy of three wagons rolled onto Rangelands. Only Alf Grant saw them arrive and came to welcome them home. Alf suggested the first thing Mads should do was to introduce Mathilde to her new home. Mads needed no encouragement. It had been an agonising wait for Mads to show off his handiwork.

"Come this way with me, Daughter. Let me show you where we will be living as a family again."

Emil made to bolt after Mads and Mathilde as they started towards the cottage. Alf grabbed him by the arm and held him back. "All in good time, Lad, all in good time. Allow Mathilde to look around before you go belting in there."

"But it is to be my home too," Emil protested. "Why can't I look too?"

"You saw all the work as it happened. You know what the place looks like inside. Allow your uncle to show off his handiwork to his daughter without you in the way." Feeling hard done by, Emil skulked off to sit on a nearby stump and sulk.

With Emil out of earshot, Ned spoke quietly to Alf. "This isn't the building we earmarked for renovation. Wasn't the chosen building that one over there? What happened?"

"You weren't here. We couldn't check with you. When we looked at the old dairy, it seemed far too small. To make it liveable would require extensive work. Apart from that, we thought, once everyone was here, the dairy might be returned to use. It seemed logical not to mess about with it until we knew its future. By the way, the renovated building is now referred to as *the cottage.*"

"Perhaps I too should check out Mads' handiwork now. After that we need to set up for the night before it becomes dark." On entering the cottage, Mads' voice caught their attention. "… And we managed to fit in two small bedrooms. Mathilde, I thought this one would be your room – unless you prefer the other." Mathilde approved the room and wandered into explore it.

With their tour of inspection over, Mads suggested Mathilde light a fire in the kitchen fireplace to help warm the cottage before they turned in for the night. Then it was time to unload the wagons. They needed beds and bedlinen for the night, and 'kitchen stuff' to prepare breakfast in the morning. Everything else on the wagons could wait until tomorrow. Alf and Ned completed their tour of the cottage before following Mads out to where the men unloaded the wagons.

"Dinner will be at the bunkhouse tonight," Alf announced. "The boys have an enormous stew cooking. There is more than enough for everyone."

"Perhaps we might go to the bunkhouse now so I can catch up on what happened here during my absence," Ned suggested.

On their way to the bunkhouse, Alf asked the question nagging him since the wagons arrived. "Where do you intend sleeping?"

"Eh? What do you mean by that? I'll be sleeping in the … ah, I see your point."

"The cottage has two bedrooms, one of which will be Mathilde's. Mads and Emil will be in the second bedroom. I'm sure Mads will not allow anyone else to sleep in the cottage unless he is there to watch over his daughter."

That's true, Ned thought, especially after the events on the trip from Port Beauchamp. But details of that were not something he would share with Alf. Nevertheless, Ned hadn't envisaged his current situation.

"Yes, yes. I get the picture. I just hadn't thought on the matter until you asked. It's not a problem. I will live in the bunkhouse with the rest of you. There are plenty of spare bunks in there."

"Hmm … that's true. It would be okay for a short while. The chaps might tolerate your presence for a time, but the enjoyment of your company will soon wear off. The men need time away from management. It's bad enough that they can't get away *from* me now I live in there with them. They have no time away from being under management scrutiny. That is likely to create a stressful situation with potential unhelpful consequences."

"I stand suitably enlightened. Again, I had not thought the matter through. You and I must make time tomorrow to go over a number of things … not the least of which is where I am to live… and, I suppose, where you are to live in the future. The only thing clear at the moment is that the former lessee's home can never be inhabited again."

John Oakes joined Ned and Alf in a drink while they waited for the others to join them for dinner. The alluring aroma of the stew coerced everyone. All tucked in with enthusiasm. After dinner, Alf allocated tasks for the following day.

"Toby, first thing tomorrow, you will help Mads finish unloading the wagons and setting up the cottage, then join us in the bottom paddock. Now, young Emil, your life is about to become busy. You will resume feeding and watering the stock as you did in the past. The rest of your time will be spent around the cottage assisting Mathilde. There's a kitchen garden to be started, firewood to be chopped and stacked, and water to be carried from the well to the kitchen door. First thing in the morning, set up a barrel to serve as a water butt close to the kitchen."

With nothing more to do except turn in for the night, the group dispersed. The three Eriksens returned to the cottage. Ned wandered outside for a last look at the stars before deciding which bunk to claim. It was a cold dewy night again. At least we all will sleep under proper cover tonight, he thought as he went back inside.

*****

No need for alarm clocks at Rangelands, everyone rose with the sun. Emil bounced into the bunkhouse bright and early to announce that Mathilde expected Ned and Alf for breakfast in the cottage. The two men accepted the invitation and followed Emil and the smell of breakfast back to the cottage.

With breakfast over, the table cleared and the others off attending to their respective chores, Ned and Alf remained at the table. Ned took charge. "First up, we should inspect the existing buildings. Decisions are needed about future usage of the existing ones and if new ones are required. After that, I suggest we take a ride around the property to show me what has been done. There are a few other matters I need to talk over with you, but they can wait until after we inspect the property."

Their buildings inspections took longer than expected and brought them back to where they started. Emil ran out to meet them as they neared the cottage. "You are in time for morning tea. Mathilde said for you to join us." The smell of fresh baking made the offer impossible to resist.

Inspecting the cleared areas, the new fencing, and the herd, took until lunchtime. Then Ned and Alf returned to the cottage for lunch Afterwards, the two men remained at the table to talk further about the future of the place and the work required. While Alf sat waiting for Ned to open discussions, Ned drummed his fingers on the table and gazed into the distance. At last he spoke.

"Right now, my main concern is that I am operating unilaterally. That's not how partnerships are supposed to work. I'm even not sure about establishing a proper homestead. From the outset, Meadows claimed he would move onto the property and make it his permanent residence. So far, he's made no move to do so. There hasn't been sign of him and no word from him. I asked around while I was in Marathon for the opening of the new store. Nobody knew where he was, other than 'out of town'."

"As long as we don't do anything detrimental to the best interest of the business, does it matter if you don't consult Mr Meadows?" While not prepared to admit it to Ned, Alf would be perfectly happy for Meadows to stay away permanently. Too many times he had heard the man described as a *wrong 'un to* doubt the truth of it.

"Yeah, I think it does. That old homestead occupies the best place to build a new house for me and the Eriksens. Meadows might have the same intention … or, perhaps he has ideas of doing up what's left of the old place. It won't make for a happy partnership if he arrives to find I've scuttled his plans."

"Well, I still think you should go ahead and do whatever you want. In the meantime, what are your thoughts about the old dairy? It still looks to be in good condition."

"A dairy would be a nice addition to life here. It comes down to whether Mathilde wants one or not. If she is interested in having homemade butter and cheese, perhaps that's something else to add to Emil's list of duties: helping out in the dairy."

For a while, their discussions focused on the existing buildings and their use, including necessary repairs to the stores building, and the building that had become the tack shed. They were about to move onto other matters when another thing to do with buildings occurred to Ned. "I didn't identify any building worth turning into a cottage for you. After drawing my attention to the matter last night, I appreciate you can't continue living in the bunkhouse forever. It occurs to me that building a new homestead would leave the cottage vacant."

"While that would be ideal for me, it requires a decision about the erection of a new homestead. You just pointed out your difficulties associated with that."

Discussions moved onto other matters relating to the operation of the property. "Progress to date has been good, although quite slow. Losing workers to other projects in recent weeks hasn't helped. With Mads and Emil likely to be confined to working around here for some time to come, it leaves only John Oakes, Toby and I to do everything else. We are not going to be well placed when spring arrives and the rains come again. I need more men – and soon – if we are to be in a position to capitalise on opportunities over the next few months."

"Again, this is something that should not be my decision alone. It is something the partners should decide."

"In the interest of keeping the place going and making it pay its way, I doubt Meadows could argue with your making unilateral decisions when necessary. After all, his investment is at stake here as well as yours."

"It appears everything hinges on Meadows, what he wants and how he wants it to happen. I need to make a concerted effort to contact him. Perhaps, the day after tomorrow, I should head into Marathon. Maybe if I shake the tree hard enough something might fall out – if you get my meaning."

"Are you suggesting Meadows is deliberately avoiding you?" Ned shrugged in reply. Alf persisted. "Is there something to make you wonder about it?" The comment 'I told you so' came squarely to mind for Alf as they spoke. He had tried to warn Ned about Meadows' reputation. The reprimand he received then ensured he would not mention it again now.

After scuffling the dirt with the toe of his boot for a moment or two, Ned drew a deep breath and shook his head. "No, I don't have anything. I suppose it is frustration talking. I find it frustrating when I can't progress matters as I want to, especially important matters such as establishing this place properly. Still, as with me, this isn't Meadows' only business interest. The man no more spends his whole life in Marathon than I do. If I could find out where he is, I would go there to discuss everything with him." With another shake of his head, Ned changed the subject. "Let's talk about stock numbers instead for a moment."

The rest of the day slipped by without either man noticing. Their deliberations on the future of Rangelands came to an end when Mathilde announced she needed to set the table for dinner, and suggested the men might find something to do elsewhere for half an hour until dinner was served. Ned and Alf adjourned to the bunkhouse for a pre-dinner rum swizzle and for John Oakes' report on the day's work.

After dinner, the two men and Mads lingered at the dining table. Mathilde and Emil worked around them clearing it. "Mathilde, when you have finished, please join us for a few minutes," Ned said.

Still drying her hands on her apron as she sat down, Mathilde sat nervously opposite Ned. "I'm not sure if the others have spoken to you about the old dairy." Mathilde shook her head. "Right. Well, the small building beyond the well is a dairy. It's in need of a clean-up and some minor work, but would make an excellent dairy again. My question is, do you want to have a dairy? I realise it would mean more work for you, but we thought Emil might help out with some of it."

Mathilde studied the tabletop as she chose her words with care. "Y-e-e-s, a dairy would be a good thing. We will need to milk everyday anyway to have milk for all of us to use – and we could make butter. It would be nice to make some cheeses, but we could do that only now during winter. For the rest of the year, I think the weather is too hot and the cheeses will go bad. How soon would the dairy be ready to use? Have you spoken to Emil about this? He already seems quite busy with all his chores."

"Not yet; we wanted your opinion first. We will talk to Emil in the morning. By the way, where is he? He seemed to disappear after dinner."

"Mr Rixon, where do you think he went?" Mathilde laughed. "He went to the bunkhouse to be with the other men for a while. He was here with me all day and hasn't spent any time with them."

After arranging to inspect the dairy with Mads next morning to determine the work required, Ned and Alf took their leave and returned to the bunkhouse for the night. On their way across, Alf said quietly, "Mark my words, it will be only a short time before Emil comes looking for a bed in the bunkhouse with the rest of us. He has lived with us for too long now to go back to sharing a room with his uncle. I'm not sure how Mads will take it when it happens."

Alf is right, Ned thought. Emil has grown up a lot in the last few months and now considers himself one of the men. Alf will have to keep an eye on him for a bit. Having to spend his days helping Mathilde with domestic chores might not sit well with him.

Before he dropped off to sleep that night, Ned devoted some thought to those things he must take care of tomorrow before heading into Marathon the following day. He didn't know how long his trip would keep him away from the property, but suspected it would be more than a couple of days.

*****

"Ned, will you need me around here today? I'd like to give the men a hand in the bottom paddock. Will you be okay to sort out with Mads what you want done with the dairy?" Alf asked over breakfast. A short while later, Alf rode out with the others as Ned and Mads began their inspection of the dairy.

Emil was filling the kitchen water butt when Ned called to him to ask Mathilde to join them at the dairy. As Mathilde strode to the dairy, Emil hung back in the kitchen doorway. His long face a clear indication of his resentment at not being included. "Come here, Emil. We need your thoughts as well," Ned yelled.

Their inspection took no time. Mathilde assured them all it needed was a clean and a couple of minor repairs. Emil remained silent throughout the inspection. Sensing something was amiss, Ned attempted to draw him out.

"So Emil, what is your assessment of this facility? Do you think it will be okay?"

The inquiry brought a sullen look from the lad. "I suppose so. I don't see how it matters what I think. What has it to do with me anyway?" Mads went to chastise Emil for his rudeness. Ned stopped him.

"It has everything to do with you. Mathilde will be too busy in the cottage to manage the dairy as well. We were hoping that, if the dairy were up and running again, you might take charge of it. Of course, it is an important job and, if you don't think you are up to the task, we might have to rethink the situation."

"Of course I am up to the task. I can run the dairy. This was one of my jobs on our farm back home. I agree with Mathilde that making cheese in summer in this country will be impossible.

105

It would go off before it matured. What would I have to do here … the milking and the butter making?"

"Ah, that is good to hear. Yes; both the milking and the butter making, and anything else you and Mathilde think you can do with the milk you collect."

"How soon will it be ready to use? One of the cows had a calf. She is ready for milking and, now we are all here, we need fresh milk every day."

Ned dropped Mads a sly wink before replying. "If you are quite certain you can manage this, I think the dairy might be back in business again within a couple of days. What say you, Mads?"

"If it is cleaned today … make those repairs tomorrow … Yes, I'd say the day after tomorrow it should be right to go."

All trace of Emil's belligerence gone, he pushed himself away from the railing he leaned against. "I'll go fetch the buckets, brushes and things so we can make a start. Matilde, do we have any carbolic we can use to clean in here?"

With the two youngsters on their way to the cottage, Mads turned to Ned. "Nicely handled, Boss. If Emil has his way, I am about to have a busy, wet day helping him clean this place. He is right though. He would have learned all about dairies from living on the family farm. I am amazed how well he has adjusted to leaving his home and his parents to travel to a land so far from the life he knew. It is good he and Mathilde have become close. They look after each other."

A smug feeling oozed through Ned as he walked away. I do like it when things come together to deliver a great outcome, he told himself. With the dairy ticked off on his list of things to do today, Ned's next task was to join Alf and the others working in the bottom paddock. As he went into the new tack room to select a bridle and saddle, Emil called to him from the doorway of the stores building.

"Sir, could I have a moment please?" Ned detoured to Emil.

"What is it, Emil? You're not having second thoughts about taking on the dairy, are you?"

"No, Sir. I wanted to give you something. I know you plan to ride to Marathon tomorrow, so I wanted to give you this before you go. Begging your pardon, Mr Rixon, but I urge you to read what I have written before you leave … better still, before you go to join the others this morning." Emil handed Ned the report he wrote, and then left for the dairy.

Mystified by it all, Ned decided to comply with Emil's suggestion to read the rolled up document before he rode out. Perched uncomfortably on a bag of potatoes, Ned unrolled the multipage document and began reading. When he finished, stunned by its contents, Ned sat staring at the ground for what seemed a long time. In reality, it was only a minute or so before he was on his feet and striding towards the dairy. Although only halfway there, he called Emil to him. Hearing the urgency in Ned's voice, a nervous Emil ran out to meet him.

"Perhaps you could leave the cleaning for a few minutes for a chat. Let's adjourn to the bunkhouse for privacy."

Instead of entering the building, they perched on a couple of old stumps near the fireplace out front. "This is an interesting report, Emil. Are you confident everything you recorded is correct? If you are not *sure* about anything you wrote, but *think* your interpretation of what you saw is correct, please tell me." Emil strenuously denied having any doubts about the accuracy of the contents of his report. "Your uncle might not be happy about being left to do all the cleaning of the dairy, but I think you and I should take a ride to look at that stockyard in the scrub."

After a quick word to Mads as they passed the dairy, the pair was soon mounted and rode off. "Let's take the scenic route," Ned suggested as they rode out of the yard. Emil's confused look told Ned he needed to explain. "I think we should ride about all over the place as though you are showing me around. It might be better not to go directly into the scrub in case someone is watching the place." Emil's face lit up with excitement at Ned's explanation.

"Oh yes, I think you need to inspect all the work we have done in your absence … and what we hope to do next." Emil hoped Ned would understand that 'what we hope to do next' meant 'clearing another patch of scrub'. In that way, he hoped to create something that looked, to an outsider, like a natural progression of their works inspection when he took Ned into the scrub.

Half an hour later, Ned and Emil entered the scrub. Their ride through the bush would take them on a long meandering track to the stockyard. Along the way, they encountered three head of cattle. "We'll drive them into the yard," Ned said. "Then, when we are finished there, we will bring them out and put them into one of the fenced paddocks." He noted a startled look cross Emil's face. "It's all right. We will put them in a separate paddock until we work out who they belong to or what to do with them. I'll have a word with the police while I am in Marathon tomorrow."

The stockyard looked undisturbed. Once Emil dropped the slip rails and the cattle escaped, they stayed in the area but did not return to the yard. "There was no reason for them to come back here," Emil mused. "There is no water for them in the yard, and the grass growing through the scrub would give them reasonable feed."

Their time at the stockyard was brief. Emil pointed out the places referred to in his report: where the lanterns were hanging, where the various men were when he got a good look at each of them, and where they congregated at the end to discuss their operation and their 'close call' that night. With nothing more to be achieved by staying at the stockyard, they herded the three cattle out of the scrub, and locked them in one of the paddocks before telling Alf about the newcomers.

As they rode back to the bunkhouse, no one spoke for some time until Ned broke the silence. "The information in your report is vital evidence. It will be invaluable to the police. But you took a huge risk that night in investigating what was happening. You must promise me you will do nothing like that again. That night could have ended very differently if you were discovered. Your uncle and Mathilde have suffered enough grief already without something happening to you too."

"But what if I hear something happening in the scrub? Am I supposed to ignore it? Pretend it didn't happen?"

"If what you heard that night proves correct, those men will not be back here for another week or two. I will be back here before then and, after I talk to the police, I imagine they will be ready for them should they return. If you hear or see anything suspicious in the meantime, make a note of what it was and the date and time ... but do nothing else. For now, everything in your report remains between us. Do not mention any of it to Mr Grant or the other men. And, under no circumstances, say anything about it to your uncle or Mathilde. They do not need the worry of it ... and telling your uncle is unlikely to end well for you."

Ned spent the rest of the day preparing for his trip to Marathon and making a list of the things he needed to do there. When he asked Mathilde if she needed supplies brought back from town, her list was not long but included more than Ned could carry with ease in a pack saddle. He needed to take a wagon. That night over dinner, Ned announced he would be taking the dray into Marathon.

Next morning, as Ned drove out through Rangelands' main gate and onto the dirt track to town, his thoughts were with Emil. Once again he marvelled at how much the lad had matured in such a short time. "He is going to be one hell of a useful bloke to have around," he told the cold morning, "And I don't want to lose him... or Mathilde. Where did that come from?" He asked himself as a soft smile caressed the corners of his lips.

Chapter 11 Inquiries

Ned's time in Marathon was an exercise in frustration. On his arrival, he arranged to stay with Tom Croxley in his quarters under the store, and for the horses and dray to remain in the horse yard behind the store until he was ready to head back to Rangelands. There wasn't much of the afternoon left, but he wanted to visit the police station before the day was out.

Police Sergeant Donald Slattery and one police constable comprised the fledgling Marathon police force; their police station no more than a shack down by the wharves. A more senior officer was required for the embryonic township, and a proper building was mooted for somewhere in the block around the corner from Rixon's store, but all that was for 'one day soon'. The constable, on his knees rummaging for something under the counter, stood up and stretched as Ned walked in. "Sergeant Slattery is in his office and doesn't want to be disturbed," he told Ned. His arrogant tone rankled, and Ned struggled to remain civil. He peered sharply around the constable.

Adopting an amazed demeanour, Ned said, "I wasn't aware this place ran to a separate office. It doesn't look large enough to afford the officer-in-charge his own workspace. In behind, through there is it?" With that, Ned darted around the counter, past the stunned constable, and tapped gently on the wall next to the office doorway. The constable joined Ned in the doorway as Slattery looked up from the pile of paper cluttering his desk. "I'm sorry, Sir. I did tell him you weren't to be disturbed. I'll throw him out, shall I?"

"No, Constable. Move out of the way and let the man in. It's Rixon isn't it," Slattery said extending his hand to Ned. "Set ye down and tell me what brings you here upsetting my constable

110

like that." The twinkle in his eyes told Ned volumes about the relationship between the two officers. Once the constable returned to the front counter, Slattery leaned over closer to Ned and murmured, "New appointee... No brains, but trying hard – in fact, bloody trying most of the time, and bloody useless. Now what can this miserable police station be doing for you, Sir? I do hope it is something interesting ... and a crime I am able to solve. This station could do with getting a few runs on the board to bring us more officers."

They hadn't progressed past the usual pleasantries and introductions when sounds of a ruckus somewhere near the wharves broke out. It was close. The sounds from it brought conversation to a halt. A few moments later, the constable ensured any opportunity to continue disappeared when he rushed into the room. "Come quick, Sir. I think they are killing one another out there. What are we to do?"

Sergeant Slattery heaved a sigh of resignation and stood up. "Excuse me, Mr Rixon. It appears duty calls. Like I said..." he added with a jerk of his head in the direction of the fleeing constable, "...useless. Perhaps we might discuss whatever you came to see me about at some later time?"

"Of course; it can keep. I'll be off so you may sort out whatever that's all about out there."

It might be a good thing today panned out as it has, Ned told himself as he walked back along Marathon's main street. I now have a chance to make a few inquiries of my own before speaking to Slattery again. He went in to the first hotel on the street. A corrugated iron and hessian shanty with a dirt floor, it was not among the more salubrious drinking establishments he had known.

From the moment he entered, it became obvious the locals didn't share his opinion of the place. At an hour when most men were still at work, a goodly crowd kept the barman busy. It also was obvious some patrons had been there for much of the afternoon. The place was becoming rowdy and Ned detected a frantic air about the barman. Rather than add to the man's woes and risk the sharp edge of his tongue as the last customer had, Ned went to stand quietly at one end of the makeshift bar. A drinker beside him moved away, leaving a crude and wobbly barstool vacant. Ned dragged the seat over and sat down cautiously.

After a few minutes, as if by some preordained ritual, the crowd thinned out. Men left the pub in small groups. Ned found himself one of only three still at the bar. The barman, realising Ned had no drink in front of him, hurried along to serve him. Although a little early for Ned's liking, he bought a small rum. He wasn't here to drink. He was here for information. And it was information he asked for when the barman returned with his drink.

Reluctant at first, the barman's attempts to duck Ned's questions came to an end when Ned lost patience with the man. "Stop playing silly buggers with me and answer my questions," Ned demanded a little more loudly than normal. "You have two choices. You either answer my questions now, or you can answer them for Sergeant Slattery when he hauls you in for questioning."

"Why would he haul me in for questioning? I know nuthin' about nuthin'. I aint done nuthin' wrong."

I've got a right one here, Ned thought, but he persisted with his questioning of the man. "Right. Well that may be so, but I'm sure the Sergeant will find out whether that be true or not. In the meantime, I'll ask you once more: do you know of Mr Richard Meadows?"

"Sure, I've heard talk of him. What of it?"

"Have you seen him in here?"

"Mebbe; all sorts come in here from time to time. Mostly, I take no notice."

"Does Mr Meadows drink here regularly?"

"Nah; his sort don't hang about in here. Him and his toff mates think they are too good for places like this. Truth is, I think they be no better than the likes of most of my regulars."

Ned had all there was to gain from the barman. What the man said probably was true. From the little Ned knew of Meadows, this pub would not suit the man at all. Located close to the wharves, the pub's clientele comprised a rough element from among sailors and wharf labourers. After thanking the barman and leaving a small tip for his trouble, Ned was out on the street and heading for the next pub.

The appearance of the second pub differed little from the first. Ned hesitated outside. He smacked his forehead at the realisation he forgot to ask the barman at the first pub about any duffing going on in the area. On reflection, it was just as well. Ned guessed the barman wouldn't have said anything, or would have lied.

Less crowded than the previous one, the majority of this place's drinkers were still at work. He also discovered that here the publican was the barman. Again, Ned asked after Richard Meadows. The publican claimed he didn't *know* Meadows, but said he *knew of* the man. He recalled Meadows coming in a few times to drink with two or three other men. "I wouldn't say they were his mates. More like his workers, I think. A bit rough looking they were, if I remember rightly. I think Meadows is more likely to frequent the pub across the road. He probably stays there when he is in town. He might stay at one of the boarding houses, but the pub across the way would be more to his style."

As the publican finished speaking, Ned cast his eyes over the other drinkers. Something suggested not to bother asking in this establishment about duffing. While the clientele were a step up from those of the previous pub, they had the appearance of workers and hardened bushmen. Men who might well be involved in such elicit activities themselves. With nothing more to be gained there, Ned left and made his way further along the street to what looked like a third grog shop. It was new and not yet open for business. That left only the hotel across the street to visit.

This presented as a more upmarket facility than the other pubs. Of timber construction, the hotel offered travellers accommodation in a number of small rooms and basic meals in its dining room. Ned stayed there on previous visits to Marathon. The barman welcomed him like a returning honoured guest. There were eight other men in the bar area. Six he recognised as farmers or pastoralists. Two men at a table in the corner Ned pegged as business men negotiating a business deal.

The quiet, sedate atmosphere there provided a welcome change from the previous two grog shops. As the barman wasn't busy, he was happy to chat. Over his rum, Ned dropped into their conversation a casual question about Meadows.

"Yes, I know Mr Meadows. He usually stays here whenever he is in town. Come to think of it, he hasn't been in for a while now. It's probably months since I last saw him. I don't suppose there is anything surprising about that. I believe the man has quite a few business interests outside Marathon. I imagine they take up much of his time and require him elsewhere."

Feeling encouraged by the man's reply, Ned chanced asking again if there had been any chat amongst drinkers about duffing in the area.

"I don't know anything definite, and no one discussed it with me directly, but I've heard a bit of talk about it at the tables. A few of the graziers are whinging about losing stock."

After making a show of checking his pocket watch and being amazed by how late it was, Ned scrambled off his stool, and announced he and a friend would be back for dinner later. On his way back to the store, Ned ran through his mind everything he gained from his inquiries that afternoon. There was much to consider but, by the time he reached the store, he was convinced of two things: while some knew of Richard Meadows, few actually knew the man, and consensus was Meadows hadn't shown his face in Marathon for some time now – maybe months.

With the store's front door already closed at the end of the day, Ned entered through the backdoor and almost collided with Tom Croxley helping the last customer carry his purchases out to his wagon. Leaning against the back wall of the store, Ned watched as the wagon drove off. Tom came back brushing the dust off his hands and the front of his trousers. After locking the backdoor, he and Ned went down to Tom quarters below the store.

Tom was about to pour rum into two glasses he set on the table. Ned held up his hand to stop him. "You have one if you wish, Tom, but I've had a couple already this afternoon. I think I'll save myself for dinner. How about joining me for dinner at the hotel?"

You would have to be daft to knock back the boss buying you dinner, Tom thought as he poured himself a good measure of rum ... and I could do with a change from my own cooking.

Once they were both settled, Ned asked his question. "Have you heard talk of cattle duffing occurring anywhere around the Marathon area in recent times?"

"Yes, a fair bit of bellyaching about it amongst the graziers. Quite a few have whinged to me about losing stock. It's not just cattle; sheep too. The pastoralists are up in arms about the police not doing anything about it. As I see it, there is no hard evidence for the police to work with, and the police are a bit thin on the ground around here."

"I've noticed. If there is no evidence, how do they know they are losing stock?"

"I think those who are more directly involved with their stock have a better idea. It seems often a beast that stands out from the others. You know, it has a strange marking or a different coat, or something. Then, suddenly it goes missing and never returns."

"It might have gone bush and died or become feral."

"Maybe ... but the owners don't think that's the case. They look for their beasts when they go missing. After all, they are worth money to their owners. So, while the owners might be sure about what is happening, they have no evidence to prove it."

"I imagine it's almost impossible for a bloke to get cattle with someone else's brand on them accepted at the meatworks or boiling down works without difficult questions being asked."

"From what I hear, the police make a show of turning up at those facilities whenever a few head are brought in. There haven't been any arrests, so the duffers appear to be getting away with it. Anyway, most of the graziers are a bit slack about

115

branding. One bloke told me that, after being sure he lost cattle on two or three occasions, he made an effort to have every head he owned rounded up and branded. A short time later, he reckons a few more went missing. They all say the same thing: it's never a big number stolen at any one time; never more than three or four at the most."

"By the way, talking of customers, do you know Richard Meadows?"

"Meadows…? No. He's not one of our customers; must buy from the other store in town." Tom shook his head. Then Ned saw Tom's face light up as realisation dawned. "Meadows… that name rings a bell. Hang about; is he that bloke you went into partnership with to buy your property up the valley? Come to think of it, I have heard his name mentioned, and not in any good light, I might add. It's usually along the lines of what a 'rotten thieving bastard'… What have you got yourself involved with, Boss? All I can say is: take care how you go with that one."

Conversation ended when Tom turned in for the night. Ned still had something to do before giving in to sleep. Tomorrow he would attempt to talk with Sergeant Slattery again. Ned's original intention was to give Slattery Emil's report. Now his thinking differed. Perhaps it was wiser for him to hold onto the report. After thinking about it through dinner and beyond, he knew exactly what he would do. With writing materials taken from Tom's desk, Ned wrote out a concise version of Emil's work. The finished product was a more professional document and lacked anything of a speculative nature Emil included in his report. This is what Ned would hand to Slattery tomorrow.

*****

The morning was sunny and crisp and the men rose early. Over a hot breakfast Tom prepared, he and Ned discussed Ned's plans for the day. The first and most important item on their agenda was the list of items Mathilde wanted. He handed her list to Tom and asked that everything be ready to load into the dray when Ned returned later in the day.

"If you plan on returning to Rangelands after you finish in town, you will finish your journey in the dark," Tom warned. "Is that wise? Why not stay another night and leave early tomorrow morning?"

"Yes, it will be late when I arrive back at the property, but not too late. I don't have much to do today. I want to have a chat to Sergeant Slattery first thing this morning, and then I'll be back here to hitch up and load the dray. I'm hoping to be out of Marathon well before lunch."

With a salty sea breeze blowing in his face, Ned walked around to the police station. It was locked, and no sign of anyone around the place. That scuttled Ned's plans for the day before it even began. After sitting on the narrow front veranda for half an hour, still no one turned up. Ned decided there was someone else he might talk to. On his way, he called at the store to tell Tom, he would be later leaving Marathon than he intended. Then, it was on to the courthouse.

No cases were being heard. The magistrate was not on the Bench and was delighted to see Ned. After Ned asked him to do the honours at the opening of the new store, they had become friends. Conversation was light and of no consequence over a cup of tea, then Ned turned to the question of cattle and sheep duffing occurring in the district. The magistrate admitted there were numerous complaints about it.

"There's no hard evidence. That's the problem; that and not a strong police presence in the area. So far, there have been no arrests, and there are plenty of pastoralists bleating loud and long about it. My concern is, if things keep going as they are, there could be a major incident. Graziers are starting to patrol their herds at night. If they catch duffers in the act, they are likely to shoot. Then all hell will break loose."

Reassured by his discussions with the magistrate, Ned decided to try his luck again at the police station. This time the front door was open. The counter was unmanned. Although Ned half expected him to bob up from under the counter, there was no sign of the constable. He continued through to the rear of the building and knocked on Slattery's door.

A harsh voice barked, "Come in…"

Ned cast a cautious glance around the door. Slattery was its only occupant. "Am I interrupting, or might you spare me a few minutes of your time?"

"No, no. You're not interrupting anything. Come on in; it's Mr Rixon from yesterday, isn't it?" Ned nodded and drew up a chair across from the sergeant. "Before we begin again, let me apologise for the way things turned out yesterday. Yet another drunken brawl; that's all we spend our time on these days. But enough of that; what can I do for you?"

"I wanted to talk to you about cattle stealing that's happening up my way. No doubt, plenty of landowners have been in to tell you about the same thing already. So I don't take up more time than necessary, I've detailed in this document what is going on." Ned slid his edited copy of Emil's report across the desk to the sergeant.

"Hang about. Your property is the store around the corner, is it not?" Ned nodded. "Well now, I haven't heard of too much cattle duffing happening in the main street of Marathon."

"What…? No, I'm not talking about my property in Marathon. I'm talking about Rangelands, my pastoral property up the valley. It's all in there," Ned said gesturing to the document lying on the desk. "I suggest, if you find the time, you read it as soon as possible. I have reason to believe things will be happening up there again in a few days' time … on the occasion of the next new moon when there will be a moonless night."

That was enough to grab Slattery's attention. Ned drew his attention to critical points included in the document before they discussed other complaints the police received about duffing. "By the way, your front counter is unattended today. What's happened to your constable?"

"Argh, don't be asking about that moron. I fired him first thing this morning. He's no loss. Totally useless he was, and then he goes and arrives late and drunk for work this morning. I'll read your report and then I'll talk to headquarters. This might be just what I need to get myself some decent officers," Slattery said as he waved Ned's report at him.

Their discussion of the duffing crisis ended, Ned rose to leave – and then thought better of it. "If you might indulge me for another few minutes, there is another matter troubling me." Slattery gestured for Ned to resume his seat. "I've made inquiries all over town about a man called Richard Meadows. People say they know of him but haven't seen him in Marathon for some time. I'm wondering if you know anything of this man."

"Are you suggesting he is missing?"

"Uhmm… no, I don't think that's what I'm saying. Do you know something that might suggest he is?"

"Me…? No, not at all. I know of Mr Meadows. I know him to be a man with a bad reputation, but I also know the police have no hard evidence against him. I doubt he is missing – unless someone he took down has done away with him. My guess is he is lying low to avoid some sort of trouble. Did you want the police to look into his whereabouts?"

"That won't be necessary. Read the document I gave you. You'll have all the answers you need. Thanks for your time. I'll be off and leave you to get on with your job."

It was well and truly lunchtime when Ned returned to the store. In anticipation of Ned's desire to be on the road as soon as possible, Tom had hitched up the dray and brought it around to the loading dock. He was loading the last of Mathilde's supplies into the wagon when Ned arrived. Time allowed for only a few words before Ned was on his way out of town.

With his mind preoccupied with all he learned in Marathon, Ned didn't notice the time rushing by as he drove the horses hard along the track. Night had dropped its dark curtain by the time the horses found their way unerringly to the home yard. The wagon was unloaded by lantern light before Alf and Ned sat down to a late dinner kept warm for them for an hour or so by the fire.

As he waited for sleep to come, Ned allowed himself to wonder how much he had achieved in Marathon. Somehow, it felt as though he came home with little to show for his time in town.

Chapter 12 Welcome Back

His late return to Rangelands, followed by a restless night, had Ned slow off the mark next morning. The others were at work long before Ned surfaced. On his way for breakfast, he noticed Emil busy in the dairy. He detoured to check on its progress. Mads was right about it only requiring a couple of days to have it operational. Ned didn't linger at the dairy. Breakfast smelled good.

Straight after breakfast, on his way to saddle his horse to ride down check on the men, he crossed paths with Mads walking towards the cottage. "Mads, hold up a moment. I want to congratulate you on the job you did on the dairy. Inside almost looks like a new building, and it's good to see it being used." Mads explained that, after giving it a thorough cleaning, the repairs required were more minor than originally thought.

"I must say, Mads," Ned began, "I am impressed with how mature Emil is for his age. He is so useful to have around the place. It's easy to forget he is so young."

Mads became serious. "I am proud of him, and I know his father is proud too. Emil is a bright lad. He knew how hard things were back home. The family farm has been in my family for generations. Once, it produced enough to feed the family and plenty to sell as well. Now, it is too small to support even the family. When my brother knew we considered coming to Australia, he begged me to take Emil with us. It wasn't an easy decision for any of us, especially Emil's mother. She, like my wife, said Australia was a land too far away. She believed she might never see her son again, and worried about what might happen to him in this new land."

"Yes, it was a hard decision to make."

"Since then, my brother had to find work away from the farm, and work is hard find. His daughter helps her mother run the farm. Emil is the baby of the family. My brother believed sending Emil with us was the best he could do for the lad."

"Is Emil happy here in Australia? Do you know what he would like to do with his life?"

"He is happy here. I have asked him several times and his answer is always the same. It helps that he is doing what he loves. A life on the land is all he has ever wanted for himself. Has something happened to concern you about Emil?"

"No. It is just that we have loaded him up with what might be considered 'domestic' work. I was concerned he might be unhappy about that and would rather be out there working with the men."

"There might be something in what you say. I think Emil sometimes sees himself as being treated like a child. I feel sure he misses the company of the men. In the short time we were on Sweers Island, he grew close to the others, particularly the young lads, Toby and Lofty."

Ned considered Mads comments before responding. "Perhaps Emil might feel happier and more settled if he were allowed to live in the bunkhouse with the men. He would live in the bunkhouse, but have the option of eating with the men or at the cottage. How would that sit with you?"

"I had not thought about such an arrangement, but Emil is now twelve years old and no longer a child. I will consider your suggestion." Satisfied, Ned started towards the horse yard again. Mads called him back. "There is a problem I need to discuss. We have too much milk. Milking every day provides us with more than we need. And, after butter is made, there is buttermilk as well as surplus milk. Do you have any plans for the excess milk? I imagine there is no market for it out here as most properties probably have their own milkers."

"I have no plans. I didn't realise there would be a problem. Do you have a suggestion?"

"You might consider investing in pigs. We could feed them milk, buttermilk, kitchen scraps and excess vegetables from the two big gardens now established here. A small piggery could be set up in that unused area down by the creek."

"Pigs, eh...? I will give your suggestion some thought. There is a good market for pigs, and the occasional suckling pig would go well on our menu. There is something to consider though: will Emil be happy looking after pigs, and does he have the time? I will discuss the matter with Alf first." Ned shook his head as he rode to the bottom paddock. "I have so many things on my mind. Now I have to add pigs to the list," he told the black clouds gathering overhead.

Dark clouds began gathering early that morning. By lunchtime, they showed real promise. It was early for spring rains but, in this land, they're welcome whenever they arrive. Ned sat and chatted with the men during their lunch break. As he prepared to ride back to the bunkhouse, the first light sprinkle fell from the heavens. "Alf, let's believe those clouds are going to deliver. Perhaps you should call it a day and get everyone home before the heavens open." He watched them pack up before riding back ahead of them.

By the time the others returned to the bunkhouse, Ned was installed at the cottage's dining table where he attended to paperwork for the rest of the afternoon. Noise from the bunkhouse drifted into his consciousness. The boys are enjoying a bit of high-spirited fun on their afternoon off, he thought as he listened to their laughter. Then Alf arrived and all thoughts of paperwork were abandoned.

"Hey Ned, come and see what just arrived." Thinking it nothing more than a new calf, Ned pushed his paperwork to one side with a sigh and followed Alf to the bunkhouse.

"G'day, Boss," greeted Ned as he entered the bunkhouse. Taken by surprise by the familiar voice, Ned stood gaping for a moment before rushing forward to grasp the young man's hand. Lofty had arrived.

"Good God, Lofty, it is good to see you. Ever since you and the last of the men left Sweers Island, I often wondered how you all fared. I dared not think there be a chance you all escaped the Gulf Fever and survived."

"Aye, some of us were lucky; so many weren't. I didn't think I would ever see you lot again … not all of you anyway."

"What did you do after you left the island, Lofty? We're all ears to hear what you did and where you've been," Toby said.

"If it's to be a long story," Alf suggested, "Maybe we need a drink to help it go down." A brief interlude ensued while tots of rum were added to pannikins.

"Truth be told, I didn't know where to go or what to do after I reached the mainland. For a while, I just followed the others heading towards the coast. Then I remembered my sister married a man on a property from somewhere out there a bit west of Townsville. That seemed like a good place to go. I thought to stay there until I got my head around what to do. Her husband needed a hand with fencing, so I pitched in to help. I was working away from the house one day, when a bull gored him … opened his innards right up. Made a right mess of him it did. They carted him off to hospital; told us he'd be there for a long time. I couldn't leave; had to stay and work the place for my sister. Gulf Fever was spreading across the top end of the mainland. He caught it in the hospital and didn't make it. Then I was stuck there on the property. My sister had two little kids and things were tough."

"Tough luck, eh Lofty? You escaped it on Sweers Island, only to have it come knocking on your door again. Things came good though, eh? You're here now. You must've got away from the place," Toby said.

"Yeah, things worked out in the end. Bloke on the neighbouring property was a widower. His wife died more than a year ago leaving him with three little kids. My sister helped him with the kids. Then, after her husband died, the bloke next door sometimes came over to help me run the property. He knew my sister wanted to sell up. Some paperwork that I don't understand had to be done before she could sell. While that was happening, her and the bloke next door got close. With her intending to sell, I started looking around for something to do afterwards. A long cattle drive planned to move a big mob from out that way down south to some place past here wanted a few men to ride with them. I put my hand up. By the time the sale went ahead my sister and the bloke next door had decided to marry. So… the sale happened … a week later my sister remarried … the following day, I started on the cattle drive."

"It's taken you a few months to get here," Alf observed. "How did the cattle drive go?"

"All right; a bit boring after a while, but they're a good bunch of blokes. We weren't droving every day. Cattle were dropped off at places along the way; not big mobs, just a few head here and there. Whenever we stopped at a property, we spent a day or two out of the saddle. It gave the horses and our arses a bit of a rest."

"Which way did you come?" Alf asked.

"…Sort of inland; followed a track heading this way. While stopped at a small property, when the owner and droving boss were yarning around the fire, I heard mention of Port Beauchamp. I remembered Mr Rixon had business in that place. I pulled the owner aside and asked him the way to it. When we reached where that track turns off. I told the boss I was leaving. He wasn't too happy, but I headed for Port Beauchamp. I found Mr Rixon's store and talked to a Mr Kincaid there. He told me everyone had moved to Marathon. I never heard of Marathon before, but he gave me directions. In the meantime, there was a few days' work going at the stockyards at the wharves, so I took it. Then a bloke who bought some cattle from the stockyards wanted a hand to move them to his property about three quarters of the way towards Marathon. I left him at his property line and rode on to Marathon."

"Did you look up Tom Croxley at the new store?" Alf asked.

"Yes sir, Mr Grant, I did. He told me you were all living up the valley somewhere. I did a few days' work around the wharves to get a bit of cash and think about what to do next. Anyway, the work ran out, so I rode up here to see if you needed a hand with anything."

"You did well to find us, Lad," John Oakes said.

Lofty chuckled. "Yeah, well, I knocked on the door at three places before the last bloke gave me proper directions. So, here I am. Is there any chance of a job going up here? I'll take whatever you've got." Lofty turned to direct his question to Ned.

Alf, now standing behind Lofty, gave Ned an enthusiastic nod. "Well now, Lofty, as you know, Alf is the manager around here. It's up to him who he hires." Lofty spun round to face Alf. Alf fought to stifle a giggle at the beseeching look on Lofty's face.

"Pick your bunk, but not one of those there. They are already spoken for."

"Do you mean I've got a job, Mr Grant? If you be offering me a job, I'll have that bunk over there, thanks."

The bunkhouse erupted into laughter at Lofty's relief and enthusiasm. He wasted no time throwing his swag onto the bunk he'd selected.

In something of a welcome-back tribute to Lofty, Alf and Ned dined with the men in the bunkhouse that night. Even Emil was allowed to join them for dinner and to stay on for a while afterwards. Stories were swapped and a serious quantity of rum drunk before everyone turned in for the night.

While swapping stories, Lofty asked, "Do anyone remember Tommy Tyler from our Sweers Island days?" Everyone nodded.

"What happened to Tommy? He left Sweers early after the fever broke out. Did he survive?" Toby asked.

"Yeah, seems he did," Lofty said. "I didn't know about him till I ran into him in Marathon. He's been in town for a while. Found a job at the boiling down works. Not a great job but it's all he could get. He looks after the animals in the yards until they're processed; finds it a bit difficult when really nice ones are killed. And that place stinks. He's looking for a proper job... a job on a property somewhere. Hasn't been able to find anything though. If you be looking for another man, he'd be ever so grateful if you thought of him." Lofty gave Alf a nervous look before asking, "Do you think there might be a chance of a job for Tommy anytime soon?"

"Tommy was a good lad; a good worker. If I needed another man, I would consider Tommy but, I need to think about whether someone else is required," Alf said. It wasn't that he needed to think about it. He needed to ask Ned about it first. If they took on Tommy as well as Lofty, he would have enough men until they expanded the herd.

After the others turned in for the night, Ned and Alf shared one last drink beside the fire. The night was cool after the afternoon showers and the welcome heat coming from the embers made both men a little drowsy. "We should call it a night before we fall asleep out here," Ned suggested.

"There's one last thing I wanted to tie up before the night ends," Alf said, before launching into a spiel about why they should take on Tommy Tyler. "It will give me a full complement of men to complete the clearing and fencing on time."

He was taken aback when Ned replied, "So ... hire him."

Next morning, as Lofty saddled up to head off to work with the others, Alf gave him the good news. "I've given the matter of employing Tommy some thought, and I see that I do need one more man. If Tommy is interested, the job is his. How do we get in touch with him?"

"He'll be interested, Mr Grant. Tommy only gets Sundays off, and only if there are no cattle in the yards to look after. If you could spare me for a day, I'd ride into town to talk to him." Alf agreed, but suggested Lofty spent that day and the next getting to know the property before heading into town.

Just when it seemed everything was in place for Lofty's trip to town, Ned scuttled the plan. He announced he needed to go into Marathon again. Although he didn't elaborate, everyone believed it was associated with all the paperwork he had been ploughing through in recent days. The trip is timely from Alf's point of view. He needs more fencing material. With the extra hands on board work will progress faster, and fencing will increase. He suggested Ned and Lofty take one of the wagons. Lofty could talk to Tommy while Ned attended to his business, and they could return with a wagon load of fencing materials.

*****

As they unhitched the horses in the yard behind the store, Ned explained to Lofty. "My business in Marathon might take the next two days. We will bunk down here in the quarters with Tom Croxley. It's late, but this might be a good time to catch up with Tommy to ask if he still wants a job. My business will keep me busy all day tomorrow. You will help Tom in the store. If I finish my business earlier than expected, everything should be in place for us to leave around lunchtime the day after tomorrow. If that's not the case, we will leave first thing the day after. You should give Tommy that information. He needs to be here at the store to leave with us. I suggest you take one of the horses and to talk to Tommy now."

By the time Lofty saddled a horse and rode out to the boiling down works, the working day was over. He waited near the gate until Tommy came out on his way home. They rode into town together and stopped at the pub opposite the hotel. Tommy looked miserable and admitted to having 'a rotten day'. All the way into town he went on about a couple of beautiful horses to be put down, and what a waste of perfectly good horseflesh it would be. Lofty hoped his news might put a bit more spark into Tommy.

Once they were seated in the pub, Lofty delivered the news about a job available Rangelands if Tommy was interested. For a worrying moment, Lofty thought Tommy was going to hug him. How would that look in a grog shop? But Tommy managed to restrain himself and rushed to assure Lofty he would leave with them whenever they were ready. "I'll go into work tomorrow, and then see what the next day looks like. If Mr Rixon wants to leave sometime during that next day, come and get me. I'll move my few things over to the store tomorrow night ready to load onto the wagon."

While Lofty spent the last of the working day talking to Tommy, Ned took advantage of the time to call on his bank manager. He spent the last couple of days developing some ideas. Turning any of them into a reality depended on the state of his finances … and another couple of important factors. The bank manager's news was all good. Port Beauchamp store's trade was down a bit but remained solid. On the other hand, the Marathon store added plenty to the coffers. So, in spite of recent spending, plenty of cash remained in the bank accounts.

Buoyed by news of his financial situation, Ned's next port of call was the courthouse. The magistrate was only too happy to dine with Ned at the hotel that night. While waiting to go to dinner, Ned mulled over the topics to discuss with the magistrate. There was nothing in any of what Ned wanted to discuss that might compromise the magistrate. Dinner tonight was to seek a legal opinion on a troubling matter.

The dining room was almost deserted, only three other men at a table at the other end of the room. With the initial niceties over, Ned sought clarification on issues relating to partnership and property ownership. He posed his questions without any reference to his personal situation or to Rangelands ownership. The magistrate was no fool. In spite of Ned's careful wording, the magistrate realised the matters discussed were close to home for Ned.

"If a property is held by a partnership under a Homestead Lease agreement for ten years, and one of the partners wants to freehold the property by paying any outstanding monies, is it possible for him to do so?" Ned asked.

"When the lease was taken on, there was indication of what an outright sale price might be. The normal arrangement is for lease monies paid as rent over the ten year life of the lease to amount to about half of that nominal sale price. It is possible to convert the property to freehold at any time during the ten years or at the end of the lease by paying whatever money is required to achieve the nominal sale price. I'm sure you already know all that, but I thought it worth mentioning anyway. Now, you were asking about what might happen in the case of a partnership where one partner wishes to freehold property. The necessary paperwork also requires the signature of the other partner. In effect, it confirms both partners' agreement to the proposed change."

While Ned suspected this would be the case, it was not what he wanted to hear, so he added complexity to the supposedly hypothetical situation. "What would happen in the event one of the partners was convicted of a serious crime? Could the other partner have the partnership dissolved on those grounds?"

"Yes, but it would require an application to the court to have the matter heard and receive a ruling for the dissolution of the partnership."

Dinner dragged on longer than intended. In the end, as Ned walked the magistrate out of the hotel, he couldn't help feeling a bit deflated by the outcome of the evening. Everything was possible, but nothing was straightforward. From his perspective, none of it was easy to achieve. After a carriage collected the magistrate, Ned went back inside for another word with the barman.

Meadows had not stayed at the hotel since Ned last asked after him. A couple of others drinking in the bar also had not seen Meadows for quite some time. They were happy to answer his questions, but Ned noted a reaction to mention of Meadows' name. He had little doubt Meadows somehow was operating on the wrong side of the law. Ned accepted his choice of a partner was a mistake.

*****

Items remaining on Ned's list of things to do while in Marathon: further enquiries around town about Meadows, and a visit to the police station. By the time he went to bed last night, Ned scrapped the idea of making further inquiries about Meadows. Why waste time asking questions when you already know the answers? That left only the visit to the police station to deal with this morning. He felt sure they could leave town by lunchtime.

Over breakfast, he discussed the list of fencing materials Alf required, and instructed Lofty to have the wagon hitched and loaded by lunchtime. "I see Tommy brought his belongings over last night. Before you do anything else today, Lofty, you need to make sure Tommy knows we might leave town about lunchtime. He needs to be here and ready to go."

"I'll ride over first thing. I told him we might leave today, but I'll make sure he's here."

Lofty left straight after breakfast. Ned and Tom discussed matters relating to the store until it was time for Tom to open for the day. That was Ned's cue to head to the police station to see if Sergeant Slattery was there.

Slattery tells him things had improved since Ned's previous visit to the police station. "I've three new constables, all of whom seem to know a bit about the law and how to be police officers. I passed on your information about what happened on your place, and stressed the urgency of having something in place before the next new moon. Well, like I said, three new officers arrived, and a detachment of the Native Police is due in town tomorrow. Theirs is a permanent posting to Marathon."

"That is good news. My visit today was to maybe draw up plans for those forthcoming critical nights."

"Excellent idea … and the first thing I'm putting in place is for the Native Police to camp at your property. They will arrive tomorrow. The next day they will ride to your property and camp there until the critical period is over. Their presence should be kept low key, but they will be on the lookout for any activity in the days leading to the new moon. My constables and I will arrive the day of the new moon. If anything occurs before we arrive, one of the Native Police officers will gallop into town to tell me. Now, what else do we need to think about?"

Plans covering every possible aspect of what might occur, as well as contingencies, were developed over a couple of hours. Then, Ned had nothing more to do in town. It was still only mid-morning. For want of something better to do, Ned strolled back to the store. Both Lofty and Tommy were there with the wagon loaded and ready to go. This is better than I had hoped for, Ned thought. We might even get back to Rangelands at a reasonable hour this afternoon. A particularly beautiful horse in the horse yard caught his attention. It had a classic Arab head and a finely marked roan and white coat.

"What a magnificent looking animal! Does either of you know who owns that horse? It must have arrived sometime this morning. Maybe I should ask Tom if he knows."

"There be no need to be bothering Tom about it," Lofty said. "He belongs to Tommy and me. A farmer being forced off his land by the bank sold all his animals to the boiling down works. He would rather get a few shillings for them that way than give the bank the satisfaction of auctioning them off later for higher prices. We couldn't let this one be put down, so Tommy and I pooled our money and bought him from the works. I'm sorry Mr Rixon, Sir. I never thought to ask first if it would be okay for us to bring another horse onto the property."

"Such a fine looking animal would always be welcome at Rangelands. Perhaps I should buy him from you. That way you would have your money back and Rangelands would own a good-looking horse. We can discuss it later. Now that you both have horses, perhaps you might ride back ahead of the wagon. You could leave now. I need to spend some time with Mr Croxley before I follow you." Ned's suggestion accepted, ten minutes later Ned stood on the loading dock waving the two lads off on their way up the valley. "Lofty, try not to get lost this time; I don't want to have to come looking for you," Ned called after them.

In between dealing with customers, Tom and Ned spent the next hour or so discussing matters relating to the store's operation. Tom reported business improving faster than he anticipated. He raised the likelihood of needing someone to assist him in the not-too-distant future.

The two lads arrived back at the property in the early afternoon and were met by Alf Grant. Alf had just managed to convince a young pig to go into a cage he had positioned under one of the trees. "What's with the pig?" Lofty asked.

"Well, it was going to be dinner tomorrow night. I wasn't expecting anyone to come back today. I thought roast suckling pig on a spit would be a nice change."

"There is still enough time to cook it if we started soon. Let's get it dealt with," Tommy suggested.

By the time Ned arrived with the wagon, the sun already was sliding behind the distant hills. The aroma of roasting pork welcomed him home. While the lads unloaded the wagon, Ned went to tell Mathilde he was back. She was putting the finishing touches to decorating a cake. "Gracious, what's the occasion? Have I forgotten some important event? Roasting pork … A fancy cake … What's going on?"

"It's supposed to be a surprise. We wanted to have a welcome back party for Lofty and Tommy … And of course for your return from Marathon. You don't mind, do you?"

"What an excellent idea; of course I don't mind. I'm just wondering how long we have to wait before I can finally taste that pig that smells so good."

The party went well. The pig on a spit was cooked to perfection, and Mathilde's cake had everyone moaning with delight. Emil complained about spending all afternoon turning the spit, but nobody took any notice. During the evening, Ned took Alf aside to ask him about the pig and its origin.

"A farmer, a couple of properties from here, raises a few pigs. I knew he had some young ones, so I rode across today to buy one."

"Mads and I spoke about getting a few pigs. I'll tell him to make a start on a piggery. As soon as it's ready to accommodate three or four animals, you should see what the farmer has to sell."

As he settled in his bunk that night, Ned acknowledged the bunkhouse was now almost filled to capacity. The time had come for him to take a firm stand and do something about erecting a proper homestead.

Chapter 13 Unsettling Times

The first few days after the group's return from Marathon seemed close to chaos. In amongst settling Lofty and Tommy into life on Rangelands, reallocating chores and workloads, the contingent of Native Police arrived. Even Emil wasn't immune from the changes happening. During Ned's absence, Mads decided to go ahead with establishing a small piggery down by the creek. By the time Ned and the others returned, one pen was complete and awaiting occupants.

During a quiet 'recovery' after the welcome home party the night before, Ned managed to have a few quiet words with Emil. It was only fair the lad knew the role his report had in events that might occur over the next few days. While keen for Emil to know about it, Ned was economical with the details. He did not want the boy coming up with any independent heroic ideas of how he could become involved.

Over dinner that night, Ned raised the matter of establishing a piggery. Mads admitted he had taken the initiative of setting up one pen already, and would now proceed with constructing the rest of the infrastructure. What was already in place, although only a basic pen at this stage, was ready to accommodate its first pigs. "I'll have a word to Alf tomorrow about finding you some 'occupants'. Will two pigs do for a start?"

As indicated by Slattery, in the afternoon of the second day they were back, a contingent of Native Police, comprised of two white officers and four indigenous members, arrived to set up camp. Their instructions were to find somewhere out of sight and close to the bunkhouse. The officer in charge, Fredrickson, asked Ned to indicate such a place. Ned suggested the officer look around for somewhere suitable. A few minutes later, the officer sought out Ned again to ask if they might camp in the 'derelict building over yonder'. He indicated the former homestead.

Concerned about the safety of the building, Ned insisted on an inspection before agreeing to the request. After a brief wander around inside, Fredrickson pronounced the building safe and suitable, and Ned invited them to go ahead and settle in. As he walked away, Ned shook his head in wonder at how eager they were to move into the old building. Still, I suppose it offers more comfort than spending the next few days in the close confines of small tents on cold dewy nights, he thought.

Ned talked to Alf about acquiring a couple of pigs. Mads indicated the piggery, when finished, would comprise three pens and a separate small shed to hold various pieces of equipment such as buckets and shovels.

"You want me to buy only two pigs now?" Alf asked. "What should they be?"

"Eh? What do you mean? Just buy two pigs … Oh, I see… We probably should start with a couple of sows, and then add a boar when the other pens are completed."

"When I bought the piglet the other day, the farmer did ask if I was interested in buying fully grown animals. I might have one of the lads help me load a cage onto a wagon before we ride over to see what's on offer." Half an hour later, Ned watched Alf and Lofty head out to buy pigs.

"I better find Emil and warn him his workload is about to increase," Ned murmured with a wry grin.

Late in the afternoon, Ned checked on how setting up camp in the old homestead was progressing. In spite of being in the building, their tents were being utilised. A closer look at the condition of the thatched roof suggested they would not be dry if it rained. They unfolded their tents and hung them by all four corners from the rafters to create a false – and hopefully waterproof – ceiling. While the men busied themselves with setting up their new accommodation and clearing the fireplace to set a fire for the night, Ned suggested he take Fredrickson on a familiarisation tour of the property.

Their tour provided Ned with his first look at the new piggery. Then onto the area where the men were clearing scrub. This took them adjacent to the scrub where the action would take place if the rustlers returned as anticipated. As they cantered along the edge of the scrub some distance away from the area with the bush stockyard, Ned suggested, "Perhaps you might have a better idea of the work involved in clearing land if I take you for a short ride in there. You could see for yourself how thick the trees are and how dense the undergrowth." Ned reined his horse around and gave Fredrickson a wink as he started towards the scrub.

Walking their horses through the dark, cool scrub, made it easier to carry on a conversation. At one point when they came close together to ride through a narrow gap between two large trees, Ned said quietly, "Speak on any safe topic that enters your mind, but talk loudly. If anyone should be hanging around in here, they will hear us coming and should move away." Ned wanted to show Fredrickson the stockyard, but didn't want to be observed doing so.

They didn't linger long at the yard, just long enough for Fredrickson to familiarise himself with the layout of the area. As they emerged from the scrub, Fredrickson reined in his horse and studied the edge of the scrub immediately in front of where the stockyard was located. "Right, those two large trees that stand out from the rest are my markers. If we come down here at night, I'll use those to locate the stockyard. With a new moon, it will be dark, but those two big ghost gums will stand out in what light there is."

Ned asked Fredrickson if he had enough men. "We have sufficient men for the job in hand. There will be two shifts patrolling every night. I and my second in command, both of us accompanied by two constables, will each cover one shift every night. Thank you for your time, but now I must join my men. We need to have our evening meal before the first patrol heads out."

After dinner, Alf asked about the Native Police. "The Native Police mob seemed to have settled in okay. I saw one of the officers and two constables ride out as I went across for dinner. Where were they off to at this hour of the night? It already was dark when they left."

"They are on patrol. Each night, they will split patrolling the property between two shifts, each with one of the officers in charge. I have no idea how or where they intend patrolling. I confess I'm a little concerned about people riding around the property in the dark. No self-respecting rustler would come near the place if he saw someone moving about at night. The whole operation could be jeopardised. Nevertheless, Fredrickson and his men intend patrolling the place tonight and tomorrow night. Sergeant Slattery of the Marathon police will arrive the following day. That is the night of the new moon, and is when we think there will be activity at the bush stockyard."

*****

Fredrickson sought out Ned to report nothing happened during patrols on the first night. Ned expressed his concerns about the possibility of the patrols jeopardising the operation. His concerns were dismissed. Fredrickson assured him his men were well trained and knew what they were doing. He also told Ned there would be no interaction between his men and Ned's. They wanted to remain invisible and would spend most daylight hours out of sight in the derelict building. Fredrickson went to lengths to explain that, as part of maintaining their invisibility, none of his men would wear uniforms while engaged on this operation.

Emil, churning butter in the dairy, witnessed the conversation between Ned and Fredrickson. As Ned walked past on his way to the horse yard, Emil called him over. "I saw you talking to that bloke in charge of that mob, and I also saw him and a couple of his men ride out last night after dark. Where were they going?"

Ned thought about how much to share with Emil. Realising Emil knew more than anyone else on the property about why the native police were there, and had kept what he knew to himself,

Ned decided to share all he knew. "They will be patrolling every night. I don't know what that entails, but it will continue up to and including the night of the new moon."

"They will ruin everything! If Meadows and his men see people riding around at night, they'll disappear and will never be caught. I let myself believe what was going on would stop after the new moon. Now I'm not so sure." It was hard for Ned to say anything to calm Emil's misgivings when he shared those same doubts himself.

After their second night of patrolling the property, Fredrickson again met with Ned to report. "…A quiet night again last night, Mr Rixon. Nary a sound or sight of anything untoward happening on the property. The clear night with almost no moon would have made anyone with a lantern anywhere near that scrub easy to spot. Tonight is the key to it all. Slattery will arrive sometime today. All of us will take up our positions soon after nine o'clock tonight. If nothing happens, we might continue our surveillance for an extra couple of nights."

His report delivered, Fredrickson returned to his men. Ned pondered what Fredrickson said. His uneasy feelings about the likely success of the operation escalated. He was still considering what he should do when Emil galloped up to him.

"Sir, you know how Alf collected the last of our pigs from the farmer yesterday…?" Ned nodded. "Well, that gave us a boar, two sows and four piglets…" Emil paused, waiting for Ned to confirm he knew about the number of pigs they had acquired. Ned nodded again. "I went to the piggery to feed and water them. Two piglets are missing. I searched everywhere. All I found were a lot of horse's hoof prints around the piggery, and a few boot prints in the pen where the piglets were with their mother."

"Were they your boot prints by any chance?"

"No, Sir. They were much too big to be mine, and no one else from the bunkhouse goes there."

"Emil, when did you last check on the pigs?"

"Last thing before I came home for dinner last night."

So much for the quiet night when nothing happened, Ned thought. He thanked Emil for bring it to his attention and told the lad not to mention the missing piglets to anyone else. All Emil's information had done was clarify in Ned's mind what he must do … and it must be done before tonight.

A gallop through the paddocks brought Ned to the new area where his men were working. "I know it's a bit early for a morning cuppa," he told Alf, "But could we take tea now, please? I have something urgent to discuss with all of you, and it may take a while."

Tea break stretched on longer than usual that morning as Ned acquainted his men with all that happened over the previous couple of days, and speculated on what might eventuate that night. By the end of their break, a plan was in place and each of the men knew his part in it. As Ned rode back to the bunkhouse, he felt more relaxed about *the night of the new moon,* as he had come to think of the events that night might bring. At the horse yard, he encountered Fredrickson tending his horse. He felt sufficiently belligerent about the native police's activities so far to warrant a few words to him.

"While you and your men were having a quiet time last night with nothing heard or seen, two piglets went missing from my piggery. The culprits left behind plenty of hoof prints and boot prints. I am prepared to accept – for the moment – those prints were not made by your men. Have you any thoughts on the subject?" In reality, Ned wasn't confident the native police members hadn't seen fit to supplement their ration with fresh pork.

Fredrickson's initial blustering denial earned him a hard stare from Ned. That worked; Frederickson backed down. "I assure you my men had nothing to do with it. My men and I rode past the piggery but did not go close. I'm confident the same is true for my other team. I will discuss the matter with them, and I will post one of the constables in the scrub overlooking the piggery to keep watch all day." Although Ned thought such action a waste of time and manpower, he said nothing. He might have reacted differently if he knew the man keeping watch had instructions to 'shoot to kill' anyone attempting to reduce the piggery's number of occupants.

Slattery and his three constables arrived late in the afternoon. After fussing around and checking out every conceivable campsite, he and his men moved in to share the former homestead with the native police. In a few words to Ned before setting up their camp, Slattery said, "I anticipate we will be here for two nights if there is to be action at this time. We expect it will be tonight. In the event nothing happens tonight, we will remain here for the following night in the off chance it might occur then. Perhaps I might dine with you and your men tonight...? I thought it might be useful for them to know who I am, but not necessarily to know why I am here. "

Ned vetoed the idea of dining together, citing the need for secrecy and an early night for his workers. Slattery's red and veined nose suggested he was partial to more than the odd tipple, and saw sitting with Ned's men as an opportunity to indulge. Ned wanted his men and Slattery with clear heads if the need arose to act later in the night.

With his plans for a night on the grog thwarted, Slattery returned to his camp to brief the men on the night's plan of action. His first move was to cancel the native police's usual night patrols. Fearing that men seen moving about the place at night might deter the rustlers, he opted for a more covert approach. Once it was dark, all the men would take up positions to hide in the scrub. Those positions would be some distance away from the stockyard. "If tonight follows the same pattern as the previous event, we will be warned something is happening by the sounds of upset cattle. We must wait until all activity is focused in and around the stockyard before moving in to apprehend the rustlers."

During their brief discussion after Slattery's arrival, Ned indicated he wanted to move cattle from their present paddock into the newly fenced bottom paddock. Slattery asked they be moved just on dusk. He and his men would help move them, his intention being for the police to slip away from the paddock to take up their positions in the scrub ready for the rest of the night.

After moving the cattle, Ned and his men returned to the bunkhouse and went through the motions of settling in for an early night. Although Ned was tense and had difficulty dropping off, he was sound asleep at one o'clock went Emil shook him awake.

"Mr Rixon, Mr Rixon!" Emil hissed. "Wake up, please. Listen! Something is upsetting the cattle. They are making a lot of noise – just like the last time."

After telling Emil to go back to bed and stay there, Ned woke Alf and the other three men. In accordance with their plan and on foot, they headed to the scrub beyond the bottom paddock. They carried no lanterns. None were needed. They knew the terrain so well, and horses would alert people to their approach. Once they reached the bottom paddock, they mingled with the cattle for a few minutes while watching for any sign of activity in the scrub.

It wasn't long before they caught the first glimpse of lanterns moving through the trees. This was all they needed to see. Ned and his men moved into their planned positions spread out along the edge of the scrub and just a couple of paces inside it. Then the waiting game began. The lanterns and the voices drew nearer, but were still some distance away deep in the scrub. Ned knew the others – the police and native police – were focused on the stockyard. As soon as the activity moved to their area, they would pounce. Ned saw he and his men as a last line of defence should any of the duffers decide to make a break for it from their side of the scrub.

Ten minutes slipped by before they saw any action, but it felt like they waited more than half an hour. Alf caught sight of a figure at the gate into the bottom paddock, where a few minutes earlier, Ned and his men had hidden themselves amongst the cattle. He saw the figure struggling to open the gate. The deliberately fancy way Alf chained the gate closed after the cattle were in that paddock was doing what it was designed to do: make it difficult to unchain and open the gate.

His training with the Fusiliers recalled to the forefront of his mind, Alf snuck up behind the man at the gate. Suddenly, a dark figure appears beside Alf. In the belief it was another of the rustlers, Alf drops to a defensive position and spins around to face this second man. Then he realises the man beside him is one the native police constables. Alf returns his focus to his original mission.

The man hears something and starts to turn around as Alf lunges at him. He grabs the man and, positioning himself behind him, Alf wraps an arm tight around the man's throat while clamping his free hand over the man's mouth. The constable skips around to stand in front of the man. As the constable thrusts his rifle barrel hard against the man's stomach, Alf whispers in the man's ear, "I suggest you stay quite still. My mate here is itching to pull the trigger. One wrong move from you, and I won't be able to stop him." As they cuff the man and tie him to a fence post, all hell breaks loose in the scrub.

Shots and shouting fill the air. Ned and his men surge forward towards the stockyard where the commotion is centred. From the light of many lanterns, they see one man is dead and another on the ground appears seriously wounded. Off to one side, another man is tied to a tree. But there are no police there. The action has moved away from the stockyard; is moving further into the scrub. Confused by what is happening, Ned tells his men retreat to their original positions.

As they make their way back to the edge of the scrub, Ned notices the sounds of people crashing through the scrub becoming louder. The sound now is coming towards them. Figures ooze out of the darkness to pass Ned and melt into the scrub ahead of him. "Hurry, Lads!" Ned yells. The Rangelands men break into a run. Another voice yells a command.

It's Alf. "Come right through to the open ground." Ned and his men obey, and break out of the scrub onto the narrow strip of open ground between the scrub and the fence line. A moment later, a man races out of the scrub a short distance away from them. Ned and his men prepare to give chase ... but there is no need. Two dark figures capture and wrestle the man to the ground. When Ned and the others reach the man, he is face down on the ground and the cuffs are being snapped on. Before anything else can happen, Slattery and one of his constables emerge from the scrub and race to join them.

Slattery's constable hauls the man to his feet while Slattery thrusts a lantern in the man's face. It's Meadows. In a moment of rage, Ned steps up and slugs Meadows, who ends up in a scrambled heap on the ground again. "Dear me, Sir, you need to take more care rushing around in the dark like that. You see how easy it is to trip and do yourself a nasty injury," Slattery tells Meadows and as he hauls him to his feet again. "Come on, let's have you. Up you get. Lads ... Help this gentleman onto the wagon and secure him safely. We don't want him wandering about and injuring himself again."

The action is all but over. The police wagon arrives. Meadows and the man tied to the tree, both still handcuffed, are bundled into the cage on the wagon. Ned instructs John Oakes to take a lad with him to deal with the cattle in the bush stockyard. "Put them in the paddock we just moved ours out to keep them separate.

Slattery sidles up to Ned while he is speaking to John Oakes. "We've got one dead and one wounded to take back to town. Might we borrow your dray to transport them?" he asks.

Alf volunteers to fetch the dray. By the time he returns with it, the cattle from the stockyard are in the paddock. He tells John Oakes, "They want to use the wagon to transport the bodies back to Marathon. You take charge of the wagon. The police will bring the remaining two men out of the scrub and load them on. Once that's done, take the wagon home, before driving it into town tomorrow. Bring the wagon back when it's all done. If you are not free to return to Rangelands until it is too late to complete the journey in daylight, spend the night with Tom Croxley in the quarters at the store and return the following day." With a constable perched up beside him, Oakes headed for home. As they follow some distance behind, Slattery tells Ned they will leave with the wagon at first light.

Four o'clock was but a memory by the time everyone returned from the night's operation. "Just time enough for a decent breakfast before you head off, I think," Ned suggested to Slattery. Two constables guarded the prisoners while everyone else from the old homestead joined Ned and his men for a hearty breakfast eaten around the outdoor fireplace. Then the two guards were relieved and came for breakfast. Reliving the night's adventure and tucking into a hearty fried breakfast lasted through to first light.

There was a flurry of activity for a period while the camp was pulled down, gear was packed and horses saddled before the wagons rolled out of Rangelands. Slattery and his constables rode with the Rangelands dray, while the native police contingent accompanied the police wagon.

By lunchtime, as close to normalcy as possible had returned to Rangelands, but the adrenalin generated by the night's activities lingered. After breakfast, Ned decided a day off for everyone was the wisest move. Having eaten with the others earlier, when the normal hour for breakfast at the cottage ticked round, Ned went across to join them for toast and tea ... and to tell them of the night's events.

A petulant Emil wanted to know every last detail and made it known he is disappointed and offended at not being allowed to participate. Mads demanded to know what it is all about. Ned carefully explains both the events leading up to, and those of last night. Somehow he manages not to mention Emil's name in the process. But it remained clear Mads was not happy. Things have not improved by the time breakfast is over and everyone heads off to their respective chores. As Ned leaves the cottage, he makes a mental note to check later with Emil that nothing Ned said reflected on the lad in such a way as to incur Mads' anger. The last thing Ned wanted is for Emil to be in trouble with his uncle.

When halfway back to the bunkhouse, Ned remembers something. Something important he must tell Emil, and something he hopes might help lift the lad's spirits and restore the relationship between them. As he enters the dairy where Emil is working, the look Emil gives him is not welcoming.

"Emil, I know you are not happy, but that's the way it had to be last night. But I do have something important to tell you. When it's time to feed and water the pigs today, you should take a wagon with a cage down to that bush stockyard in the scrub. Two piglets are tied up there, and they will be desperate for their mother by now." The boy's eyes lit up and he rushed out of the dairy. The next time Ned saw him, Emil was halfway to the scrub and driving the horses so hard the wagon rocked and bucked over the uneven ground. Well, at least I've made someone a little happier today, Ned thought. I doubt I've done the same for Mads.

Chapter 14 The Partnership

Mads remained unhappy. His main complaint was that he was the only man not told about, or involved in capturing the rustlers. "I have been slighted, in spite of everything I have done for the man and this place." Mads told the universe as he wandered around the derelict former homestead. "He chooses to treat me like an outsider; like someone he can't trust. I won't be treated like this." His inspection of the old homestead after the police's use completed, Mads marched across the paddocks to join the others working on clearing the next area of scrub. Alf had a more inclusive approach. He always welcomed another pair of hands to help.

The trip to town with the prisoners was slow. After dropping off the body and the wounded man at the primitive medical facility, John Oakes took Sergeant Slattery and the constable riding with him to the police lock-up. Slattery became a ball of bureaucracy, ordering his constables about and overseeing every detail of processing of the prisoners before locking them in their cells. To John Oakes, the processing seemed as slow as the trip to town. At last Slattery was free. John approached him. "It's getting late. I should return to Rangelands. If you don't need me, I will head off."

"Don't be silly, Man. It's too late to start back now … and you were told to stay overnight rather than travel in the dark. I would be remiss to let you leave at this late hour. Besides, I need your statement about what you observed last night." Slattery saw a look of alarm flash across John's face. "Don't go getting yourself in a dither. All I need is for you to tell me what you saw and who from the property did what – if anything. It's just so the paperwork is straight, and we don't lose the case against these villains because I slipped up on some blessed paperwork. Take me to the station now and we will have it over and done with in a blink. Then, spend the night with Tom Croxley and head back up the valley first thing in the morning." Reluctant, but not in a position to refuse, John complied.

It was lunchtime the next day before John Oakes arrived at Rangelands. As he drove the wagon between the bunkhouse and the cottage on his way to the horse yard, Ned happened to wander out of the bunkhouse. "Deal with the wagon and horses, and then have some lunch. I'll catch up with you in the bunkhouse as soon as I have eaten," Ned told him. The men ate quickly and soon settled opposite one another at the table in the bunkhouse.

John gave his report. "Nothing happened on the way into town. The prisoners in the cage were quiet; didn't misbehave at all. Your Mr Meadows was sullen. The other bloke stayed as far away from him as possible. On my wagon, it was the coppers doing all the yapping. The 'passengers' said nothing. Well, one said nothing being dead as he was. The other one – the wounded bloke – made a bit of noise, mainly yelping and moaning at every bump on the track. At Marathon, all the 'processing' – or whatever that technical stuff be called – took just as long as the trip. I wanted to come back when it was done, but that big-shot copper wouldn't let me."

"Good to hear. Now, tell me what has happened with Meadows and his mob."

"Nothing much to tell; I dropped my two at the hospital, and then took Slattery and the constable to the lock-up. Meadows and his mate were locked in the cells. Then Slattery made me give him a statement before I spent the night at the store."

"Do we know when they are likely to appear in court?"

"Yesterday was the end of the week. The magistrate claimed it was too hard to bring a court together on Saturday, so the prisoners will appear in court on Monday."

"I expected everyone wanted them tried as soon as possible. The magistrate does sometimes hear cases on Saturdays."

"Aah, but not this Saturday; Marathon's new Turf Club holds its first big race meeting this weekend, if you see what I'm saying. Nobody gives up a day at the races to be in court … including the magistrate."

"It does suit me better for the hearings to be on Monday. I want to sit in on them. I'll ride into Marathon tomorrow to be in the courthouse first thing Monday morning."

"From what I've heard, those hearings might drag on for a few days. How long might depend on how well Slattery and his mob tell their story. Oh, I suppose Slattery might be asking you to say something too; to tell the court what you know."

As Ned left the bunkhouse, John's last words stayed with him. That's true, Ned counselled himself. I might be called to give evidence. Best I take the right clothes with me so I am appropriately attired to stand up in court.

First thing Sunday morning, Ned went in search of Mads. Things had not improved. Mads remained distant. Ned wanted the problem gone before he rode into town. After breakfast, and after telling Mathilde he might be gone for a few days, Ned found Mads repairing to one of the wagons. His reception decided Ned it was not the right time for the discussion he wanted. Mads mood was not right. Ned confined himself to asking about the piggery.

"I'm impressed with the way the piggery has developed. I can see it adding a valuable string to our income flow in the near future. To my untrained eye, it looks almost complete. Is there much work left to do?

"No, not much; a day or maybe one and a half days' work. Was there anything extra you wanted added?"

"Not at all; I'm very happy with it … and I see Emil has taken a liking to looking after the pigs." Mads grunted in reply, turned his back to Ned and started work on the wagon again.

Frustrated and concerned by Mads' continuing bad mood, Ned strode away. Best walk away now, he told himself, before I say something I will regret. He has a few days to get over it while I'm away. If his mood persists when I return, I will have it out with him. This situation between us can't go on much longer. It will impact on the others and the running of the place.

The court case against the cattle rustlers opened on Monday morning as expected. Richard Meadows and his two men were in the dock. Procedural matters and the swearing in of jurors took up most of the morning. As the jurors traipsed into the courtroom, the man sitting next to Ned nudged him in the ribs. "This should be over quickly," he murmured. Ned gave him an inquiring look. "All except two of the jurors are local farmers or graziers. That solicitor chap representing the duffers will have a hard time convincing those jurors his clients are innocent."

"Surely their verdict will depend on the evidence presented."

"They done it! We all know what they been up to, but no one could prove it. Too clever by half, that boss bloke. I feel sorry for the blokes he had working with him. Sorry lot they are. Not the brightest lot, and happy to take any work for a crust. Still, that be no excuse for stealing another man's livelihood. They are not so dumb as not to know the law." Ned felt relieved the conversation ended when the magistrate called the courtroom to order.

Although Ned expected the hearing to last a few days, by the end of the afternoon's session, he felt encouraged by the progress made. Most pleasing was the fact that he hadn't been called to give evidence. It wasn't that he didn't want to. Because of his association with Meadows, Ned preferred to remain inconspicuous during the trial.

Tuesday saw the prisoners appear individually in the dock. Meadows was up first. Sullen, he refused to answer questions until a few stern words from the magistrate. The threat of a contempt of court charge changed Meadows stance to one of denying everything. He was held over for further questioning and cross-examination later.

Next in the dock was the uninjured man. His nervousness was clear. In spite of it, he maintained his innocence and denied any wrongdoing. He claimed on several occasions he *was doing nothing more than helping Meadows round up some cattle on*

Meadows' own property. The prosecutor had a grand time with that claim. The man returned to his cell to await the jury's verdict.

Last in the dock was the wounded man. Ned was shocked. Now shaved and washed, the man looked much younger than Ned first thought. Injured and so nervous he could barely speak, the lad remained seated throughout his time in the dock. After a few minutes of questioning, he fell apart and told the court everything. He even went so far as to explain in detail how the gang doctored brands on some animals and rebranded others so the owners couldn't claim the beasts were theirs.

By Wednesday afternoon, only the sentencing remained. The prisoners were brought to the dock in the same order as they appeared the previous day. When asked by the magistrate how they found the prisoner, the foreman of the jury's announcement had a triumphant ring to it. Both the uninjured and the wounded men received hefty prison sentences. Sentencing Meadows took a lot longer than for the other two. He was found guilty. Because of the serious nature of the crime he organised and perpetrated, Meadows was ordered to stand trial in the Brisbane Supreme Court.

"Why would they do that? He is as guilty as the others … more so than them," The man next to Ned exclaimed. "He organised and ran the whole operation. Why isn't he being put behind bars too?"

"It is for those reasons he has been sent to the Supreme Court. The operation he masterminded and ran is a hanging offence. What his final sentence will be is now up to that higher court to decide." As Ned finished speaking, he noticed the shocked look spreading across the man's face. It was obvious the man had no understanding of the severity the law placed on such activities.

With the trial over, Ned planned a quiet drink alone at the hotel to ponder everything that happened, and consider his own position in relation to it. In no hurry, Ned was last to leave the courthouse. As he stepped out onto the street, the magistrate caught up with him. "Wait up, Mr Rixon. I wager you'll be heading to the hotel. If you don't mind, I'll walk some way with you." They fell into step and headed for the main street in silence.

Once on the main street, the magistrate spoke. "Get your solicitor to draw up the application to dissolve the partnership. He will want facts and figures to support the argument for dissolution. Tell him to make it quick. I have a quiet week next week…" The magistrate tapped the side of his nose and dropped Ned a conspiratorial wink before peeling off and crossing the street.

Now Ned had something else to contemplate over his solitary quiet drink. That last piece of advice required little consideration. He would take the magistrate's advice and talk to his solicitor. The sooner the partnership with Richard Meadows was no more, the sooner Ned could move forward. He would now stay in Marathon for as long as required to do whatever necessary to dissolve that partnership.

*****

Ned marched into his solicitor's office as soon as the clerk threw open the door this morning. His strategy paid off. The clerk advised Ned his solicitor, Mr Fallon, was in early today, but their first client wasn't due until ten o'clock. Ned expected the process he was about to embark upon would be a protracted and complicated affair. He drew a chair up to the solicitor's desk and began a detailed explanation for his visit. He need not have bothered.

Marathon is a small embryonic township. Word spreads fast. The outcome of yesterday's trial was the talk of the town. …And why not? Cattle duffing was a serious offence impacting the lives of the people who were this community. An end to the problem was a relief for the whole community. While the process was demanding, even exhausting at times, it was better than Ned anticipated.

At the end of the day, the necessary documentation was complete. "My clerk will lodge the paperwork at the court-house first thing tomorrow," Fallon assured Ned. "There is no need for you to wait for the application to be heard. I believe

150

I can safely say it will be a mere formality now. After Meadows' conviction, your application to dissolve your partnership with him will be expected. The court might query why you are taking this course of action when it is possible your partner may not be long for this world anyway. I shall argue it is about dignity and reputation – yours, that is, not Meadows'. There is also the need to keep the business running and progress it. The partnership could present some obstacles in that regard. Do you object in any way to that approach?"

His quiet reply of, "No, I have no problem with that," required major self-restraint and did not reflect Ned's inner turmoil. He really wanted to shout, "Of course not! Do what you must; just make it go away and quickly."

"Very well; we shall lodge your application in the morning. I believe there is every possibility it will be heard within the next week or two As soon as we have a decision, I will write you. If you have heard nothing in the meantime, on your next trip to town, it may be worth inquiring after the status of the application. There will be more paperwork to complete once the partnership is dissolved, not the least of which will be changing the name on the lease of the property to only your name."

With his business in Marathon completed, except for having a conversation with Tom Croxley before leaving town, Ned treated himself to dinner at the hotel. The magistrate and his wife also dined there with another couple. During the evening, the magistrate, on his way to the bar, stopped at Ned's table. "I see you are still in town. Would I be right in assuming you spent the day with your solicitor?"

"You would be. In the morning, his clerk will lodge the application we discussed earlier."

"I have it tentatively booked in for hearing next Thursday … assuming it is lodged tomorrow, of course." He dropped Ned another knowing wink before continuing to the bar.

A smile tugged at the corners of Ned's mouth. With that information, he could head home as soon as he spent a few minutes with Tom Croxley in the morning. The only issue left for Ned to consider was whether to return to Marathon to be present at the hearing next Thursday. He mulled it over all the way back to the store before finally deciding he would return next Wednesday.

Things did not go according to plan next morning. Instead of his early departure, it was ten o'clock before he rode out of town. One train of thought predominated all the way home: what would Mads' mood be like after these few days to get over his ill feelings towards Ned? After arriving home around mid-afternoon, it didn't take Ned long to find out.

His first task was to let Mathilde know he was back and would be joining them for dinner. Mads came into the cottage while he was speaking to her, providing an ideal opportunity to test the atmosphere. Mads is unlikely to be anything but civil in front of his daughter, Ned assured himself. "I came to see Mathilde as soon as I arrived home to let her know I would be joining you for dinner. Anything of import happen while I was away?"

"Ask Alf. He will know." Having delivered his response, Mads stormed out, leaving Mathilde looking shocked.

"I am so sorry. I don't know what's wrong with him. I tried asking Papa what was bothering him, but he told me it was disrespectful for me to question my father. I think I have done something to upset him, but I don't know what."

"No, Mathilde, it is nothing you did. I will speak with your father to try to sort it out. It has gone on too long, but it can't go on any longer."

"Please don't upset him or make him any angrier. Both Emil and I love it here and are happy with our new lives. We don't want to leave Rangelands."

"Has there been talk of leaving?"

"No, but … if Papa continues to be unhappy here, he might decide to leave."

After a few hollow, but he hoped reassuring words to Mathilde, Ned went in search of Mads. No more kid gloves. This nonsense must stop now. He sent a mental apology to Mathilde. Ned knew that before the day was over, he might make Mads a whole lot angrier.

Ned found Mads placing timber offcuts in his new lumber rack behind the tack room. "Mads, if you could spare me a few minutes, I'd like you to accompany me to the bunkhouse." Mads looked up but made no move to go with Ned. "There is something I want to ask you about," Ned continued without hesitation. "Now would be a good time, thanks Mads." The tone of Ned's final comment left Mads little room to manoeuvre. He threw the length of timber he held into the rack and started after Ned.

It was a short walk that provided little time for Ned to sort out how to initiate the conversation they would have. They sat facing each other. Ned made a start. "We have this place to ourselves, Mads, so both of us may speak freely. It's obvious you are unhappy – angry even – about something. Please tell me what troubles you." Mads growled, but made no attempt to reply. Ned took a moment to control his rising anger. This situation can't go on. He knew he must force Mads to talk.

"It can't go on like this, Mads. No one, especially me, can help you or fix whatever the problem is if you don't tell them about it. Now, for me this has become an untenable situation. I have something important for you to do, but I am not sure you are interested in it. There is no point wasting time telling you about it if you don't want to do it. And I would be reluctant to start the project if I'm not sure you will even be here long enough to finish the work. It's obvious you do not want to talk to me, and it seems you would prefer I didn't speak to you. If that is the case, how is having you here on the property going to work? Over the last week, your behaviour is that of a sulking four-year old. For god's sake, grow up and behave like a man." As Ned spoke, he watched Mads' face turn bright red.

Ned had hit a nerve and he intended attacking it until Mads opened up. It took more needling of Mads before Ned achieved that – and with spectacular results. Mads' pent up anger erupted and, once freed, it kept flowing.

"You criticise my attitude…! Well, my attitude is what you have made it. It is due to you and the way you operate – and the way you treat me." The story simmering for several days began to unfold.

"It is true; at first I was angry I was the only man on the property you did not tell what was happening on the night of the new moon. I wasn't told and I wasn't asked to participate. Did you think me too old? John Oakes is no longer a young man, but he was involved."

"I did not think you too old to be involved. That had nothing to do with it. The reason I kept you out of it was for the sake of Mathilde and Emil. Nobody was certain anything would happen that night or, if it did, how bad it might be. Mads, you are the only one of us who has a family to worry about. You have two young people who need you; depend on you. They have been through too much already. What if something happened to you out there that night? Maybe I was wrong, but I thought to save you worrying about what might happen by not mentioning it to you."

For a few moments there was silence as Mads digested Ned's explanation. Ned let the silence drift on. It was Mads' turn to comment. Ned would give him all the time he needed. The tension evident in Mads over the last few days began to disappear. The 'old' Mads began to emerge. But then, Mads was off again on another tangent.

"Yes, you are right. I have two young people who depend on me. They depend on me to keep them safe. I think it is not safe for them to be here anymore. Things could have gone differently that night. None of us might have survived to talk about it. … And what about the pigs that were stolen? I saw Emil drive the wagon with a cage on the back into the scrub. Then I watched him go to the piggery. I followed him to the piggery and demanded to know about the pigs. He told me about them being stolen. The men stealing the cattle might be in jail, but I think there are other bad men about as well … like the ones who steal pigs.

What if they come back? Will we be safe here? I think, maybe it is not safe for Emil to go to the piggery on his own anymore."

"Mads, it was all the same mob. The men who stole the cattle were the same ones who stole the pigs. They won't be coming back again." In spite of Ned's best efforts, Mads remained unconvinced, and reiterated his belief it was not safe for them to continue to live at Rangelands. "We all are safe here, Mads. Where would you go that is safer than here?"

"I am thinking to move to Marathon; buy a house on a bit of land, set up a home, and work at my trade there. Maybe it will be better there for Mathilde. She will have other women to talk to, and soon, maybe find a husband."

"While you built the new store, you saw the men in Marathon. Did you see anyone you would be happy for Mathilde to marry? Anyway, you won't be able to buy a house." Mads spluttered the start of a fiery response. Ned cut him off. "Are you a British citizen?"

"I am Danish. You know that, so why do you ask a silly question?"

"Because, unless you have taken the Oath of Allegiance to become a British citizen, you cannot buy or own land. It's the law. Of course, you could rent somewhere to live, I suppose. But is that what you want for yourself and your family?"

Another silence. Ned saw Mads shoulders drop and an almost imperceptible shake of his head. But the silence remained.

"I thought I felt like a mug of tea," Ned said, "But now I think I would like something a little stronger. Will you join me?" Mads nodded and Ned set about pouring them both a measure of rum. "Mads, if you decide to leave here, I cannot stop you. I would not try to stop you … but I would be more disappointed than you could know to see you go. I too depend on you, Mathilde and Emil for so much. More than that, I think of you as a friend. You are a free man and free to leave if you wish but please, before you make that decision, ask the young ones how they feel about such a move. Ask them if they think it is unsafe to live here. If Mathilde is missing the company of other women, whenever anyone goes into Marathon, they should take a wagon and Mathilde could go too. Think about it, please Mads."

Then silence again. It remained while they sipped their rums. Their mugs sat empty on the table for a couple of minutes. Ned accepted he had asked Mads to think things over, but now he wondered how much longer he should allow the heavy silence to continue. Should he try saying something humorous, or something profound to reignite conversation? Mads ended Ned's dilemma.

"I am old; a silly old man. I don't really want to leave here; none of us do. I don't have to ask the young ones if they feel safe here or if they want to leave. I know their answers. They would fight with me to stay here. Maybe you are right and I have been acting like a four-year old, but I have been so worried for them ... and for me. Worried that something might happen to them and I would lose one or both of them. Some nights I still can't accept I will never see my wife and the rest of my children ever again." Ned looked away as Mads blinked back the tears that welled up.

"Ned, earlier you spoke of an important project you had in mind. I am interested, I will be here to work on it and I will be here to finish it. Please end the mystery and put me out of my misery. Tell me what this new project is to be. I have been curious to know since you mentioned it."

Ned walked around the table and placed a hand on Mads shoulder. "Come with me and I will show you as I tell you about it."

Mads stood, shook Ned's hand and followed him out of the bunkhouse. Like two old friends out for a stroll together, they made their way across to the derelict homestead.

Chapter 15   Future Plans

It was time to acquaint Mads with Ned's next major project. They stopped in front of the derelict homestead. "This is our next undertaking. Sit for a minute while I tell you about recent events and what I plan to do now. I haven't told any of the others – not even Alf." Ned told Mads of Richard Meadows' conviction and the likely outcome of his appearance in the Brisbane court. He then explained the lease arrangement under which Rangelands is held and the conditions attaching to that lease. "While I was in Marathon this week, I took steps to dissolve the partnership between myself and Meadows. I will set in motion the process to purchase the land outright and convert it to freehold. There now is no impediment to my establishing a proper and permanent home for myself here on the property."

"But you do not own the land yet. It remains leased. Is it wise to begin building so soon? What happens if you cannot purchase the land?"

"I am given to believe only the formalities are required – and payment of the money, of course. If all goes according to plan, the process should be complete within the next month. The timing will depend on when the local Land Board meets again." Mads nodded to signify he understood, but the concerned look on his face remained. Ned sought to further reassure him. "I thought we might make a tentative start only on a new home-stead now."

"What is a 'tentative start'? You are either constructing a new building, or you are not."

"Yes. Well, this is the best place on the property to build a homestead. The former lessee thought so too. That's why he built here. It's on top of a little rise, so it looks out over most of the property, and there is a well close by at the back. To build here requires demolition of this building. That much we can do while waiting for the legal processes to be completed. We need to develop a design. I have some ideas of what I want, and no doubt you will have some thoughts about that as well. Mathilde, as the housekeeper, should have input. It will be good to incorporate a woman's perspective into designing the building."

"The demolition can start straight away. There might be some suitable timber in the existing building to reuse in the new homestead. Perhaps an inspection of the old place will provide information on the timbers used in its construction."

A significant amount of material appeared suitable for re-use. Mads cautioned some of it might need discarding once demolition occurred and he could better assess it. "I'm not sure how much spare time Emil has these days, but any free time he has should be spent assisting you here," Ned said.

"Who will live in the new building?" Mads asked. "It's important to know as it will inform the design process."

"I haven't thought too much on that. My thinking was for a return to something like the homestead on Sweers Island, with you and the young ones living in the house with me."

After a moment's thought, Mads nodded. "Yes, that would work here too ... but only if Emil and Mathilde agree. If we are to live in the homestead, what is to become of the cottage?"

"I suppose, from the outset, I saw the cottage becoming Alf's residence once we moved into the homestead. There is one other thing involving both the cottage and the new homestead. We need water supplied to both buildings. Carting water every day can't continue, especially when there will be two buildings to supply. I noticed what looks like an old well out the back. We need to investigate that, and the spring coming down from the hill behind the buildings."

Discussion of the new homestead complete, the two men ambled back to the cottage. Ned again complimented Mads on the piggery. "It is an excellent facility. My hope is it will not be too difficult to expand it if needs be in the future."

"You plan to have more pigs?" Mads asked, and Ned heard the hint of excitement in his voice.

"I refuse to give the matter any thought until after the homestead is built. After the first sales of our pigs, I will decide whether to expand or not. In the meantime, while we wait to start on the homestead, adding another pen to the piggery would be useful. I'm thinking of acquiring another sow to have another litter coming along."

"Another pen will not be a problem. If I may suggest something else you might consider. In my country, pigs are allowed to forage in the paddocks, eating whatever they find. It breeds a better pig; more meaty and with a better flavour. They still go into the pens at night and when they have their litters. If you want to try this, we could fence an area off from the piggery for them to forage in." Ned agrees to trial the idea after he purchases the additional sow, but stresses any work at the piggery beyond the extra pen is secondary to building the new house.

At dinner that night, Ned advised he will be returning to Marathon on Wednesday afternoon next week to attend the dissolution of the partnership hearing on Thursday morning. "It is likely I will stay an extra day or two as I'm sure there will be the usual mountain of paperwork to complete afterwards. Mathilde, perhaps you could prepare a list of things you need." Then another thought occurred to him. "It occurs to me, Mathilde, that you too might like to visit Marathon, for shopping or simply to familiarise yourself with the township."

"Oh, yes please. I confess to being curious about what the township is like and what it has to offer."

"She would be in town for two or three nights. Where will she stay while she is in town?" Mads asked. "I do not think it appropriate for my daughter to stay in the quarters under the store with you and Tom Croxley."

"Good Lord, no. I would take a room at the hotel for Mathilde. I assume you don't object to her staying there on her own." While Mads thought about it, Ned sought to reassure him. "Of course, if you would prefer, I also could take a room at the hotel to be close and watch over her. Regardless, I am unlikely to be available during the day to chaperone Mathilde."

"I do not require a chaperone, thank you," Mathilde growled, "...Not during the day or at night."

It appeared the issue was resolved when Mads agreed to a room at the hotel for Mathilde. As Ned began to relax, Mads threw in another suggestion. "Perhaps I too should go to Marathon with you and Mathilde. I could talk to Tom about supplies of materials for the homestead. My presence would remove from your shoulders responsibility for Mathilde. I could stay at the hotel in case she needed protection during the night. That way, you could stay at the quarters as planned."

Ned saw the look of disappointment – or was it horror – cloud Mathilde's face. "It is too soon to be talking to Tom about materials. When we have a firm design, you will have a better idea of what's required. That will be soon enough to talk to Tom. You could take a trip then." Mads wasn't happy, but he accepted Ned's decision.

A range of emotions crossed Mathilde's features during the discussions. With the matter now settled, Mathilde could not hide her excitement about the trip to town. All Ned could think about was developing a more definite itinerary than he usually worried about for such a trip.

With that occupying his mind, sleep was a long time coming that night. But, by the time he fell asleep, he had his itinerary. Thursday: in court for the partnership hearing, and discussions and any paperwork with his solicitor in the afternoon. Friday: anything to finalise with the solicitor, followed by catch-up with Tom, before leaving Marathon around lunchtime to arrive at the property before dark. That sounded reasonable. Satisfied with his deliberations, a sound night's sleep followed. Before falling asleep, Ned made a mental note to talk to Alf about the impending demolition of the old homestead. He couldn't risk having another man offside because he wasn't kept informed about happenings on the property.

*****

Ned's first stop on their arrival in town was the hotel. With only one other guest booked in, there was no problem securing a room for Mathilde for at least two nights. Then Ned called on his solicitor. He caught Mr Fallon preparing to leave his office at the end of the day. Their brief conversation confirmed hearing of his application was scheduled for nine o'clock next morning. "I intend sitting in on the hearing. If my application is successful, I will need to talk to you again about my next move," Ned told Fallon.

"If the hearing is successful, I will need you to come to my office to complete some paperwork, and I will need to talk through other matters with you," Fallon replied. On the assumption the hearing would be over by lunchtime, they agreed to meet in Fallon's office at one o'clock.

Not wanting Mathilde left alone on her first evening in town, Ned planned to dine at the hotel with her. As Tom was busy with customers when Ned put the horses and wagon in the horse yard behind the store, there was no opportunity for the two men to speak. When Ned returned to the quarters after leaving the solicitor's office, Tom was closing up for the day. He welcomed Ned's invitation to join Ned and Mathilde for dinner at the hotel. It was a hectic day in the store and Tom was exhausted. I must talk to Ned about hiring more staff, he thought as they strolled to the hotel.

Dinner was a pleasant affair. The food, basic but good, was accompanied by light conversation in an almost deserted dining room. After Ned booked her in, Mathilde took a stroll along the main street, noting the various businesses operating close to the hotel. On returning to her room, she made a list of the shops she thought to visit the following day. She took the opportunity over dinner to question the two men about those establishments. Tom proved a wealth of knowledge about who sold what, the quality of the goods sold and customer service – and places best avoided.

Thursday morning, Ned arrived at the courthouse well ahead of the time for the hearing of his application to become the sole lessee. By the time nine o'clock rolled around, the gallery was full. Surprised, Ned expected no more than a handful of people to share the space with him.

In the end, it all felt like an anticlimax. After only a few questions to the solicitor to clarify various details of Ned's application, the hearing was over in about twenty minutes. Fallon had other applicants to represent that morning, so Ned settled back to watch his solicitor in action. It filled in the morning, but didn't achieve much. Ned accepted that, with his solicitor involved in court all morning, there was nothing he could do anyway until their one o'clock appointment. With no further matters to be heard, the court rose for the day at eleven o'clock.

Ned allowed the court to empty before rising to his feet. As he wandered out of the courthouse, he wondered what to do with himself until his one o'clock appointment. On his way, he made a spur of the moment decision to drop in to the police station on the off chance Sergeant Slattery was in his office.

Slattery looked up and frowned as Ned entered the office, his overall demeanour not particularly welcoming. "Well, Mr Rixon, what brings you to my office again so soon? I'm not keen to hear of more strange goings-on happening on your property."

"No, nothing like that brings me here. My intention is nothing more than to check with you on outcomes from the operation that occurred at Rangelands."

"Aah, I see. Well, no doubt you know Meadows was committed to stand trial in Brisbane. That is set down for next week. Unofficial sources tell me it is likely a capital punishment sentence will be handed down."

"No surprises there, I suppose. Have you received any further reports of cattle duffing in the area since rounding up Meadows' mob?"

"Nah, nary a murmur since then, and I'm hoping it stays that way. I still struggle to comprehend how a handful of blokes could cause so much havoc throughout the area. It would be nice if it turns out they were the only mob operating here. Perhaps that is too much to expect." That last comment of Slattery's is something to think about, Ned thought as he took his leave of the police sergeant. Maybe, after Meadow's mob was rounded up, any others active in the area decided to lie low for a while.

With spare time still before his one o'clock appointment, Ned decided to check on Mathilde and maybe lunch with her at the hotel. When she didn't answer his knock on her door, Ned enquired after her at the bar. "No, I haven't seen her come back in. She went out shopping earlier this morning; stopped by the bar on her way out to ask about the shops in town." Ned waited at one of the tables until about 12.15pm. When Mathilde still hadn't returned, he went back to the store for a bite of lunch before meeting with his solicitor.

His session with Mr Fallon lasted a couple of hours, during which the partnership paperwork was finalised in accordance with the court's decision that morning. That dealt with, Ned moved onto the matter of purchasing and freeholding Rangelands, briefing the solicitor, and generating more paperwork. After spending most of the day indoors, Ned returned to the horse yard at the store and saddled one of his horses.

Tom told him impounded stray cattle remaining unclaimed were to be auctioned the following morning. Having dealt with everything else scheduled for that day, Ned rode to the pound to inspect the impounded cattle. The animals were an impressive looking lot and all in good condition. Two things convinced him to attend the auction the following morning. First and foremost was the appearance of the cattle. The other important factor was the timing of the auction. Set for eight o'clock on Friday morning, it probably was too early for most graziers to be in town in time. Except for those with properties close in to town, it would not be worth the hassle of coming into town so early for so few head of cattle.

Pleased with the way the day panned out, Ned returned to the store to prepare for dinner at the hotel with Mathilde again. As soon as he walked in, the barman, busy pouring drinks, gestured with one hand to direct Ned through to the dining room. He found Mathilde already seated at a table with another couple. "Mr Rixon, you remember Mrs Tomlins and her husband?"

"Of course I remember Mrs Tomlins. Good to see you again, Dear Lady." Ned introduced himself to Sam Tomlins. "I think we spoke once along the track on the way from Port Beauchamp, but were never formally introduced. I seem to remember you didn't plan on staying in Marathon, preferring to move further south."

"That's true. Our plans changed when we recognised the opportunities available in this area," Sam said.

Mathilde, unable contain her excitement any longer, cut into the conversation. "I met Mrs Tomlins in town earlier today. Over sandwiches for lunch in the tearooms, Mrs Tomlins told me they had just secured an agricultural farm lease over a block of land up the valley. It's not too far from Rangelands; only a couple of properties away."

The Tomlins did not linger long at the table after their meals. Ned suspected their polite withdrawal was designed to allow private discussions between him and Mathilde. If only I might have the conversation I'd like with Mathilde, he thought. That thought didn't progress. Mathilde killed it when she launched into details about the Tomlins' new life in Marathon.

"They both agreed they liked the place and it had great potential. So, they looked for a block of land. Luck came their way when the property owner hired Mr Tomlins. A few days later, the property owner's wife became ill. He hired Mrs Tomlins to housekeep and look after the children. With both of them working, they saved a little extra money to pay the initial fees associated with acquiring the lease of their block. The lease worries Mrs Tomlins though. She admitted she is not sure they will be able to continue to meet the lease payments and conditions, but they had to bid for the lease now before land in the better areas became scarce. Now Mr Tomlins is talking about having to find off-farm work to supplement their income until the farm is fully operational and providing reasonable returns. They are so excited about starting this new venture. It would be a shame to see them lose the land."

"That is interesting, and so is the timing. There may be some work going at Rangelands in the near future. If you speak to Mrs Tomlins again before we leave for home, please ask her to tell her husband to come by Rangelands soon to inquire about work." Mathilde's face lit up at the prospect of helping her friend. Ned had no doubt Mathilde would search out Mrs Tomlins to pass on the message. "Before I forget, Mathilde, it is likely we will leave town around lunchtime tomorrow. Please take the list of supplies you require to Tom first thing in the morning. Have a look at everything in the store while you are there. You might see other things you would like."

*****

Ned's assumptions about the auction of impounded stray cattle were correct. It attracted only two potential bidders, Ned and one other. The other bidder was interested in only two of the animals, but the auctioneer was reluctant to split the herd. Discussion and haggling between the two men stretched on with Ned becoming increasingly frustrated. Not prepared to bide his time any longer, Ned offered a solution to the stalemate. "Can we get on with business please? I am prepared to offer a bid on all ten head of cattle. The other would-be-bidder protested. "You may talk to me later," Ned told him, and gave the man a look that he hoped the other party interpreted correctly.

"Well then, what do you bid for these ten head? I have other matters demanding my attention today, so I would be pleased to have this auction done with."

The bid Ned offered was low. Lower than he thought the auctioneer would demand. Keen to finalise the deal, the auctioneer wasted no time in bringing his hammer down. "Thank you, Sir. Please finalise the financial details with my clerk. I bid you good day, Gentlemen." With that, the auctioneer gathered up his paperwork and gavel and strode off.

"If you remain interested in any of the herd, hang about until I've dealt with the clerk," Ned told the other man before speaking to the auctioneer's clerk. Once the financials were completed, Ned returned to the other farmer, who hung on a rail watching the cattle while Ned dealt with the clerk. "I assume by your continued presence you remain interested in acquiring a couple of those animals. Which two head do you prefer?"

A few minutes later, the other man had purchased his two cattle from Ned and was preparing to move them the short distance to his property. As Ned made to leave the area, the clerk rushed after him. "Excuse me, Sir. You are supposed to take those cattle with you. Now you own them, you can't leave them here."

"Oh, I'm sure that, for a small fee, they could remain here for a couple of days or so. Is that not the case?" The transaction took only moments to complete. Ned bought himself feed and water and use of a small yard at the pound for three days. He now had eight head of cattle to move to Rangelands and only a maximum of three days in which to move them out of the pound. How to accomplish it occupied his mind on the way back to the store.

There remained only to have a chat with Tom Croxley before Ned and Mathilde were free to leave for Rangelands. With the yard at the pound only available for three days, Ned felt a degree of urgency about returning home. Back at the store, Tom Croxley was busy with a customer. Then Ned noticed Mathilde standing off to one side with another woman. When they moved slightly, he recognised the woman as Mrs Tomlins. A glance back at the customer with Tom confirmed the customer was Sam Tomlins.

Mathilde asked how the auction went. Sam Tomlins joined the group as Ned replied, "Very well; I got what I wanted at an excellent price, but now I have eight head of cattle to move to Rangelands and not much time in which to do it."

"I am willing to do that for you, and am able to do so as soon as you wish," Sam Tomlins said.

"I don't think droving them to Rangelands will require more than one person."

"They were stray cattle; free for too long before being rounded up and impounded. They are quite skittish. I doubt they will be content to plod quietly along the track up the valley to your place."

The two men moved a short distance from the women to discuss the matter further. It took Ned moments to develop a plan and put it to Sam. "Okay, we are agreed we will both go home today. Tomorrow I will send John Oakes to fetch the cattle. He will collect you as he goes past your place. It will be an early start. The cattle need to be out of the pound yard by mid-morning at the latest. I hear there is a major cricket match taking place on Saturday afternoon in Marathon. There is unlikely to be anyone around once the impounded animals are watered and fed in the morning."

"Perhaps Mr Oakes might spend tonight at our farm. It would shorten the ride into town tomorrow and avoid wasting time collecting me on the way through." Ned agreed to put Sam's suggestion to John Oakes as soon as he arrived home.

With the wagon loaded, Ned was on the rugged track to Rangelands by eleven o'clock. The first thing Ned noticed on their mid-afternoon arrival was the old homestead now almost gone. Although eager to talk with Mads about the homestead, Ned remembered he needed to find John Oakes and send him off to spend the night with the Tomlins before heading into town tomorrow.

With Alf included in the conversation, Ned explained about the situation with cattle in the yard at the pound and Sam Tomlins' offer for Oakes to spend the night with the. When Ned finished his explanations, Oakes returned to the bunkhouse, packed a few items into a saddlebag and was on his way to the Tomlins farm by the time Ned returned from the paddock.

In Ned's absence, Emil and Mads had unloaded and dealt with the wagon. The sun was sinking behind the hills. Soon, the men would return to the bunkhouse and it would be time to go to the cottage for dinner. Again he put off talking to Mads about the homestead in favour of cleaning up and changing for dinner. He suspected the homestead would dominate conversation at the table, and he was proved right.

Ned was guilty of initiating the topic by asking Mads about the demolition. In response, Mads launched in to a progress update. Now fully immersed in the 'new homestead project', Mads asked many questions of Ned over dinner. Most of them focused on the design features Ned wanted in the new place. Discussion of the new building continued after dinner when Mads showed Ned his preliminary sketch. "It is rough at the moment and needs more work, but I thought it might help clarify what is wanted. I need to know how you see the house before I do anymore work on the drawing."

"I will devote serious thought to the matter over the next days before coming back to you with my ideas. My thoughts are not the only ones needed to determine the final plan. Mathilde, I would appreciate your input on the design of my new homestead. I'm sure a woman's point of view will highlight issues we men wouldn't think of. Please give it some thought and bring forward your ideas."

"Thank you. I will think on the matter. I suppose most suggestions I might make will relate to the kitchen area. That said, I will try not to confine my thinking to the kitchen."

It was growing late. Ned felt they exhausted the topic of the homestead. He needed something more relaxing to end the day. After arranging with Mads for a homestead site inspection straight after breakfast the next day, Ned escaped to the bunkhouse for a couple of quiet rums with Alf before turning in for the night. As he climbed into his bunk, Ned reminded himself of the importance of constructing the new homestead.

He must clear his mind of other matters and devote his thoughts to the design of the building. Mr Fallon intimated that within the next few days, he would lodge Ned's application to purchase Rangelands and convert it to freehold. Fallon expected no obstacles, and suggested the process should be complete within a month. By then, everything needed to be in place to forge ahead with the new building. ...And he had better not be the bloke holding up the work.

Chapter 16 The Homestead

An early morning inspection of the homestead site brought mixed reactions. With some pride, Mads showed Ned the stack of reclaimed timber. "I was surprised by how good much of the timber in the old house was in spite of how derelict the building looked. The new building will require more than what is stacked here." Then the two men paced out the pegged-out footprint of the new building.

"It looks small," Ned said. "I envisaged a larger house than this appears it will be."

"It is larger than the old house, and also a bit larger than the Sweers Island homestead. I will mark it out again after we agree a firm plan."

Mathilde wandered out to join the men. Contributing ideas to the design of the new house proved difficult for her. She hoped joining the site inspection might help her develop a 'feel' for how the building might look.

"Papa, I can't work out what all these pegs in the ground mean. Tell me please, where the front of the house is, and where the rooms will be."

After indicating the location of the front door, Mads pointed out the various rooms. "There in front of us will be the sitting room; behind that are the dining room and the walkway through to the kitchen. Over there is Mr Rixon's bedroom and his office. Our bedrooms are down this other side of the house."

It took Mathilde a moment to absorb the details before commenting. "That is not a good place for the kitchen. It should be over there to catch the breeze and avoid the smell of cooking filling the house. And, if this is where the front door is to be, it doesn't give much of a view. If it was over there and faced out that way, it would overlook much of the property. Is there to be a veranda anywhere? It would be nice to sit out on the veranda during summer."

"That means the house needs to be turned almost ninety degrees on the site," Mads said.

Ned turned the preliminary plan around to have it facing the way Mathilde suggested. "The problem with simply turning it around is that the bedrooms are then along the front of the house as you approach it from the track, and would block out the view."

Mads stood by Ned to study his preliminary plan. "It's no good. The house cannot be turned on its axis. I need to redraw the plan, but I will wait until everyone finishes coming up with ideas."

"Another change that's needed," Ned said, "Is the addition of another bedroom. I want at least five bedrooms. This plan only has four."

"Okay, I know; it's back to the drawing board for me."

After announcing she would give further thought to the layout of the house, Mathilde returned to the cottage, leaving the men discussing how to situate the house on the site. "Once we settle the design of the new building, how much assistance with construction will you require?" Ned asked.

"Of course Emil will help when he has time, but I will require one man to assist me fulltime once construction commences."

"That might be something Sam Tomlins would be interested in. I understand he is looking for off-farm employment to ease their financial situation. What do you think about that?"

"Yeah, Sam would be good. He would need to be prepared to work fulltime though."

The conversation regarding an offsider for Mads ended with Ned agreeing to talk to Sam ... having carefully avoided mentioning he already had done that.

Around the time Ned and Mads were discussing the new homestead, John Oakes and Sam Tomlins arrived at the Marathon pound to collect the eight head of cattle. It hadn't taken Sam long last evening to work out something was amiss. John was standoffish from the moment he arrived at Tomlins' farm and the tension continued on their ride into town. They managed to catch the pound keeper as he was about to leave the yards. He was only there that morning to feed and water the impounded animals. And he was none too happy about being there. He was in danger of missing the cricket match due to start in less than an hour's time.

With the cricket match at the forefront of his mind, he rushed to unlock the gate to the small yard holding Ned's cattle, and told John and Sam it was up to them to round up the cattle and move them out. Then, he was in the saddle and galloping off in the hope of changing into his whites in time for the start of the match.

That won't be difficult, John thought. There are only eight of them. I could do this on my own. Does the boss think I'm getting too old and need a nursemaid to hold my hand while I do my job? He had cause to revisit those thoughts on several occasions along the track.

The cattle were not inclined to co-operate. After taking longer than it should and causing all manner of curses, the two men finally rounded them up and moved them out of the yard. Then the real work began. Sensing freedom beckoning the moment they were out of the yard, the cattle wanted to make a break for it. Tension mounted as the two riders endeavoured to move the cattle out of Marathon and onto the track towards Rangelands. Once they started on the track, John heaved a sigh of relief. "Thank God we are clear of the town at last."

"...And we made it without trampling anyone or any property," Sam added.

Neither man had counted on the lure of the scrub and bushland lining both sides of the track up the valley. On the other hand, the cattle were well aware freedom lurked there on either side of them – and they were much more interested in that than whatever these two blokes had in mind for them. It proved hard work keeping the herd together and on the track. From the moment they left Marathon, it was a continual battle as the cattle tried to head for the scrub.

By the time they arrived at Rangelands, the two men were exhausted, and the beasts had gone from being skittish to downright ornery. Already late when they arrived, when the cattle were safely yarded, it was dark. Alf persuaded Sam to spend the night in the bunkhouse rather than ride back to his farm in the dark. That gave Mads the opportunity to talk to Sam about helping with the new homestead. Sam's enthusiasm for the job lifted Mads spirits.

While Ned advocated waiting until after purchase of the land before making a start on construction, he earlier indicated the transaction was a matter of form and would go ahead without problems. Rather than sit around doing nothing until then, Mads decided to begin preparations. His first task was to establish a saw pit and identify trees suitable for timber from those cleared from the property. Working alone, it took some time to create the saw pit and haul the first of the suitable trees close to his new worksite.

Emil, intrigued by what was happening, asked Mads if he might be involved in cutting up the trees. By halfway through the month-long waiting period imposed by Ned, Mads – and Emil when he had time – were stacking timber to dry. "I don't know what these particular trees are called," Mads commented, "But they produce beautiful timber; hard red wood with a beautiful grain."

"Where will you use it in the new house?" Emil asked.

"It will make beautiful floors. Depending on how much of it we end up with, it could be used in lots of ways throughout the house. Their timber will be good to use internally, to line walls and make benches and cupboards."

As the piggery expanded, Emil's time to help Mads lessened. In the week during which Ned believed his application to purchase would go before the sitting of the Land Court, Mads approached Ned about asking Sam Tomlins to spend whatever spare time he had during the week working on sawing up trees. Expecting

Ned to be reluctant, Mads was surprised when Ned told him to ride over to see Sam the following day. Sam worked full-time with Mads for the rest of the week.

Unsure what day the Land Court would sit, on Thursday afternoon, Ned rode into Marathon in time to catch Mr Fallon as he was about to leave his office for the day. "Ah, you've come to sit in on tomorrow's hearing," Fallon said. "I believe our application is first up at nine o'clock. If all goes well, we should finalise matters by lunchtime. I have no other matters before the court, so I will return to my office directly after the hearing."

This was sweet music to Ned's ears. If, as Fallon suggested, they finalised everything by lunchtime, Ned could return to Rangelands in the afternoon. Any delays or problems with the process would have him remain in Marathon over the weekend. The prospect of a weekend in Marathon did not appeal.

Fallon was correct. The hearing of his application was swift and uncomplicated. Afterwards, Ned accompanied Fallon to his office where they spent the next couple of hours finalising the paperwork. Then Fallon accompanied Ned to the bank where they waited impatiently for bank cheques to be drawn. "That's it," Fallon said as they left the bank. "All that remains now is to lodge this cheque at the courthouse. Once I'm back at my office, I will send my clerk to deal with it."

"That won't be necessary. I'll deliver it to the courthouse myself."

"If you insist," Fallon began a little tartly. "However, I will require the receipt in order to finalise the file." Ned gave him a curt nod and strode off, leaving Fallon trailing in his wake. It's not that I don't trust him, Ned told himself as he headed for the courthouse. I just need to know the money is paid and nothing more can prevent the land becoming mine. Less than half an hour later, Ned was back in Fallon's office handing over the receipt ... and signing yet another document.

"Right then, Mr Rixon," Fallon announced formally, "Rangelands is now freehold and yours. The Title Deed to the property will arrive in the mail in due course."

They shook hands and Ned left the solicitor's office. All the way back to the store, Ned wondered how he caused such a schism in his relationship with Fallon. There was no mistaking Fallon's frosty demeanour or his curt dismissal of Ned at the end.

In the store, things were quiet. Tom dashed to the quarters to grab a bite for lunch. He sliced bread to put with his cheese as Ned came in. "Help yourself to some lunch if you like," Tom said. "I'll take mine to eat in the store. I need to be there in case customers come in."

"Slice me a piece off that loaf too, please, and I'll come with you."

Undisturbed by customers, the two men sat munching their bread and cheese in silence behind the counter. His parting from Fallon continued to rankle. Tom noticed something bothered his boss and asked if he could help. "I'm not even sure what it is I need help with," Ned said. "Something that happened last thing before I returned here perplexes me." Encouraged by Tom, Ned told how his relationship with his solicitor suddenly soured. At the end of Ned's story, Tom looked uncomfortable and fidgeted. "What is it, Man? Do you think I did something wrong, or improper in some way?"

"Er ... well ..."

"What is it, Tom? Spit it out. What do you know?"

"Argh, what the hell...! Your friend, Mr Fallon, has been linked to some funny stories of late. Word is, money clients paid did not go to where it was supposed to go ... or, in some cases, it turned out to be not enough."

"Come on, Tom. What do you mean by 'not enough'?"

"It seems the clients thought they paid the correct amount based on information Fallon gave them. Then they received word the amount paid was 'a bit short' and they had to come up with more money. I don't know how solicitors work, but it seems this one puts the client's money into some sort of trust account and lets it sit there for a while before paying it out to wherever it is supposed to go. That's when it's discovered the amount paid is not quite enough. Fallon gives the client some story about the cost of legal processes being added to the original amount and asks the client for extra to cover the contingency. It's never much; just a few more pounds."

Shocked, Ned sat staring at Tom. "I see. That might explain what upset Fallon. I took the cheque straight from the bank to the courthouse. He offered to have his clerk pay it into the courthouse for me. I needed the knowledge it was done and the process was complete."

"You prevented Mr Fallon making his illegal bit on the side ... unless he adds some spurious figure to your bill to collect an equivalent amount."

"Not possible; I had two cheques drawn up at the bank: one to cover Fallon's account, and the other to pay for the land transaction. There should be no further account from Fallon. I gave him his cheque before we left the bank. Any requests for further funds will not be met and may well result in yet another visit to Sergeant Slattery's office."

Ned left Marathon later than intended, but still arrived home before dark. His mind churned over Tom's comments about Fallon's dubious practices, and he seethed about the man's attempt to rob him. Before he reached home, Ned decided the next time he was in town, he would have a quiet word with Sergeant Slattery. Ned wasn't interested in initiating any action against Fallon – after all, he had not been wronged – but he would be alerting Slattery to keep his ear to the ground for any murmurings about such practices by the solicitor.

After letting Mathilde know he would be joining them for dinner, he went to the bunkhouse to freshen up and was surprised to find Sam sitting at the table yarning with the men. On his way for dinner, Ned had a quiet word to Alf. "I see Sam is here for the night. I take it he worked here today."

"Yeah, and he is a damned good worker. He's been here for a couple of days now. It's dark when we return from the paddock so I told him to stay rather than ride back to his farm each night. I assume that arrangement is okay with you." It was okay, but

Ned was curious about what Sam was doing at Rangelands. He was about to pose that question when he saw Mathilde come to the door of the cottage to see if they were on their way to dinner. Ned parked his curiosity until later.

As they left the table after dinner, Mads said, "If you have a few minutes tomorrow, perhaps you might ride down to the bottom paddock. I would like you to see the timber we have set aside there. Oh, I forgot to ask earlier, how did the Land Court view your application?"

"Lord ... it slipped my mind as well. I intended to tell you as soon as I arrived home. I now own this place. Now we can make a proper start on our new home ... but first we must agree a plan."

"Ah well, that's for tomorrow too. I have a new plan for you to assess."

"Tomorrow will be soon enough to discuss such heavy matters. I feel weary. Perhaps an early night is in order for me ... if I can find an empty bunk!"

*****

Mads was justifiably proud of his stacks of timber for the new building. When Ned arrived at Mads' worksite, Sam was coming towards them. He walked beside a team of horses straining to haul a huge tree to the saw pit. "Sam has been incredible," Mads said with genuine admiration in his voice. "He works as hard and long as any man I know, and he has some kind of magic he uses on that team of horses to coax unbelievable effort from them." Any questions Ned had about Sam's presence on the property evaporated. To Ned's untrained eye, the timber resulting from their labours would save him quite a bit on building costs.

"If you return to the cottage for lunch," Ned told Mads, "That might be a good time to look over your new plan and maybe take another look at the homestead site." After arranging that with Mads, Ned moved on the where Alf and the other men were working.

They were boiling the billy to make tea when Ned arrived. Their morning tea break lasted a little longer than usual while

Ned shared his news of having purchased Rangelands. Once their questions stopped coming, Ned rode off in search of Emil. He guessed he would find the lad at the piggery.

Emil was bursting with pride as he showed Ned around. Another litter of piglets arrived in the last few days. The other change at the piggery was the fenced off area in front of the pens. The older piglets and their mothers foraged in the fenced area. Emil showed off his expanded knowledge of pig-raising. "Allowing the pigs to forage like this makes their meat taste better. They seem to like being free to roam around out here. All that foraging doesn't stop them eating everything else I feed them though."

"They do look to be enjoying themselves," Ned agreed. "Their numbers are increasing. We will need to start keeping records of when each litter arrives so we know when which ones are ready to sell."

"I am. As soon as the first pigs arrived, Uncle Mads told me I should do that. I think it will be a while yet before we have any to sell. They are growing fast, but are still small." Ned was about to tell him they would be selling the piglets as soon as they were the right size, which was likely to be not long after they were weaned. Then he thought better of it. Emil had become attached to his charges. It would be a wrench for him when the time came to sell some of them, and that would be soon enough for Emil to learn about it.

In the time left before lunch, Ned returned to the cottage. He wanted to hear Mathilde's ideas for the new homestead. He wasn't confident Mads would take her thoughts into account when designing the place. Mads still considered his daughter a child and often was dismissive of matters she brought to his attention. For Ned, it was more important to him than anyone knew that Mathilde should be happy and comfortable in their new homestead.

Mathilde was slicing freshly baked bread when Ned found her in the kitchen. "Could you spare me a few minutes to talk about the new homestead, please?"

"I am running a little late this morning. Perhaps we can talk while I finish preparing lunch. What is it you wish to discuss with me?"

"Have you had a chance to look at the new plan your father has drawn up for the homestead?" Mathilde nodded. "What is your opinion – your honest opinion – of how the new homestead will look? As the housekeeper and the woman of this house, how does the design suit you?"

"I had a quick look at the plan while Papa worked on it. It looks very big and I think it will be quite nice. I'm not sure the verandas are what you had in mind, but you can judge for yourself when you sit down with Papa to go over the plan. There is one thing… Oh, no; it doesn't matter."

"Come now, Mathilde. I asked for your honest opinion. What is this thing you tell me doesn't matter?"

"Well … You asked for five bedrooms in the house. Emil told me he does not want to live in the homestead. He wants to stay in the bunkhouse with the men. I tried telling him he wouldn't have to share a room with Papa in the new place. There will be plenty of bedrooms. He will have his own room. It seems he is set on sleeping in the bunkhouse. He has not told Papa yet, and I have not mentioned it either. I do not think Papa will be happy with such an arrangement. He does not accept that his nephew is no longer a child; that he is growing up fast and now should make some decisions about his own life."

"I see. Thank you for alerting me to this situation. You are right, Emil is now of an age where he would prefer to be with the other men, and perhaps he should have the right to choose. I think we might leave fighting that battle with Papa until we come to it. It makes no difference to the plan for the new building. I still wish to have five bedrooms. So, I think this conversation should remain between us for now."

As Ned stood to leave the kitchen, Mathilde stopped him. "Mr Rixon, I have had no opportunity to speak to you alone until now. Ever since we arrived, I have wanted to thank you."

"Thank me…? What have I done to warrant your thanks?"

"You were such a gentleman about what happened on the way from Port Beauchamp; what happened to me, I mean. It seems it did not turn you against me, and for that I am grateful. More than anything else, I feared losing your respect."

"My dear woman, that could never happen. What you suffered at the hands of an absolute reprobate has not changed my feelings towards you in any way. In fact, the way you handled that event and its aftermath only served to strengthen my admiration of you. I hoped this place and the solitude it offers might help you in some way recover from all that."

As she felt the heat rising up her cheeks, Mathilde could not meet Ned's eyes. "Thank you, Sir. Your kind words mean a lot to me."

The arrival of Mads and Emil for lunch provided a timely interruption to the situation in the kitchen. With a nod to Mathilde, Ned turned on his heel and went to join the others in the dining room. Emil dominated conversation over lunch with news of his pigs and how well they were doing. To bring lunch and Emil's babble to an end, Mads suggested he hurry down to assist Sam Tomlins at the sawpit for the rest of the afternoon.

With the table cleared, Mads produced his new sketch of the homestead for Ned examine. It only took a quick glance for Ned to realise everything they discussed was there in the new drawing. They spent some time examining and discussing the various aspects of the building. Then, with nothing more to discuss, they headed for the homestead site.

On their way, in what he hoped was a casual tone, Ned said, "I'm a little unsure about the verandas on the plan. Perhaps we should pace them out so I have a better appreciation of how they will be. On the plan, they looked a little inadequate to me." Mads stiffened beside him, but made no comment. When they reached the site, the first thing they did was pace out the verandas as on the plan.

It is going to be an impressive house, Ned thought as he stepped back a few paces for an overall view. Mads did an excellent job on its design. As he stood looking over the site, Ned felt an excitement surging within him and an impatience to see the building finished. It was not only the prospect of moving into the new place that excited him. It was his other intentions – secret intentions – associated with moving into the new house that really excited him.

As they turned to leave the site, Ned asked, "Do you think Emil will want to live in the new house?"

"Of course; why would he not want to live in the lovely new house we are building? Why do you ask such a strange question?"

"Is it strange? Emil is no longer a child. He might prefer to stay in the bunkhouse with the other men. It might be good for him to do that. Being amongst the others might help with his progression to manhood."

"You no longer wish for Emil to live in the same house with us…?"

"No. That's not the case. It was nothing more than an idle thought that came to me about how much and how fast Emil has grown up in the short time I have known him. It was not my intention to question your care and upbringing of your nephew." That's not strictly true, Ned thought, but Mads doesn't need to know that – not right now anyway.

Ned's words gnawed at Mads for the next couple of days until the slow realisation of their wisdom sunk in. That night after dinner, as Emil was about to go to the bunkhouse to spend time with the men before coming back to bed, Mads stopped him. "You enjoy spending time at the bunkhouse with the men. What attracts you there every evening?"

"Most days, I don't see the men until the evening. Their work is at the far end of the property, while mine is around here. I enjoy their company, listening to their stories, and hearing about the work they do. Mr Tomlins turns out to be an excellent storyteller too."

"There are not too many spare bunks over there at the moment. Of course, that will change once the new homestead is finished. Mr Rixon and Mr Grant will move out of the bunkhouse. Mr Tomlins will spend only the occasional night there. When bunks become vacant, would you prefer to move into the bunkhouse rather than the new homestead?"

"At least two bunks are vacant. I could move in there now. I would sleep in the bunkhouse. My duties wouldn't change and I would still help Mathilde with the chores in the cottage. I even would continue to eat with you in the cottage … like Mr Rixon and Mr Grant do. Please can I move in with the men?"

"So, you no longer want to live with your family. What have we done to deserve this?"

"It's not that, Uncle Mads. You and Mathilde are my family and I love you, but I need to be with the men; to learn from them if I am ever to be able to look after a property."

"I shall give the matter some thought." Although there was nothing Mads needed to think about, he didn't want to appear eager for the lad to move out. Emil waited a whole week before Mads gave his blessing to his moving into the bunkhouse.

Ned struggled to keep a straight face when Emil, with all his belongings, arrived at the bunkhouse and claimed one of the two vacant bunks as his own without as much as a by-your-leave to the other occupants.

Chapter 17 Consolidation

Life, Ned hoped, would be an ordered routine after the purchase of Rangelands. He did not take into consideration length of construction, or vagaries of the weather. After several more trips to collect material as it arrived, building work began in earnest. With what looked like an incredible amount of timber stacked in neat piles around the site, Mads and Sam started the building.

It would sit on low posts to elevate it a few inches above the ground. During that waiting period for the posts to consolidate, Mads and Sam measured and cut all the heavy beams to support the building on the posts. Then, after two weeks of no apparent progress apart from a few posts in the ground, work stepped up a gear. Sam moved into the bunkhouse.

Sam and Mads worked long days, and progress reflected their efforts … until early in the second week. That's when the rains came, contrary to the belief that it rarely rained at that time of year. It rained and drizzled for four days. Although the rain then disappeared, it remained overcast, blustery and cold for the better part of another week. After a couple of days of sunshine, the paddocks were lush and green. The stacks of timber needed to dry out again. They were unstacked and spread out over every available spare inch of ground close to the building site to dry them quickly. Another week was wasted. With no building work occurring, Sam spent the time at home and caught up with work on his farm.

Ned grew impatient. How long did it take to build a house? How long before they moved into this one? Although it didn't seem like it to Ned, it was a short delay. Soon Mads and Sam were back on the job and the building started to take shape. The two men worked alone except for a couple of hours most days when Emil came to help. While they managed most things by themselves, there came a time when extra hands and more muscle were required.

With Ned away for a few days attending cattle sales, Mads approached Alf about the situation. Aware of Ned's frustration at delays with the building, Alf pulled his men from their worksite and put them to work on the house. After four days, the men returned to clearing trees and fencing paddocks, and Mads and Sam went back to working alone.

On his return to Rangelands, the first thing to catch Ned's eye as he rode up the track to the bunkhouse was something more than just the skeleton of a house. That night over dinner, he congratulated Mads on the progress made. "I don't suppose you might hazard a guess at how much longer it will take to finish the homestead," he asked. Ned's excitement evaporated with Mads response.

"Weeks... At least six weeks, although more like eight or nine if I'm honest."

"So long...? How much more is there to do?" Mads ticked off on his fingers all of the parts of the house still to complete. "By the sound of that list, it will be lucky to take only nine weeks."

Ned shared his disappointment with Alf as they sat by the fire for their usual pre-bedtime tipple. "I can't believe it will take so long. It looks so advanced already."

"What's the rush? I know it's a bit crowded in here now, but there are still spare bunks. None of us have to sleep outside under the stars. Mads and Sam have done a damn good job, but it still is only a shell ... and there are no verandas yet. It will take a while longer for the inside to be ready for you to move in. I appreciate it is awkward for you being in here with the men. I too find it that way on occasions. But it is not forever; only a few more weeks. Don't go moaning about it. You will end up with Mads and Sam offside after they have put in such long hours because they know you are impatient."

"I know, I know; but there are other things I want to do as well. I bought a few more head of cattle at the sale last week. I need you to send men to Marathon to move them to here. ...And I stopped by that place where we bought the pigs and purchased another three. The farmer will look after them until we fetch them, but I can't bring them back here until the piggery is expanded to accommodate them. On top of that, some of the first litter of pigs are ready for the meatworks. With everything that's happening, I can't spare anyone to load them onto a wagon and take them into town."

"I thought I was the manager." Ned gave Alf a confused look. "You, as the owner and boss, tell me, the manager, what you want done. Then I, as the manager, sort out the men to do it. That's the way it has always worked in the past. Has something changed without my being aware of it?"

Ned roared laughing. "Touché; you are right. I don't know what's come over me. Nothing has changed except I am impatient about the new house. And again, you are right about that too. I don't know why I am in such a hurry to see it finished."

"I think I could tell you why..."

"Well, man, tell me!"

"No, I think not. We have not drunk enough rum tonight for me to risk it. But, if this keeps up, I will be telling you what I believe is behind it ... and to hell with the consequences. Now, shall we meet after breakfast to discuss all this work you are creating for my men?" Confused about what had just happened, Ned agreed without argument. "Good; then let's turn in for the night before tackling these problems in the morning." Ned followed Alf inside and climbed into his bunk. He felt Alf's comments were important, but had no idea why. He continued to ponder their conversation until he fell asleep.

As arranged, as soon as the men left the bunkhouse after breakfast, Ned met with Alf. "Before we begin discussing work, what do you think is making me impatient about the new house? If I understood, I might be able to do something about it. I want to know your opinion."

Alf chuckled. "Oh, I don't think you do want to know … and I don't think I want to tell you. In fact, I know I'm not about to share my opinion with you; maybe sometime later, but not yet. Now may we get on with why we are here?"

About fifteen minutes later, Alf announced, "Right; that takes care of moving your recent purchases of cattle and pigs to Rangelands. The men will finish fencing another paddock by this evening, so the extra cattle will not cause a problem. I think the piggery has enough pens for one more sow. If we move the existing pigs around to leave the biggest pen empty, we should be able to put the three new pigs in there on a temporary basis – at least until one of them has a litter. It won't hurt the piglets to wait another week before sending them to the meatworks. Once all your new purchases are safely here on the property, then the piglets will go to the meatworks. How does that suit you? Everything will be dealt with before the end of next week." Ned approved without hesitation.

Later in the day, Ned questioned himself. With actions in place to deal with all his 'problems', he couldn't understand why he still felt unsettled. Deep down, he knew it was about the house taking so long to complete. "…But why is that a problem?" Ned asked himself aloud. "Buck up, man," he told himself. "The men are doing a great job on the building. Be grateful and get over whatever this thing is that's gnawing at you." Fine words and good advice, but not easily put into practice.

A few days later, when Alf returned to the bunkhouse at the end of the day, he saw Ned go inside the new building. Alf detoured from the bunkhouse to join Ned. "It's looking good, isn't it?" he said when he found Ned standing in what would be the new kitchen.

"Yes. They have done a beautiful job. I'll talk to Mads, but I think we should just about be able to move in. There is not much more to do to finish the place internally. We could move in as soon as that is done. Then Mads and Sam can continue finishing off the outside. They could construct the verandas after we move in."

"No, Ned. There is quite a bit to do before the place is ready for you." Alf watched Ned prepare to protest. "I know you are impatient to move in, but the place is not ready yet."

"Why not? It only requires a bit more work here in the kitchen. There is nothing more to do in the bedrooms, and the dining room only needs the furniture moved in. What makes you think we can't move in yet?"

"There are no bathroom facilities yet. You can't move in without a privy. And Mads still has to construct a system to deliver water to the kitchen. Work hasn't started on any of those things yet."

"As soon as the interior is finished, I will demand Mads stops work on the house, and he and Sam devote their time and effort to those 'outside' items you mentioned."

"Mads and Sam are working long days because of your impatience. They are exhausted. If you upset Mads, they might decide not to work such long days, and maybe take the odd day off to rest. Leave the men alone to get on with the job. That way, you will move in sooner."

Knowing Alf was right didn't sweeten Ned's mood. He turned on his heel and stormed out of the house, leaving a bemused Alf in the kitchen.

"For God's sake, Ned, say something … make a move … do something … start the dialogue." Alf said. Ned didn't hear his advice. Alf was alone in the empty house. He sighed and followed Ned out of the house and back to the bunkhouse.

Another couple of weeks rolled by. Spring turned into summer. The front and back verandas were complete. Structures for the verandas along each side of the house were in place. One particularly hot evening, after dinner, Mads asked Ned to stroll with him to the new house. "There is still sufficient light left in the day to see well enough, but we should take lanterns."

Intrigued, Ned fetched two lanterns and they ambled to the homestead like two men enjoying each other's company on a stroll through Hyde Park on a summer's evening. "The interior is complete now … I think! I still need Mathilde to tell me the kitchen meets with her approval," Mads said as they wandered through the building. "Is there anything that remains not right by you? If you are happy with the way things are inside, we shall concentrate our efforts on what is to be done outside."

"I see nothing amiss or anything more that needs doing in here. You say you are finished all the inside work. Does that mean we may move in now?"

"No. You must be patient for a little longer."

"How much longer? Give me your best estimate, please."

"At least two weeks; maybe three. How long depends on when the new cast iron stove arrives. The last estimate was that it would arrive in Marathon either last week or early this week. Nobody has spoken to Tom Croxley since to find out if it has arrived. It will require several men to load it onto a wagon to bring it here, and those men might be needed to help install it. While Sam and I await the arrival of the stove, we will work on the outside facilities building. The side verandas will remain unfinished until all other work is complete."

"Damn, I forgot about the blasted stove. If Mathilde needs to stock up on supplies, I will send a wagon and some men to town as soon as we have a list from her."

"Perhaps the stove has not arrived yet..."

"Well, at least we will know one way or the other. If nothing else, Tom might have more definite information about its arrival. I will speak to Mathilde at breakfast tomorrow."

Night closed in while the men stood talking. The two men left the building together, before saying goodnight and parting to go to their separate sleeping quarters.

As Alf wandered out of the bunkhouse to enjoy his nightcap beside the fire, he saw Ned coming towards him. The look on his friend's face caused him concern. In an attempt to lighten Ned's mood, Alf said, "Cheer up, me old Mate. Whatever it is, the world won't end because of it. Grab yourself a drink and sit a while with me out here."

Ned hesitated. He wasn't in the mood to be sociable, but it would not be good form to reject the invitation. A few moments later, he too was perched on a stump beside the fire. "There's nothing important looming here on the property is there?" he asked.

"Not that I am aware of. Everything seems to be trotting along nicely. I'm thinking we will clear one more small area and fence it, and then leave the rest of the scrub for a while. The herd has increased to the point where we need to be devoting more time to the stock and preparing them for market. Emil can't do everything. Over the last little while, Rangelands has become a sound grazing property. My men and I need to change our focus from establishing the place to managing its operation. I don't see anything in that transition requiring your personal input. So, why do you ask? Do you have plans I need to be aware of?"

"No, but it is a while since I was last at Port Beauchamp. I'm thinking I should see how things are doing up there. Maybe I should take myself off to annoy Mr Kincaid and others for a few days … get away from this place … give everyone a break from me."

"Oh, I see. So, what did you learn from tonight's inspection of the new homestead? It's obvious it wasn't anything you wanted to know. Were you pressuring Mads about moving into the new place? If that is what this is about, maybe the best thing you can do is to go away for a few days. A couple of weeks probably would be better."

"Thank you for sharing your insights," Ned snarled. "Christ, you're probably right. I should stay away for a while. I'm beginning to suspect my moving into the new place is deliberately being stalled. Why am I still told I can't move in? This is my property, and that is to be my house. Surely I have some say in how things happen around here. How can it take so long to build a house?"

"I've lost count of the number of times you have asked that question. Open your eyes. Look at the building. It is huge. It is beautifully constructed and well-finished. …And you have only two men working on building it. Of course, it is going to take time before it is ready to be lived in. You have never told me why you are so impatient about moving in. I'm not sure you have admitted to yourself why that is." Ned threw his hands in the air but, before he could say anything, Alf continued. "Okay; what's the urgency? Come on, tell me."

Ned glared at Alf but said nothing. Alf needled him further. "No...? Can't tell me? Don't know why that is? Would you like me to explain it to you? Come on, answer me. Shall I tell you what's wrong with you? Maybe I should. It might put us all out of our misery. For weeks now, you have found fault with everything, criticised where no criticism was justified, and snarled at everyone around you – with the possible exception of Mads and Sam. And that probably is the only wise thing you have done lately."

Alf's listing of Ned's shortcomings was interrupted. Ned, with fists clenched, jumped to his feet. For a brief moment, Alf thought he had gone too far and was about to pay the price. Then Ned wilted and collapsed onto his stump again.

"I'm sorry, Alf. Have I been so bad?" Alf shrugged and then nodded. "I don't know what is happening to me. I feel so angry all the time, although I know I have nothing to be angry about. Everything is going well for me. The last while has been a period of consolidation and transition that resulted in Rangelands becoming a sound commercial enterprise. Yet, in spite of all the good that has happened, I feel so restless."

"Jesus, Ned; are you so naive? We have been friends for a long time. So, as a friend, let me give you some advice." Ned look wary and considered it for a moment before agreeing. "It is really quite simple, my old friend. You are frustrated. There is something you want to do – something you want to make happen – but you can't. I don't know why you can't ... or why you haven't done what needs to be done, but here is what you should do. Tell Mathilde how you feel about her. See if she shares those feelings. If she does, then, for God's sake, start planning your future together. Oh, and yes, a part of that will involve discussing it with Mads. Now, is there anything in all that you don't understand, or don't believe?"

There was no response from Ned. He sat in a state of shock with his jaw hanging slack for a moment, before bounding to his feet and striding off into the night. What have I done, Alf wondered? I have either helped solve a problem, or wrecked a lifelong friendship ... and a perfectly good life to boot. He made no move to follow Ned, reasoning that time alone with his thoughts might help Ned gain a better understanding of himself. When Alf fell asleep that night Ned's bunk remained empty. As his eyelids drooped, Alf's last thought was whether he should worry that Ned still had not returned from his walk in the dark.

While that last thought did not disturb Alf sufficiently to have him go to investigate, when Ned's bunk was empty and unslept in next morning, it was time to worry. No one at the cottage had seen him that morning. Mathilde was concerned he had not arrived for breakfast. "When Papa came to breakfast, I asked if something happened last night while they were at the new homestead. Papa said no. Mr Rixon seemed his usual self when they said goodnight. Where could he be? Where did he spend the night?"

Mathilde became agitated. Alf tried reassuring her Ned was all right. "Knowing Ned, he would have gone off to see something on the property and fell asleep out there somewhere." It didn't sound convincing to Alf, and it was clear Mathilde wasn't buying his explanation either. "I will take a ride around the property to look for him."

"What if he came off his horse and has been lying injured out there all night?"

"He went for a walk. He wasn't on horseback." Again, not very reassuring, Alf told himself as he turned to leave the cottage. He wished Mathilde hadn't asked that last question. Although he knew Ned hadn't ridden off last night, that same thought plagued him since he found Ned's bunk unslept in this morning.

Alf was at the door when Emil rushed in. One look at the lad and both Alf and Mathilde knew something dreadful had happened.

"Come quick," Emil yelled, and beckoned for Alf and Mathilde to follow him.

"What is it, Lad?" Alf asked. "What has happened? Tell us." Emil raced on without responding to the urgency in Alf's voice.

It's Ned. I know it's Ned, he told himself as he galloped after Emil. Good God; what have I done; what have I driven him to do, he silently asked The One who supposedly knows all. He didn't have to wait long for answers. As the approached the wagon shed, Emil slowed to a halt on one side of the doorway to where the wagons were stored.

"In there," he said, and indicated where with a jerk of his head towards the wagons.

Alf didn't hesitate, but rushed on into the shed. He caught his breath at the sight that greeted him. Then let out a strangled wail. "No o o; he can't be." They had found Ned. His head and torso were on the ground, while his legs hung over the drawbar of a wagon. One glance was all Alf required to assume Ned fell from the drawbar. Perhaps he sat there in the peace and quiet of the dark to think things over. Maybe he fell asleep sitting there. Alf became aware of Mathilde rushing into the shed behind him. "Do not come in here. Go back outside and wait there," he yelled at her without turning around."

"No! I need to…"

"Do as you are told. Go outside and wait with Emil." Alf heard Mathilde catch her breath at the reprimand. He would deal with that later.

Picking his way carefully over to Ned, Alf noted Ned was physically sick during the night. There was a pulse. "Sweet Jesus; he's not dead, just drunk," Alf whispered. The rum hogshead on its side near his friend attested to what happened last night. Ned hadn't fallen off the drawbar because he fell asleep. It happened because he was blind drunk. The hogshead was the one from the bunkhouse with the burn mark Lofty made on it when he placed the pan straight from the fire on top of it. Alf couldn't remember how much of its contents remained after their nightcaps last night. He nudged the barrel with his boot: empty. "You've done a good number on yourself, Old Mate," Ned murmured to his comatose friend. "What's to do with you now? When you finally wake up, you will not be fit to be around other humans for some time." Alf sensed a presence behind him. He turned to look over his shoulder and found Mathilde standing about a metre back.

"Is he dead?" It was a simple question. The anguish etched into her face said much more.

"No, he is alive, but very drunk."

"We must get him into bed. How can we move him to the bunkhouse?"

"We don't. Fetch a rug, Mathilde, so he is comfortable here in the shed."

"No. It is not right to leave him here. He needs looking after. I must care for him." As she spoke, Mathilde came close and knelt beside Ned. Alf watched her run her hand up over Ned's cheek to brush the hair back from his face. "Emil," she yelled, "Fetch me some water in a clean pail, please... and a cloth." Soon Emil came into the shed. Laden with Mathilde's requirements, he stood just inside the doorway and refused to come closer. Alf went to him to relieve him of his load and bring it to Mathilde.

"He is all right, Emil. It is okay to come closer." Emil shook his head. "There is nothing to be afraid of here. Come closer and see for yourself."

"There has been so much death," Mathilde whispered to Alf. "Seeing Mr Rixon like this brings back all the horror associated with what happened to our family. He is frightened. Give him time. When Mr Rixon is up and about again, Emil will be fine. He will accept that all is well and there is nothing to fear here, but it might take a couple of days for him to settle down again. He is so young to have seen so much tragedy."

Alf heard the words she spoke but his attention was focused on her actions. The tenderness with which she sponged Ned's face and his shirt front spoke volumes. This was not the tenderness of a nurse caring for her patient. It was the tenderness of an emotion that ran much deeper than that. In some strange way,

Alf felt vindicated. His words to Ned last night were justified. As he watched Mathilde at work, Alf sent Ned a non-verbal message. You are such a fool Ned Rixon, he thought. If only you would tell this woman of your feelings. Her actions today give me clear indication she shares those feelings.

At last, Mathilde finished and dropped the cloth into the bucket. "What happens now? I can't leave him here like this," she told Alf.

"He will be out to it for quite a while I think; probably all day. When he wakes, he will be so hung over, he will feel lousy. He'll be sick and have a terrible headache, and he won't want to have people around him. With his swag and a rug from the cottage, we will make him comfortable in one of the wagons. That way, the other men are less likely to see him like this, and his dignity will remain intact."

It took all three of them to load Ned and make him as comfortable as possible in the wagon. "Perhaps we could all do with a cup of tea after what happened this morning," Mathilde suggested. Alf and Emil followed her to the cottage and soon the three of them were seated at the dining table with steaming mugs of tea.

"Why did he do it? I've never known Mr Rixon to do anything like this before. What happened to make him do this?" Emil asked in a voice heavy with anxiety.

"Who knows...?" Alf said and shrugged. "Ned has plenty to worry him: this place, the store in town, and everything he owns at Port Beauchamp. There's plenty in all that to weigh him down, I shouldn't wonder. Anyway, it is not our place to ponder such matters. Our job is to support him and to try to avoid creating situations that add to his worries." As he finished speaking, Alf looked at each of his companions in turn to check if his words had sunk in. Emil nodded his understanding. Mathilde gave a dismissive flick of her head.

"It's that house! That's what caused it," she exclaimed. "It has been a concern to him ever since they started the place. I don't know why, but I have watched it eating away at him.

I should have asked. Maybe there was something I could do to ease matters for him. Mr Grant, you would know. Are there problems with the new house?" Ah, the astuteness of one so young, Alf thought as he searched the appropriate response.

"I don't believe there are problems with the house. Ned is quite impressed with the building. The only problem, if there is one, is the waiting involved before he can move in. Ned has always been a person who, once he gets an idea, wants to see it through, done and finished almost the moment after he thought of it."

"If he is so satisfied with the building, why has he not been himself over the last couple of weeks?" Mathilde asked. "He is not eating much, seems interested in little that is happening around him, and is short tempered. So, if it is not the house, what else is bothering him?"

If only I – or Ned – could tell you, Alf thought as he felt the corners of his mouth twitch upward in an attempt at a smile. He made sure they returned to their normal position before replying. "Perhaps it is a personal matter that occupies his mind. Some-thing we are not privy to and have no right to know. Best we not mention to the others what happened to day, and that we don't discuss it further. Like as not, today will leave Ned most embarrassed when he recovers. Those of us who know about it should not discuss it, and should try to forget what happened – if that's possible." Murmured agreement came from the others at the table.

Alf pushed his chair away from the table and stood up. "I think there is no more to say or do in relation to this morning's events. It is time we got back to what we are supposed to be doing, instead of sitting around drinking tea." While his words seemed a little brusque, his grin told the others all was well. "Mathilde, if you have a few spare minutes during the day, I'm sure you wouldn't mind checking on Ned from time to time." Mathilde nodded and turned away in the hope Alf would not notice her blush.

As Alf strode to the horse yard to saddle his horse, he told the universe, "Now all we do is wait until he recovers. Then we will deal with whatever comes next."

It wasn't until mid-morning of the following day when Ned staggered out of the shed. His back was stiff, and he ached all over. It would be a relief if my head fell off, he thought as he made his way to the cottage in search of tea … and maybe dry toast.

Chapter 18 Severing Ties

With the men busy about the property all day, Ned opted to spend the rest of the day in his bunk, only emerging shortly before the men were due to return in the evening. Unsure who knew about his recent 'event', Ned was not looking forward to facing the others. Aware he would have to sooner or later, he looked for ways of delaying the inevitable for as long as possible. To this end, Ned strolled across to the new homestead.

As he approached, he saw no changes. He remembered Mads saying they would concentrate on external works next. At the rear of the house, the progress became apparent. The bathroom facilities looked well advanced. Sounds emanating from inside the building confirmed work continued on the interior. Steeling himself for whatever reception he might receive, Ned stepped quietly through the open door.

Both Mads and Sam were engrossed in installing the toilet facility. A quick look in the small room at one end of the building showed it set up for bathing. A small hip bath was located at one end of the room, while a shower arrangement was installed at the opposite end. The sight of the bathroom lifted Ned's spirits. He thought the facilities almost completed. Once the last of the installations were done, there would be no obstacle to his moving into the new homestead.

Mads looked up startled when Ned spoke to him. "I'm sorry. I did not hear you come in. Was there something you wanted, or were you here to inspect the building?" Ned assured Mads he came to check progress.

"I'm amazed at how much you have achieved in such a short time. What is left to do in this building … and what is the intended use for this middle section of the building? Is it to remain open-fronted as it is now?"

"My original plan was for two separate building: a bathhouse and a privy building. Then Sam and I got talking. We came up with this idea of one building with a bathroom at one end and the privy at the other. The middle section you asked about is where Mathilde's mangle and other laundry paraphernalia will be housed. That area still requires some work, but it won't delay moving into the house."

"What more is there to do in this area?"

Sam chuckled. "We are going to build in one of those new copper things for boiling clothes. Have you seen them?" Ned looked confused and shook his head. "It is like a big copper pan or dish sunk into a brick base that includes a fireplace to heat the water."

Mads paced out the area and waved his arms about to show Ned where it would be installed, and described how it would function. "The pan, or whatever it is called, should have arrived at Marathon this week. We won't start the brickwork until the pan is here to confirm its measurements."

"It sounds like a substantial woodheap is needed close by," Ned suggested.

"Emil has started collecting wood for it. Tomorrow we will start work on providing a water supply to the homestead and to this building. We will check that existing well first thing tomorrow morning before making any decisions about the work required," Mads said. "We have only a few minutes' work to complete here. May we get on so we might finish the building before it becomes too dark to see?"

With a renewed spring in his step, Ned returned to the bunk-house to freshen up before dinner. He felt hungry, and realised he was looking forward to the evening meal. Amidst the usual end-of-day chaos in the bunkhouse, nobody noticed Ned's presence, except for Alf who surreptitiously studied his friend from a distance. So far, so good, Alf thought. There doesn't appear to be any residual problems from Ned's drinking binge. Later, when the two men sat outside by the fire, Alf raised the matter with Ned. "You seem fully recovered. Unless I don't know you as well as I think I do, I would say you look your old self tonight."

"I believe I am. The world looks rosier tonight than it did a few days ago. I need to thank you for your words of wisdom the other night ... even if I didn't respond well to them at the time. As always, you are the wiser man. You made infinite sense. I shall take your advice on board and act on it in due course – without rushing into anything though."

"Anytime, Old Friend ..."

"I see things with increased clarity now. Solutions to problems haunting me for some time come easily to me. It is likely I will visit Port Beauchamp again within the next week. It is time to close the book on that part of my life I think." Although not sure what Ned meant, it sounded like a positive move – especially if it prevented another meltdown.

After spending the next morning inspecting the property and spending some time with Alf, Ned announced he would be away for the next few days. He told Alf, "I will ride into Marathon this afternoon in time to catch the afternoon boat to Port Beauchamp. How long I will stay there depends on how things go. Once my work there is finished, I will return to Marathon on the first available boat." Alf nodded. At last Ned had seen the light.

It was a mystery to Alf why Ned insisted on spending at least four days in the saddle and camping out under the stars at night in order to check on his operations at Port Beauchamp, when he could take an overnight boat ride. Ned lunched early to accommodate his intention of spending some time with Tom Croxley at the Marathon store before joining the boat for the trip up the coast.

Ned's discussions with Tom were fragmented and sandwiched between customers, but everything was dealt with in time for Ned to be amongst the first passengers boarding the coastal vessel. Having secured one of the few small cabins on board, Ned settled in for a peaceful sleep before they docked at Port Beauchamp at first light the next morning.

Too early to call at the store, Ned went to his Port Beauchamp cottage. He lit a small fire and rummaged around to make a pot of tea. As soon as the store opened, he would go to meet with Mr Kincaid. In the meantime, while he sat drinking his tea, he ran through what he needed to tell Kincaid and how to say it.

The early morning sun on the front veranda induced mellowness. In spite of adequate sleep the previous night that mellowness slid into drowsiness. It wasn't until the sounds of the township coming to life for the day intruded that Ned realised he had been dozing. After splashing cold water on his face, he strode to the store. Kincaid was unlocking the door when Ned arrived. Their time together at such an early hour allowed for uninterrupted discussions before the arrival of the day's first customers.

Kincaid acknowledged trading slowed over recent weeks. While Beauchamp remained an active port, Marathon was becoming the major regional centre. "Larger enterprises now base their operations in Marathon. They provide a wider range and more reliable supply of goods to the whole region than is possible from Port Beauchamp," Kincaid told Ned. "Customers' orders placed on Marathon businesses are delivered overnight by boat to Beauchamp. Three or four boats sail north from Marathon every week, so there are no major delays in delivery."

This did not come as news to Ned. Although lacking evidence to support it, he suspected trading through the two ports had become exactly as Kincaid described it … and hence the reason for his visit to Beauchamp. "Thank you for that information, Mr Kincaid. The reason for this visit is to ask if you might consider relocating to Marathon. Mr Croxley is in need of an experienced assistant in my store there. You would be an asset to that store's operation."

"I would need to give the matter some consideration. What is to become of this store? While business has diminished, we still have customers, and the yards at the wharf are still in occasional use."

"I would welcome your thoughts on leaving your most senior clerk in charge of operations here. I cannot guess for how long that might be. I am certain that, at some time in the future, it will be prudent to shut down operations here in Port Beauchamp."

"May I think on this overnight?"

"Of course, but I would appreciate the outcome of your deliberations by tomorrow afternoon. I anticipate boarding tomorrow evening's boat to return to Marathon."

The reason for his visit now dealt with as much as possible, Ned went to the hotel in search of breakfast. There remained only one last matter to deal with: his cottage at Port Beauchamp. His dilemma was whether to put it up for sale now, or wait until he finalised operations there and severed his connection with the town. Although tending towards the latter as the wisest option, Ned remained undecided. Late in the day, he visited a local agent for advice. The agent was less than enthusiastic.

"The town has slowed down in recent months, resulting in not much demand for properties. I could put your cottage on my books, but it might be some while before it sells or there even is any interest in it." After promising to make a decision about the cottage before leaving town, Ned left the agent's office with no more definite idea of what to do than before. But, he had promised to think it over, so that's what Ned did while inspecting his stock yards at the wharf. Only one small yard held three head of poor-looking cattle. The yards' attendant, seeing Ned's interest in the cattle, wandered over to talk to him. Ned did not recognise the man.

Instead of introducing himself, Ned said, "You must be new to the job. I don't think I've seen you around here before."

"Nah, only bin 'ere a few weeks... grazier I worked for up the coast went bust and walked off the property... left me in the lurch a bit. I was lucky. The day I arrived in town, the bloke who 'ad this job quit. ...Not much of a job though. Nothing much 'appening at these yards of late. Don't suppose the job will last long. My tip is, bloke what owns them will close 'em down. No good trying to sell 'em; nobody would buy 'em."

"I hear tell things are quiet all over town."

"Yeah, lot o' people 'ave gone bankrupt. Lot o' others left town afore they went the same way."

On leaving the wharf area, Ned took a stroll through town. There was no denying Port Beauchamp seemed much quieter than he recalled, and certainly a lot quieter than the embryonic township of Marathon was already. His stroll through town ended at the hotel where he indulged in a pre-dinner drink at the bar before moving to the dining room for dinner. While the barman was kept busy, there seemed fewer drinkers than he remembered seeing in that bar most evenings in the past. By the time he had eaten, the future of his Port Beauchamp operations was clear in his mind. Decisions made, he slept well that night.

*****

First item on the agenda this morning was a return visit to the agent he visited yesterday. It did not take long to arrange to add the cottage to the agent's list of properties for sale. If it sold tomorrow, so be it, Ned told himself as he left the agent's office and headed for the store. It took a few minutes before Mr Kincaid was free to meet with Ned in the office. Before Ned could begin discussions, Kincaid said his piece.

"After your visit, I devoted much thought to your offer to relocate to Marathon. In the end, it wasn't a difficult decision. This job is the only thing holding me at Beauchamp. That being the case, and the way things are going around here, who knows how much longer there will be anything for me here. I'm not blind or stupid. I can see the future lies with Marathon. So, Mr Rixon, I am favourably inclined towards your offer of employment at your Marathon store. Perhaps you might share details with me of what such employment might entail."

"That is good news, Mr Kincaid. The past twenty-four hours have provided me with the wherewithal to more fully assess my future association with this town. Earlier this morning, I spoke with an agent regarding selling my cottage here. Yesterday, I spoke with the attendant at my yards at the wharf. He tells me they are seeing little use. There is no sense in maintaining the yards and paying a man to look after them if they are not paying their way."

Kincaid, who nodded throughout Ned's speech, interrupted Ned. "I agree, Sir. Not only are they not bringing income into the business, they are costing us money."

"Good; you agree we should divest ourselves of that part of the business. Now, let us talk about this store and its operation. How many people, other than you, does it employ now?"

"...A senior clerk, a junior clerk, a salesman, a storeman, and assistant storeman, and a lad to help out wherever he is needed."

"How few people would it take to run this store? I'm talking about with the reduced trade being experienced now and with the likelihood of further loss of business in the future. What is your realistic assessment, Mr Kincaid?"

"As difficult as it is for me to say, Sir, because of the likely implications, the store could manage with perhaps no more than the senior clerk and the storeman ... and I would be tempted to retain the lad."

"Ah, we think alike, Mr Kincaid. I will tell you what I propose. I would appreciate your honest opinion on all or any of it when I am finished."

It did not take long for Ned to outline his proposed plan: offer the yards at the wharf for immediate sale; give the junior clerk, salesman and assistant storeman notice that their employment would terminate at the end of the month. Ned explained further.

"That will leave three staff to manage any trade that comes to this store. Further, I suggest advertising the store for sale and, in the event it isn't sold after four months, all remaining stock to be disposed of at the best price offered. The sale of stock should last no more than one week. Every endeavour should be made to clear all stock from the premises if possible during that time. If still no buyer comes forward by the end of the 'sale' period, I will close the place down and walk away from it. At the time of closing it down, any stock remaining unsold to be transported to the Marathon store. How say you to all that, Mr Kincaid?"

"I see the logic in your thinking, Sir, and I accept it as an inevitable outcome. But ..."

"…But it is difficult to see men put out of a job?"

"Yes, Sir. All are good workers who have served the place well. The storeman has a wife and young family, but it will be just as hard on the others."

"I am aware, Mr Kincaid. By giving them until the end of the month, my hope is they find work elsewhere, even if that means moving on from Port Beauchamp. There also is the possibility the storeman, who we intend to retain for an extra three months, may decide to seek other more permanent employment and also will move on. That is the risk we must take."

After further discussion, and with the proviso that it depended on how things worked out, there might be an opportunity to offer the storeman a similar position at the Marathon store if he and his family were prepared to relocate. By the time Ned finished outlining the future of the Port Beauchamp store, a dejected Kincaid sat opposite him. "Right, cheer up, Mr Kincaid. We have other important and more exciting matters to finalise." Kincaid pulled himself up straight in his chair but, in spite of his best efforts, he could muster no enthusiasm for whatever the boss wished to discuss next. "Come now, Kincaid. We haven't discussed your new job and how soon we will see you at Marathon."

By the time their meeting ended, Kincaid was smiling and the germ of excitement began making itself at home in his stomach. By the end of the month, Tom Croxley would have his much needed help in the Marathon store.

That left only the man looking after the yards at the wharf to consider. Ned stopped Kincaid on his way out of the office to discuss one more issue with him. "The man recently employed at the yards, what can you tell me about him?" Kincaid recited details of the man. "Good; I'll call by the yards now to tell him personally of what has been decided about the future of those yards."

His business at the store completed, Ned strode along the street towards the wharf area. He had two tasks to attend to before boarding the boat this evening to return to Marathon, and he was about to deal with the first of those. From some distance away, Ned stopped to watch the man at the yards. The gaunt, bowlegged worker with deeply tanned leathery skin was repairing rails in one of the yards. Not only is this a good stockman, Ned thought, but he appears to be one who likes to keep busy. Just the kind I like.

As Ned explained the future plans for the yards, he watched the man's face fall, but there was no malice in his voice when he spoke. "No surprise there I s'pose. Things are pretty quiet here; same all over town really. Good of ya to be tellin' me early like. Nothing much 'appening around here, so I s'pose I'll be movin' on again."

"That's the other thing I wanted to talk to you about. Am I correct in assuming you would prefer a job on a property working with stock?"

"Yeah, that's what I done all my life. Reckon I'll move on from here and try to find a place that wants a stockman."

"I know a place that could use you. When you decide to leave Port Beauchamp, there is a job in the Marathon area. When you arrive at Marathon, go to Rixon's Store there and ask for directions to Rangelands. It's up the valley about four hours' ride from the township. Do you have a horse?"

"Aye, those two over there are mine."

"Excellent; as I said, there is a job for you at Rangelands if you want it."

"Sir, are you offering me a job on this Rangelands property you mentioned?"

"Yes... Is there a problem with that?"

"No problem, Sir. How soon might I start?"

After a brief discussion, it was agreed Jimmy Carter would work another two weeks at the yards before heading for Marathon. By the time Ned headed back to his cottage, there were at least two happy men in Port Beauchamp. While Jimmy's excitement grew by the moment at the prospect of his new job, Ned became sombre as he let himself into his cottage. This might be the last time he would be in this place. He purchased it almost as soon as he arrived in Port Beauchamp and it had served him well.

They left little in the cottage when they relocated to Rangelands, but this might be Ned's last chance to salvage anything else he wanted to keep.

A thorough search of the place produced little to take back to Marathon with him: a set of branding irons from Sweers Island somehow overlooked when they relocated, a couple of maps, and a bible he rescued from his brother's room at the hotel after Thomas' death. An old sack bag that served as a mat at the backdoor of the cottage, after a good shake out, served as an adequate container to carry those few possessions. With the bag and its precious cargo slung over his shoulder, on the front doorstep, Ned took a few moments to reflect before locking the door and strolling back to the hotel for a late lunch.

There was a quick visit to Kincaid at the store to apprise him of the outcome of discussions at the yard with Jimmy, followed by an equally quick visit to the agent to drop in a key to the cottage. Then it was down to the wharf to wait for the boat for Marathon.

*****

Tom Croxley had barely scrambled out of bed when Ned pounded on the door to Tom's quarters under Rixon's Store. "Geez, Boss; I thought the hounds of Hades had come for me. I couldn't think of any other reason someone would be banging on my door so early in the morning."

"I just wanted to tell you I was about to collect my horse and head back up the valley. I do have a few things in this bag that I brought back from Port Beauchamp. I thought to leave the bag here until the next time we send a wagon into town." Tom indicated where to leave the bag, and then saw Ned out as he went to his horse already saddled and hitched to the loading dock.

As Ned rode out of town that day, his spirit was lighter than it had been for some time. He was excited about going home, and he couldn't help but wonder about progress on the new homestead in his absence. The bright, cool morning made for a pleasant ride through the valley. All seemed right with the world; his world.

Arriving home before lunchtime, he went straight to the construction site to check on progress. He heard a stream of swearing before he saw the men. Mads and Sam were struggling to push some form of ducting into place. With Ned's extra weight helping, they finished the task in minutes. "What is this anyway?" Ned asked as he stood back for a better look.

"It brings water from the hand pump to the house," Mads explained. "There's a similar arrangement at the back of the ablutions building to take water into there."

Ned tried reconciling that information with the overall planned construction work. "If this is for the water supply, how much work remains to complete the whole construction project?"

"Only installation of the copper," Mads and Sam chorus in unison. "No one has been into town to see if the pan for it has arrived," Mads added.

"Ah well, I can tell you about that. I called at the quarters before I left town. A large crate with the property's name stencilled on it occupied much space in the loading dock area. I'm guessing that might be your awaited copper."

"I might take a wagon into town first thing tomorrow to collect it," Sam volunteered.

"It might need two of us to load it. I'll come with you," Mads said.

"That's good, but what I want to know is, if only the copper remains to complete, are we now able to move into this new building?" Ned asked.

"Of course," Mads said. "The building is ready. It is up to you when people move in. The copper won't prevent that happening."

Yes, Ned thought, the gods are back in my corner once more. One step at a time, he cautioned himself. First, move into the house.

Chapter 19 The Future

The next few days were a blur of frenzied activity, with everyone pressed into helping with the move into the new homestead. Such little progress achieved on the first day surprised Ned. After announcing last night that they were moving today, he expected Activity to hit full speed first thing this morning. It didn't happen that way.

When he announced it over dinner, only the Eriksens were at the table with him. They responded to the news with appropriate excitement. He and Mads indulged in a couple of rum swizzles to celebrate the impending occasion. Whether due to the rum or excitement, Ned left the cottage that night in something akin to a euphoric state. Then, when he went across to the bunkhouse, he forgot to mention tomorrow's big event.

On the morning of the 'big day', as he sat down to breakfast, Ned ran his eyes over the table and then around the room. This probably is the last time I will eat here, he told himself. After his Port Beauchamp trip, it felt like he was severing a connection with yet another significant time in his life. When the others arrived and the usual breakfast babble was in full swing, all trace of melancholia disappeared.

In accordance with their plan, after breakfast, Mads went to collect Sam before heading into Marathon. Ned rushed to intercept Mads on his way out to remind him to collect the sack bag with the bits and pieces Ned brought back from Port Beauchamp. As he watched Mads disappearing along the track, it occurred to Ned that today was supposed to be the 'big day'. The day they were to move into the new place. It wasn't happening. Alf and the men went to the far end of the property at their usual time.

Emil attended to the dairy before going to feed the pigs, and Mathilde was in the kitchen kneading today's bread.

For want of something better to do, Ned took himself on a tour of the new homestead. Well-constructed and a fine piece of craftsmanship, it was better than he imagined. So, why wasn't everyone rushing back and forth moving belongings into the place? He needed to stir people to action. That's when he realised the only one available to 'stir' was Mathilde. He strode across to the cottage.

"Mathilde, are you not interested in moving into the new homestead?"

"Of course; I am excited about it. Why do you ask?"

"Why…? Because, instead of packing things, you are flapping about here in the kitchen. Do you intend to do anything today towards making this move happen?"

"But, of course I am. That is the next thing I intend doing. We will still be eating here today and maybe tomorrow too. There needs to be bread and meals to put on the table when the time comes. I need to attend to those preparations before I think about the house. As soon as I finish preparing this stew, the bread will be ready to bake. I will put them both onto cook. Then I will look at the house to see what should go where before we start carrying heavy furniture over there."

How like Mathilde, Ned thought; so methodical and always so calm and in control. She is an amazing woman. She interrupted his thoughts. "I will finish here in a few minutes. You could wait in the sitting room. Then you might show me around the new house." Ned hurried from the kitchen. Although he could be thick at times, even he knew when his presence wasn't wanted.

The few minutes Ned thought required to acquaint Mathilde with the new place turned into an hour and a half. She inspected every square inch, paced out every room, and dithered about where to place furniture. Then, he introduced her to the ablution block and explained about the new copper yet to be completed. The laundry area received her utmost approval. Her excitement over the new copper was beyond Ned's comprehension. It almost was on a par with her excitement over the new cast iron wood fired stove in the kitchen ... although that item also caused some nervousness. "I've never cooked on one of those. I don't know how it works," she admitted.

With the tour of the new buildings completed, Ned shepherded Mathilde to the cottage. "Perhaps an early morning tea might be permitted today before we begin the serious business of moving things." Mathilde had other ideas. On her way out of the ablution block, the new water supply arrangement caught her eye. She demanded a detailed explanation of how it all worked, and insisted on a practical demonstration. To humour her, Ned worked the hand pump a few times so they could watch the water flow along the duct to the kitchen. "That is amazing," Mathilde declared. "Pump more, please. We should fill the system so it is ready for us when we move in." Ned would need a strong mug of tea after so much pumping.

When they returned to the cottage, it was closer to lunch than morning teatime. To move things along, Ned opted for only tea and dispensed with the customary slice of cake or bread and jam. Emil had no such inclination. After whining about morning tea being late, he had every intention of paying due homage to Mathilde's baking. As soon as Ned drained his mug and told Mathilde he would be back for lunch, he saddled up and rode to where Alf and the men worked.

Ned's intention was to have the men down tools and return to the bunkhouse. Then, after lunch, they would begin moving furniture. Alf shot that idea down before it went anywhere. They were pulling wire through the new fence line and could not just down tools in the middle of it. As it was, their lunch would be delayed until the work reached a stage where they could stop and leave it. "The best I can offer you, Ned, is that we will return to the bunkhouse as soon as we can leave the job we are doing," Alf said.

A dejected Ned returned to the cottage for lunch. His gloomy disposition did not go unnoticed. Mathilde and Emil exchanged glances across the table. As soon as they finished eating, Mathilde tried improving the situation. "Emil, please help me clear this table so we can get on with more important matters."

Surprised, Emil shook his head before responding. "I always help clear the table. What's different today? And what are these 'important matters'?"

"Preparations for our move into the new homestead," Mathilde snapped. "Mr Rixon told us last night we would move in today. There is plenty to do. Let's get started." Ned sent a silent prayer of thanks to whichever god had intervened.

Contrary to Ned's expectations, their 'move' did not begin by moving anything. It began with Mathilde's sorting out those things that could be packed and moved now without creating problems later that night. Something important became obvious early in the exercise. "Excuse me, Mathilde, but I have heard no mention of a bed for me to sleep in."

"We only looked at the furniture here in the cottage. You do not have a bed here. You sleep in the bunkhouse. I'm not sure where your bed ended up after our move from Port Beauchamp. Now Emil... please fetch one of the wagons for us to use to move things."

"Why do you need a wagon? Won't we just pick things up and carry them across?"

"That would involve many – *many* – trips and things might be dropped or broken."

Emil went to protest but the look from Mathilde silenced him and sent him scurrying for a wagon.

About mid-afternoon, Alf and the men arrived back. Alf found Ned going through the contents of a cupboard with Mathilde. "Right, Boss, we are here. What do you want us to do?"

"Ah, Alf, I need a word..." Ned pushed Alf out of the room and walked him outside. "My bed seems to have gone missing. Do you recall what happened to it?"

"It's over in the stores shed ... along with my bed and several other pieces of furniture that didn't fit in the cottage."

Ned slapped his forehead as the memory of storing stuff there returned.

"Let's take a look shall we? I imagine everything stored there will be dusty at best, and maybe worse than that." He was right. A thick blanket of dust covered everything in the stores shed but nothing worse had befallen any of the furniture. "Perhaps your men might start by finding my bed amongst this lot, and then cleaning it ready to move into my new bedroom."

In the short period of daylight left, Ned's bed was cleaned and, under Mathilde's close supervision, went into the homestead's master bedroom. A cupboard and the array of kitchen paraphernalia it contained were relocated to Mathilde's new kitchen. Pots and pans not earmarked for use that night or first thing the next morning also went into their new home. Not much else made the short journey to the homestead that day. Nevertheless, when Mads and Sam arrived back from town, the whole place seemed in a state of chaos.

At the bunkhouse after dinner that night, Ned reminded the men tomorrow is the big day. No one will work in the paddocks tomorrow. While the excitement lingered, for Ned frustration set in. The day had not gone as he planned. "Come hell or high water," he told Alf as they enjoyed their usual nightcap together, "I intend sleeping in my own bed in my own room tomorrow night."

*****

The sound of a light shower of rain woke Ned in the wee hours of the morning. The day dawned grey and threatening. Moving things from cottage to homestead happened between annoying light showers throughout the day. While Mads, Mathilde and Ned slept in the homestead for the first time that night, a solitary piece of furniture remained in the cottage: the dining table.

Mathilde struggled to prepare lunch, dinner and breakfast the next morning out of the cottage's much depleted kitchen. In spite of ample encouragement to abandon the cottage in favour of using the new kitchen, she insisted on staying with what she knew. Tomorrow would be soon enough to tackle her fear of that new-fangled stove, she told herself.

All morning, while the other men slaved at relocating furniture and other household items, Mads and Sam worked on installing the copper pan in the laundry. By lunchtime the job was finished except for some tidying up for Mads to complete, so Sam returned to his own farm. Perhaps not so invested in the relocation as the others, Sam noticed something the others didn't. His astuteness was revealed early next morning, when he arrived on a wagon with Mrs Tomkins perched up beside him.

"My missus be an expert on those wood-fired stoves," he told Mathilde as she and the others breakfasted at a lonely looking dining table. "...Thought it might be helpful for you to have some firsthand advice before you try using that new one of yours to cook something to feed this lot." Mathilde's face lit up. She bounded up from her chair and rushed to hug Mrs Tomlins.

After telling Emil to clear up after breakfast before he went to the dairy, Mathilde took Mrs Tomlins by the arm and walked her to the new homestead. "I am so pleased you are here," she told Mrs Tomlins. "It is such an unexpected but wonderful surprise."

"I hoped you wouldn't mind. When Sam told me last night he thought you might be worried about using the new stove, I told him he had to bring me here this morning."

The sight of the two women disappearing into the new kitchen was the last anyone saw of them until Mathilde called them to morning tea – in the new dining room. While Mrs Tomlins explained and demonstrated the intricacies of the new stove, Mads and Sam quietly moved the dining table across to join the rest of the furniture. After morning tea, the next part of Mathilde's day was spent getting acquainted with her new copper.

While most of the day's activity focused on the new homestead, another quiet change took place. Alf and the men moved furniture from storage into the cottage in readiness for Alf to move in. It was a long tiring day for all involved but, by the end of it, the new order of things was established. Alf joined Ned, the Eriksens, and the Tomlins for dinner in the homestead before retiring to his own bed in his cottage ... and those remaining in the bunkhouse welcomed their world being back to the way it should be.

*****

After two weeks, the same routine as everyone remembered from Sweers Island was in place at Rangelands. While no one commented openly on it, all found it comforting after everything that happened during that year. The rhythm of life remained unchanged only until the following week, when Jimmy Carter arrived late one afternoon.

He brought news that Ned's stockyards adjacent to the Port Beauchamp wharf were sold. Now out of a job, he was following Mr Rixon's instructions to come to Rangelands, he told Alf, who met him when he rode up to the bunkhouse. Ned came out of his office to see who the stranger was as Jimmy was explaining his presence to Alf. "Jimmy, find yourself a spare bunk in there, dump your belongings, and then join Mr Gant and me on the veranda."

While Jimmy complied, Ned explained Jimmy's story to Alf as they strolled to sit on the veranda to wait for Jimmy. "I must say his arrival is damn good timing," Alf said. "If he hadn't showed up, we would be in a real bind by the end of the week."

A farmer close to Rangelands went in too deep with the bank. The bank was threatening to foreclose. Rather than lose everything, the farmer was selling off all he could in a bid to repay the debt. If he could achieve that, he would be able to sell the lease on his farm and be able to walk away with some cash to show for his efforts.

Ned and Alf inspected the farmer's small herd of cattle. A couple of days later, Ned bought them. Although high for the quality of the animals, the price was reasonable. The farmer threw in for almost nothing extra the few pigs he had. While it was a good deal that gave Rangelands almost its ideal sized herd, Alf had his own concerns. When the new cattle arrived, the herd then would require at least one man, and probably two to tend it fulltime. He couldn't spare the men to look after the herd because he needed them clearing and fencing to provide sufficient paddocks to accommodate the larger herd … and they had to extend the piggery yet again. Jimmy's arrival was the answer to Alf's dilemma.

Several days after Jimmy's arrival, Alf took his men to collect the herd Ned bought. The delay in moving them was due to completing the extension to the piggery to accommodate the new pigs coming with the cattle. They would be gone for three or four days. On the first day, they discovered Jimmy was an excellent camp cook. With the men gone, Emil's workload increased, not by much, but enough to render him too busy to help Mathilde.

While the men were away, life was strangely quiet. After a day that provided the first taste of summer, Mads and Ned took their drinks out onto the front veranda. The stars seemed extra bright in the clear night sky and the cool south-easterly breeze was welcome after the heat of the day. Ned noticed Mads seemed in an unusually mellow mood. In a bid to avoid asking directly if something bothered him, Ned tried steering conversation around to a topic that might encourage Mads to open up. It didn't work and the men lapsed into silence until Mads found his voice again.

"When we spoke some time back, you mentioned I needed to become a British citizen to own land." Ned nodded as he recalled that conversation. "How do I do that? What is involved in it?"

Ned explained the process as he knew it. The whole time, Ned felt his stomach tightening. Was Mads still determined to buy a house in town? When things were going so well and the future looked rosy, Ned did not want that. At the end of his explanation, Ned asked, "Why the interest in becoming a British citizen? Do your plans require it?"

"I have been thinking about the future," Mads said slowly as he searched for the appropriate words. "Many of the large properties are being subdivided. Smaller portions of good land become available more regularly now. I could never hope to afford a big property, but I might manage a smaller one."

"You explained your interest in Naturalisation, but why this sudden interest in becoming a landholder? Are you unhappy here?"

"No, no. This is not about me. It is Emil I'm thinking of. I am responsible for him now, and have an obligation to my brother to do the best I can for his son. Like generations of my family before him, Emil loves being on the land; loves being a farmer. I would buy a farm and, when I grow too old to manage it, Emil would take over. Then, when I am gone, it is Emil's land. I have given the matter much thought and believe this is the best thing to do for the boy."

Mads' logic was sound. He was right about Emil's love of life on the land. After the two men discussed Mads' proposal from all angles, Ned realised something was missing. "I understand your motives, but I have heard only mention of Emil. What about your daughter? What of Mathilde's future?"

"Matilde is a girl ... a woman now. She will marry. Her future will be her husband's responsibility. Until then my responsibility to my daughter is to ensure she chooses the right man to take care of her; to make sure she doesn't marry some wastrel who runs out on her or treats her badly."

"The difficulty I see with that is, what you see as the 'right' type of man for your daughter, might not be who Mathilde chooses for herself."

"This is a depressing conversation. The truth is, I worry about her chances of ever getting married at all. What are her chances of meeting a prospective husband here? Maybe I do need to buy a cottage in town so she can meet people ... eligible bachelors, I mean. I wish her mother was here to guide me in this matter."

"May I speak frankly, Mads?" Ned's request received a nod. "I am pleased we are discussing Mathilde's future. For some time now, there is something I have wanted to ask you." Mads gestured for Ned to go ahead and ask. "I ask your permission for me to court your daughter. At this time, I have no idea of her feelings towards me, but I know I am more than fond of her. My feelings for Mathilde are strong and honourable, and I seek your permission to find out what hers are towards me." Mads looked stunned. Ned's heart sank. Had he blown everything by being so forthright?

The silence between then seemed to stretch on for an eternity before Mads shook his head as if to clear the very idea of Ned's courting his daughter from his memory. After another few moments' silence, Mads picked his words carefully before making his slow response. "I... am ...stunned. This is so ... unexpected. Thank you for asking my permission, and for being so open and honest in this matter. I find you treat my daughter with the utmost respect, and are a complete gentleman. Beyond that, I realise that in the end, I will have little say in the matter. It is for Mathilde to decide the direction of her feelings. I give you my permission on this matter, Ned, but I will observe closely what happens. How and when you progress this matter is up to you. I will say nothing to Mathilde or anyone else. This conversation shall remain between the two of us... but, remember, I will be watching."

Ned reached across and grabbed Mads' hand and shook it. "Thank you. I promise you I will do nothing that might upset or hurt Mathilde in any way." They agreed another drink was needed to toast their agreement. Ned was sure his feet never touched the floor as he went to refill their glasses.

Although wracked with nervousness, the next day, Ned began his campaign to woo Mathilde. After breakfast, with Emil in the dairy and Mads on his way to complete the extension to the piggery, Ned seized his chance. He gathered up the breakfast dishes and carried them through to the kitchen where Mathilde was preparing to wash up. "Mathilde, I have been remiss in that, after all the time we have been here on Rangelands, you have not had a tour of the place. I propose we correct that situation. As soon as you free up some time this morning, I propose taking you for a drive around the property. What do you say to that?"

"That would be wonderful. Oh, I won't have to ride a horse, will I? I don't know how to do that."

"No, of course you won't have to ride a horse. I will drive you around in the buggy."

"It should take only ten minutes for me to finish here."

"That will give me just enough time to organise the buggy."

That was the start of what turned out to be a much shorter courtship than Ned ever imagined, and one beyond Mathilde's wildest dreams.

*****

About two months after their conversation that fateful night, Ned and Mads found themselves alone on the veranda again. Mads had watched his daughter bloom as the relationship between Mathilde and Ned grew stronger by the day. There were other changes Mads noticed as well.

While still young, Mathilde had learned to handle four-in-hand and was as capable of handling a wagon as any lad, but she had not done so in over a year. She had lost her confidence. Mads observed her secret 'refresher course' with Jimmy. On two occasions, Jimmy took her to the paddock closest to the piggery. After checking there was no one around, he handed over the reins. Mathilde drove the wagon around for a while before handing the reins back to Jimmy and then, sitting demurely beside him, they returned to the homestead.

He didn't know how often this happened, but Mads observed it twice. Even the first time he saw Mathilde take the reins from Jimmy, it was obvious she had lost done of her skills. It was the day after the second time Mads watched Mathilde handle the horses under Jimmy's watchful eye when she asked Emil to hitch up the buggy. While not entirely sure it was the right thing to do, Emil did as he was asked and, a few minutes later, was surprised to see Mathilde heading along the track away from the homestead.

Concerned he might have done the wrong thing, Emil went to tell Mads about it. In response, Mads told Ned. With no knowledge of where Mathilde might have gone, the two men allowed their concern for her safety to grow as they paced the homestead veranda. When Mathilde hadn't returned after about half an hour, they found Jimmy and demanded to know what he knew. "I 'ave no idea where she would go. All I know is she asked me to teach her 'ow to 'andle the wagon. Thing is, she didn't need no teaching. She's as capable as I am. Lost a bit of her touch from lack of practice I think, that's all. She never said anything about going anywhere. Should we go look for her?"

"We wouldn't know where to begin," Ned said.

"We wait an hour or two and then, if she is not back, we go looking. We look everywhere until we find her," Mads decided.

It was almost two hours later when they saw the distant cloud of dust kicked up by the buggy returning along the track. And it was no more than seconds after she arrived home that the interrogation began.

Chapter 20 Changes

It was some time after her first escape from Rangelands that Mathilde confided in Ned, not that he and her father hadn't quizzed her about it often in the interim. "I went to see Mrs Tomlins. There are some things you want to talk only to another woman about. So, I went to see her and had afternoon tea with her."

"That's fine, but you had us worried sick about what was happening and if you were all right. Is something wrong; something you cannot discuss with me or your father? Are you all right?"

"I am fine. There is nothing wrong with me. And, no, there is nothing to discuss with either you or my father." Ned noticed the pink creep up Mathilde's cheeks. Suddenly he felt awkward and wished the floor would open and swallow him. Even a dullard like him could work out Mathilde had some 'woman's thing' she needed to discuss with another woman.

Ned hugged her. "Please forgive all the questions. You are so precious to me. I cannot stand to think something is wrong and not be able to help you." She blushed a deeper shade of crimson and shook her head. "If you are sure there is nothing bothering you – that I have done nothing to upset you…"

Mathilde giggled and shook her head. "Everything is perfect. Nothing is wrong, and I doubt you could do anything to upset me."

"It gladdens my heart to hear that, but there is something I must ask." Dropping to one knee, he continued, "Mathilde Eriksen, will you do me the honour of becoming my wife?"

"Oh, yes! Yes, please," she squeaked as her eyes brimmed with tears. Ned wasn't prepared for tears. His silly grin turned to concern.

"You are crying. What is it? What did I do?"

Mathilde hauled him to his feet and kissed him lightly on the cheek. "Dear Ned, all you did is make me the happiest woman in the world." Ned, decidedly shaken, heaved a sigh of relief.

"That's the easy part done," he quipped with a wry grin. "Now I need to talk to your father." Ned spent the rest of the day engineering a quiet meeting with Mads that night.

It did not take long to ask Mads for Mathilde's hand in marriage, but Ned ended up wondering if he were talking to a Mads doppelganger. The man's brusque attitude surprised Ned, as did his response.

"No. I cannot give you what you ask. However, I will be discussing this matter with my daughter at the first chance I get."

Jesus, what has gone wrong, Ned wondered. There was no objection up until now. Should I try to warn Mathilde? Yes, I must. That proved impossible. Mads seemed never far away, thereby eliminating any opportunity to warn her.

In the end, it was Mads who outsmarted Ned. He waited until Ned was out checking on the men. Whatever Mads' plan was, it didn't work well for him. He demanded of Mathilde to know what had been going on between her and Ned. Mathilde was taken aback. Ned had told her of his earlier conversation with Mads and how Mads had consented to their courtship. So, not only was her father's demand confusing but, combined with his gruff demeanour, it produced a surprising reaction in Mathilde. "You know very well that, over the last while, Ned and I have been getting to know one another on a more personal level. Your question seems pointless."

"So, it is 'Ned' now is it and not 'Mr Rixon' anymore? What is this 'personal level' you speak of and how would I know what you have been up to? The only way I know something is going on is because *Mr Rixon* asked to marry you. Of course I said no to such a nonsense."

"Did you now? Well, whom I marry is my choice, not yours, and I am telling you I intend marrying *Ned* with or without your approval. How we progress from here is up to you, but I will accept *Ned's* formal proposal when it comes." Mathilde watched a smug look spread across her father's face and, in an instant, she realised why. "I don't doubt that, in your present mood, you refused Ned's request for permission to marry me. He was being gallant. His intention was no more than to do the right thing and formally approach you. If you feel smug because you believe Ned will not propose against your wishes, you should know this: now that I know Ned has spoken to you, if he does not propose to me, I will propose to him. He does not require anyone's permission to marry."

Mads was lost for words. Who was this woman? It can't be his daughter, not someone being so defiant. He opened his mouth to say something but closed it again. His second try to respond ended the same way. Before he could try again, Mathilde spoke again. "Do you understand all that?" Mads stared at her. "If there is something you do not understand, now is the time to clarify it." Mads shook his head. "Good! We will get on with planning a wedding ... Well, we will, after I speak to Ned later today." Having said her piece, Mathilde flounced off leaving a stunned Mads in her wake. Deciding it might be wise not to be around Mathilde for a while, Mads wandered aimlessly from the homestead.

Ned, having returned from the bottom paddock, unsaddled his horse in the horse yard. As he carried his saddle and bridle into the tack room, he noticed Mads detour in the same direction. Mads waited in silence until Ned hung up his gear before approaching him. "What is it Mads? What do you want?" Ned demanded. "If you are looking to continue our earlier conversation, don't bother. I have nothing to say to you on that matter at the moment." Mads looked sheepish and scrabbled the dirt floor with the toe of his boot.

"Forgive me, Ned. I am a silly old man. Of course I will be happy to see you marry my daughter. But, as I suggested, I needed to know how Mathilde felt about it … really felt about such a big move. I know my daughter better than anyone. At least, I thought I did. I told her she did not have my permission to marry you. If she put up no argument, I would know her heart *t*ruly was not in marrying you. On the other hand, if she pleaded her case, I would know her feelings for you were strong."

"That's as strange an approach as I ever heard; and how did that work out?"

"At first I thought it did not go well, then I realised it did exactly what I wanted it to."

"How was that?"

"Well, she did not plead her case." Ned looked shocked. Mads chuckled. "Instead, she made it clear she intended marrying you regardless of what I said or did. She guessed you had asked my permission and I refused. Because of that, she believed you would not propose. My daughter was not about to let that get in the way. If you did not propose to her, she would propose to you. It was clear to me she wanted to marry you."

Unsure how to react to all that, Ned shuffled self-consciously on the spot. "I'm sorry, Mads, but I am not sure where that leaves me or where it leaves the matter of marriage to Mathilde."

"If you care for my daughter as much as you say … and to maintain your dignity … I suggest you rush to the homestead now and propose to the woman. I have no doubt that, if you do not propose, she will propose to you … and your dignity in this matter will be lost. I am tempted to tell you to think on whether you are doing the right thing. I have never known my daughter to be so forceful or determined. Perhaps you will have your hands full with Mathilde as your wife." There was something fiendish about Mads' chuckle as he left the tack room.

To hell with warnings and thinking about it any longer, Ned told himself as he strode out of the tack room and across to the homestead. When Ned burst into the kitchen, Mathilde was stirring that night's dinner. He wrapped his arm around her waist, swung her around to face him and kissed her hard on the lips. Her attempts to prevent the large spoon she held from dripping gravy down Ned's back were to no avail. He didn't seem to notice the hot gravy. "Will you marry me?"

"Of course I will. I told you that. Nothing has changed, not for me anyway."

"Good. How soon can it be?"

"What about Papa? How shall we deal with him?"

"I have done that. He consented." Not quite the truth Ned knew, but close enough for him to be comfortable with. "Now, my dear Mathilde, you must give me a date for this wedding, and then you have work to do. I hope you know about organising weddings, for I admit I know nothing at all."

*****

For Ned, the next few weeks crawled past at sloth-like pace. He knew preparations for the wedding were in full swing. Mrs Tomlins was a regular visitor and spent many long days at the homestead. If the lady wasn't at Rangelands, there was a good chance Mathilde would be at the Tomlins' farm. What they did together was a mystery to Ned and, if he asked, the standard reply was: wedding preparations.

Soon after the waiting period began, one night as Ned and Mads sat in silence on the veranda, Ned detected a hint of melancholia in his soon-to-be father-in-law. Perhaps that's not what it was. Maybe Mads was dejected about something that happened during the day. After inwardly debating what to do, Ned went ahead and asked the question. "You seem a little down tonight, Mads. Is everything all right? Is it something you can talk about … maybe something to do with the wedding is bothering you?"

"I suppose it is true to say it is the wedding that causes me sadness. My eldest daughter, my only remaining child, is about to marry. Her mother and her siblings will not be here to witness the day. My wife is not here to support her at this time … was not here to support Mathilde after that terrible thing happened to her on the ship."

"Forgive my insensitivity, please. I did not think about this at all, when I should have done. If it affects you this way, then how must Mathilde feel? Amid all that is happening at this time, she must miss her mother. Mads, what should I do to ease the pain of the memory of losing her family this wedding must cause her and you?"

"There is nothing to be done. In some ways, it is good to think again on the family and the life we shared before that terrible night of the shipwreck. They are sweet memories with a tragic end."

It was noble of Mads to assure him he need not bother himself about the matter, but Ned knew that until the wedding was over, he would watch all the Eriksens closely for any signs of distress.

A few weeks later, as he sat alone on the veranda one evening, a strange thought occurred to Ned. After their usual nightcaps, Mads retired to bed and Alf returned to the cottage, leaving Ned alone with his thoughts. In a somewhat melancholy mood, Ned realised none of the bunkhouse crew, nor Alf, had congratulated him on his forthcoming nuptials. Did their silence indicate disapproval? Surely they saw no wrong in his marrying Mathilde. His concern about the situation went to bed with him and kept him awake for some time. By the time his eyelids closed, he had resolved to explore the matter first thing next morning.

"Good morning, Mads. Before the others join us for breakfast, I wish to seek your opinion on a matter that bothers me." Mads gestured for him to continue. Ned voiced his concern at the lack of reaction from the men to his forthcoming marriage. "I know men do not show the same level of excitement about weddings as women tend to, but surely I might expect some congratulations. Not a murmur has come my way. Have you heard if something is amiss in the camp as a result of this situation?"

Mads slapped his hand down on the table as he roared laughing. "Nobody congratulates you because nobody knows. You have not shared your good news. It is not for me to do it for you. I am not a woman. I do not indulge in such gossip. Anyway, you must tell them soon. You need to choose someone to stand up beside you as your best man."

Ned slapped his forehead. Of course he needed a best man. He had not devoted one second's thought to the matter. Not that it required much thought. It must be Alf, his friend since his earliest school days. Just when I need to speak to him, he decides to have breakfast in the bunkhouse with his men this morning! Alf was surprised when Ned called out and rushed over as Alf left the bunkhouse after breakfast. "Are the men gone?" Ned asked.

"Yeah, they are on their way to the bottom paddock. Has something happened?"

"You might say that. I find myself in need of a best man in the near future."

"A best man...? Why do you need ... what job do you need this chap for? Does he have to be special in some way? I need to know more if I am to select one for you."

Through his laughter Ned managed to croak out, "You don't have to select anyone, that's my job and I've done it. I picked you." Ned watched Alf's eyebrows draw together in confusion. "I want you to be my best man at my wedding to...." Alf's whoop of shock interrupted Ned before he finished the sentence.

There followed a moment's delay while Alf took on board what Ned said, and before he demanded to know, "To whom...?"

"To Mathilde; who else could there be? Alf shook his hand and slapped him on the back. "I assume you're up for it." Confirmation via Alf's enthusiastic nodding. "Excellent; thank you. By the way, feel free to share the good news with the others ... but not until this evening. I need to share the news with Emil before you tell the men."

*****

Two days before the big day, Mrs Tomlins took up residence in one of the spare rooms, and she and Mathilde commandeered another for whatever women need to do before a wedding. The aroma pervading the house for the past couple of weeks suggested there was to be a wedding cake, and a boozy one at that by the smell of it. As for Ned, he had been banished from the homestead to spend his last couple of days of bachelorhood sharing the cottage with Alf.

Sam Tomlins arrived the day before the wedding, and opted to move into the bunkhouse rather than risk venturing into the homestead. Emil sacrificed his favourite and fattest piglet for the occasion. Well, he picked it out and Sam did what needed to be done. Painful as it was for him to watch, Emil insisted on watching to learn how to do it. Ned felt himself at a loose end. He was one of the principal players but had no real role to play.

While the day of the wedding began early for some, others staggered out much later than usual and nursing their throbbing heads. Sam and Emil were up before dawn to put the suckling pig onto roast. The 'last night of freedom' drinking session at the bunkhouse resulted in a sorry looking lot trying to become human again before the minister arrived at around ten o'clock. They might have slept through had Mrs Tomlins not stood outside the bunkhouse banging on a pan with a wooden spoon. "Get up you drunken lot," she shouted. "There's work to be done. Chairs need setting out and the place needs a tidy up. Come on, look lively."

"Fat chance," Alf thought as he sloshed cold water over his head. A solid breakfast, aided by a blazing December sun, had them in reasonable condition by the arrival of the minister.

A few minutes after the minister, other guests from surrounding properties began arriving, along with Tom Croxley who came in the store's wagon. He closed the store early the afternoon before and camped along the track overnight in order to arrive in time for the ceremony.

Under Mrs Tomlin's stern eye, chairs were arranged under the trees so guests might avoid the sun. Out front, a table adorned with Mrs Tomlins' best tablecloth marked the place where the ceremony would occur. Paper chains and other fancy garlands were strung through the trees. Two large tables mysteriously appeared from somewhere and lined up end to end on the front veranda. A length of fabric stretched over them was held in place by strategically placed small rocks – not that there was enough breeze even to ruffle it.

Ned, standing at the makeshift altar waiting for his bride to appear, cast his eyes over the assembled guests. The sight of the men in what passed for their 'Sunday best' almost reduced him to laughter. Where is Alf, he wondered. I don't see him anywhere. He is supposed to be standing up here beside me. I haven't even given him the ring yet.

A few moments later, Alf trotted up beside Ned. "The big moment is about to happen," he whispered.

"What big moment would that be?" Ned asked a little tartly.

"The bride is about to appear on the arm of her father who, by the way, is so nervous he is almost incapable of speech. They will make their way down the homestead's steps, through the guests and up here to stand beside you at this table."

"Oh, Lord...! Here, hang on to the ring until the appropriate time. For Christ's sake, don't drop it. If it lands in this bulldust, we will never find it." Alf chuckled as he slipped the ring into a pocket. "And you don't need to be enjoying this quite so much."

"Oh, but I do, Old Friend. I really do enjoy it."

The next hour remained no more than a blur in Ned's memory. Mads walked Mathilde to the 'altar' and stood by to 'give her away' before taking his seat in the front row. Mathilde handed her bouquet of poinciana and cassia flowers to Mrs Tomlins to hold.

The ceremony was basic and brief. Alf produced the ring with great ceremony when it was asked for, and then it was all over. The new Mr and Mrs Rixon signed the register, as did Alf and Mrs Tomlins as their witnesses. Then, with the important part of the day over, guests rushed to the veranda to partake of the luncheon spread set out by Emil and Mrs Tomlins ... and to ensure their cups held something with which to toast the bride and groom.

Soon after midday, the first guests departed. That triggered a steady stream of departures until, by one o'clock the last guests were being waved on their way. Tom brought the store's wagon up to the homestead. Suitcases were loaded, and the bride and groomed climbed up to occupy makeshift seating in the back.

With a flick of the reins, the wagon was on its way to town where the couple would spend their wedding night at the hotel.

Next morning, Tom collected them from the hotel and took them to board the boat about to leave for southern ports. Only Tom knew they were heading south. Nobody knew their destination or their return date, although Ned told Alf it was likely they would be away a few weeks.

After a couple of nights in Brisbane, they again boarded a boat, this time for Sydney, where they would be based for the majority of their holiday. There were a few days enjoying the cool clean air at a guest house in the Blue Mountains before returning to spend a few more days in Sydney, and then boarding a boat again to return to Brisbane. By the time they were to board the boat to return to Marathon, Mathilde's fear of boats had diminished somewhat, but she remained nervous and tense for the entire voyage.

They booked into the hotel for two nights. After their mid-afternoon arrival at Marathon, Ned paid a visit to Tom Croxley at the store before returning to the hotel for dinner. The following day, while Ned talked with stock and station agents and his bank manager, Mathilde indulged in what passed for shopping in Marathon. She saw nothing she wanted and nothing she liked, but it filled in part of the day before returning to the hotel to while away the afternoon with a book she purchased in Sydney.

Straight after breakfast next morning, Ned commandeered the store's wagon, collected Mathilde and headed up the valley before the sun developed its December sting.

Nobody came to meet them when they arrived at the homestead. An excited welcome came at the end of the day when the others returned to find the boss and his new wife returned. As they sat down for dinner that night, Alf, Mads and Emil were especially pleased Mathilde was back. That wonderful aroma of good cooking was back to tease their tastebuds until they sat down to eat. No conversation occurred until plates were cleaned. After that, questions about where the couple had been and what they saw and did flowed for some time. In accordance with their previous routine, after dinner, the men adjourned to the veranda with their drinks while Emil helped Mathilde clean up.

Alf, wanting to talk to the men about the next day's work, said goodnight as soon as he finished his drink. Mads' sombre mood intrigued Ned. The man was happy to see them home again, but seemed to disappear into a black hole once dinner was over. "You seem in a dark mood, Mads. Would it help to talk about what bothers you?"

"No, I was deep in thought; nothing more. We talked before about my becoming a British citizen. I wish to go forward with that. Perhaps you might direct me to someone who can help with the process."

"Are you still considering buying a farm? You know you are welcome here for life, if you wish to stay … and that applies to Emil as well?"

"Thank you. Yes, you have said so before, and we are settled here now. A terrible accident happened while you were away. It created a whirlpool of thinking for me. Sam Tomlins is dead."

"Sam…? Dead…? How can this be? What happened? I must break this news carefully to Mathilde, but not tonight. She will be upset, as am I, and will demand to know all the details."

"Sam went into town. He wasn't sure how long his business in town would take, so he told Mrs Tomlins he would stay the night if it finished late. If his business was completed early, instead of going back to the homestead, he would go to that area of the farm he was clearing and work there until dark. When he didn't return at the end of the day, his wife assumed he stayed in town. It wasn't until next morning they found him on the side of the track. It seems something spooked the horse and it bolted into the scrub, throwing Sam from the wagon. A short distance from Sam's body, they found the wagon wrecked against a tree and the horse nearby with a broken leg."

"Mrs Tomlins must be beside herself with worry about her future. The farm was starting to pay its way. They began thinking it might be safe to believe they wouldn't lose the place because they couldn't meet the lease payments. That looks unavoidable now. She surely can't manage the place on her own."

"She is a remarkable woman, and not afraid of hard work. I have been going to help her whenever I have nothing pressing to do here. She has been a great friend and support to Mathilde. It is the least I can do."

"Feel free to continue as you see necessary, Mads. I share your concern for the woman ... as will Mathilde when she learns what happened." After a few moments of discussion of Mrs Tomlins' situation, conversation moved on to other topics.

"On my way through the valley today, I noticed considerable acreage planted with that sugar cane everyone is talking about. Some excellent pastoral land is now under cane. I am not sure how I feel about it encroaching on the valley's grazing country. Perhaps I should devote time to investigating this new industry before I wake one day to find it at my gate."

After Mads retired for the night, Ned remained on the veranda until Mathilde, finished in the kitchen, came to join him. Those few minutes alone provided a chance to ponder the future. Much had changed in just a month. How much change would the future bring? In the past, always one to welcome new ideas and challenges, Ned now found himself uncertain about the possible impact of change on their lives in the years to come.

Chapter 21 Time Goes By

The years rolled by. Life was good for all both on the property, and in the wider Marathon area, over the next ten years. In spite of Ned's concerns about it, the sugar industry took off. Huge swathes of land went under cane or coffee. Hopes of establishing a coffee industry evaporated. The sugar industry went from strength to strength until the Rust disease almost wiped it out in the mid1870s. It recovered and expanded to be well established by the end of that decade. New milling companies were established and new mills built. Sugar cane wasn't the only major event occupying the minds of those at Rangelands during the 1870s.

Mads continued assisting Mrs Tomlins with her farm. He sometimes spent two or three days at a time there. Ned and Mathilde noted with some amusement that to Mads 'Mrs Tomlins' became 'Rose'. It almost came as no surprise when, a couple of years after Sam's death, Mads announced he was to marry Rose.

Soon after Mads and Rose were married, Ned and Mathilde shared the news that Mads' second grandchild was on the way. Over the decade of the 1870s, five children were added to the Rixon family, all daughters. The once peaceful homestead became a place of noise and chaos. To avoid the tragedy Mathilde experienced previously, Ned insisted on household help as soon as she became pregnant with their first child. They didn't have to look far to find someone.

After a short courtship, Alf married the daughter of a farmer from further along the valley. Widowed after only a few weeks of marriage, Elizabeth returned to live with her parents. Alf met her when, on their way home from town, she accompanied her father to look at pigs. Alf admitted later to Ned to being smitten at first sight. They were married at Rangelands and made their home in the cottage. Elizabeth and Mathilde got on well immediately. It was a smooth transition when Elizabeth became housekeeper.

As the number of Rixon offspring increased, it became necessary to engage further help. Another young girl, Ruby, was employed as a nursery maid. She stepped into the role of housekeeper for a while when Elizabeth and Alf welcomed their first child. When Elizabeth returned to work, her son joined the Rixon children in the nursery each day.

One night, as Alf and Ned occupied their usual chairs on the veranda while Alf waited for Elizabeth to finish work for the day, Ned was surprised to hear Alf give a soft chuckle. "What do you find so amusing? We were enjoying a moment's silence, so it couldn't be anything I said."

"No. I was thinking there might be another marriage at Rangelands before too long." Ned's eyebrows shot up to his hairline. Alf continued. "Every night, after the children are asleep, a certain young lady sneaks across to the bunkhouse."

"What...? Are you suggesting...?"

"Eh...? No. I'm not suggesting anything. Young Toby has won a heart, that's all. Most nights, Ruby goes to meet him and they sit by the fire for a while, much as we used to do when you lived in the bunkhouse. They don't stay up late, so it isn't a problem, and those in the bunkhouse allow them their privacy."

Alf's prediction proved correct, but it took a further eighteen months before Rangelands was in the grip of wedding preparations again. And, this time, there were four women involved, Ruby, the bride-to-be, least of all. Her role revolved around considering, approving or rejecting suggestions for her big day put to her by Mathilde, Rose and Elizabeth. Toby demonstrated great wisdom and discretion by staying right out of the whole preparations fuss, and by keeping his distance from the women involved – except for Ruby.

*****

As the decade progressed, Rangelands and life on the property settled into a steady measured routine. The property, now at maximum production level, netted a substantial income each year. With the piggery side of the business so expanded, several acres were under pumpkins and other vegetables just to feed the pigs. But the march of the sugar industry across the region continued up the valley to leave Rangelands marooned among its neighbours as the only property not trying its luck with at least a plot of sugar cane.

While the outbreak of Rust Disease in 1876 dampened enthusiasm for a while, interest soon reignited and more land went under cane. A group of businessmen, diversifying to varying degrees into the fledgling industry, worked quietly behind the scenes to develop a solution to a major problem facing the industry: a factory to crush the cane, extract the juice and turn it into sugar.

Some larger plantation owners constructed small mills to process their own cane, but smaller growers had no way of turning their crops into cash. The solution devised by that group of entrepreneurs: construction of a large 'central mill' to process the cane of any surrounding farmers prepared to transport their crop to the central mill. The advent of the central mill concept generated interest and many more properties placed varying sized pieces of land under cane.

Mads continued to work at Rangelands when required and when it didn't interfere with work on the Tomlins' farm, including staying over at night when a project required it. On one such occasion, after dinner, Alf and Mads sat by the fire outside the bunkhouse. "Things have changed over the years," Mads mused. "All those bedrooms Ned wanted in the new homestead I thought excessive and ridiculous at the time are now occupied – by his children. Now, I find it more comfortable – restful even – to stay in the bunkhouse. How is Ned these days? He seems to spend increasing amounts of time in town."

"Yeah, things have changed. You have nothing to worry about where Ned is concerned. Now that things are going well here, he involves himself in other interests. He is on the executive of the local Farmers and Graziers Association, and is involved in establishing an annual pastoral and agricultural show for the district. And, let's not forget that, since he became a Justice of the Peace, he is regularly called to sit on the Bench to hear various cases."

Mads nodded. "I can't understand why he wants to spend so much time in town. Has he lost interest in this place?"

Alf laughed. "Not a bit of it. He remains as interested as ever; wants to know every detail of what happens here. I admit he spends some days of almost every week in town, but he is always here at home on weekends. I know he refused membership of the turf club because it would mean being in town quite a few weekends over the year. No, he hasn't lost interest in Rangelands. It's more a case of the place not offering challenges anymore."

"I hear tell he is still as vocal as ever about good grazing land being sacrificed to the district's new sugar industry."

"Not quite so vocal these days. In fact, I half expect you're in for a shock when he returns on Friday from this trip to town." Mads, not about to leave it hanging like that, pumped Alf for more information. "I won't be surprised if, on his return he announces he has purchased *Trevallyn Farm.*"

"Trevallyn Farm...? ...Bert Reynold's farm running along the western boundary of Rangelands?"

"That's the one. Bert's in too deep to the bank and they are threatening to foreclose. It's only a small farm but has good soil. Negotiations between Ned and Bert have been ongoing for a while. The price was close to being settled before Ned left for town ... and the Land Court sits in Marathon on Thursday."

"Ned owns a huge chunk of land already. Why does he need another small farm? Anyway, they might not agree a price. Ned won't buy unless he gets his own way on that."

"Bert would rather sell than have the bank foreclose. He would lose everything to the bank. If he sells, even at a low price, he could pay off the bank debt and still have a little to use for a new start somewhere. I think they will settle a price, as long as it covers the minimum Bert needs."

"But why buy the farm?"

"Ah well, it's the new challenge Ned needs."

"Bert put most of the farm under cane, didn't he?"

"That he did. And Ned had opportunity to invest in the consortium that's building the new central mill. He needs to be involved with cane to maintain his credibility within the industry ... and Trevallyn Farm already is all about cane." Alf tapped the side of his nose and gave Mads a knowing wink.

"You and your chaps know a lot about growing cane, do you Alf?"

"Not a bloody thing; we've spent our lives with livestock. As Ned doesn't know any more than we do about cane growing, I am concerned about this new investment if it happens."

"Well, well ... I don't put much belief in coincidence as a rule, but maybe there is something in it after all. Rose and I have a guest coming to spend a few days with us after he arrives in Marathon on Friday. Friendship between their two families goes back to Rose's grandparents' time. Young Lachlan, now in his early thirties, got himself in a spot of bother when he was about seventeen. Something to do with a young girl, I believe. Anyway he was packed off to his uncle who owned a plantation in the West Indies. I think he was happy enough and learned all about sugar cane while he was there. That is, until things went bad in that part of the world. He fled to Java; worked there in the industry for a short while, then a short stint in Mauritius, before now coming to Australia to try his luck in our new industry. Perhaps he might prove useful if Ned adds Trevallyn Farm to his landholdings."

"I shall keep that in mind. It would be helpful if you made the young man feel welcome long enough for me to sort out what's happening here before he moves on ... so we don't lose his expertise."

"Oh aye; I will endeavour to keep him as long as possible. I need to learn all I can while he is here. I too have put one of my paddocks under cane."

Ned's return to Rangelands on Thursday afternoon instead of on Friday as expected came as a surprise. His news of the successful purchase of Trevallyn Farm came as something of an anticlimax. Mads returned home on Wednesday night, so only Ned and Alf occupied the veranda after dinner on Thursday night. That's when Ned announced the purchase. He was taken aback when Alf was slow to comment. "Okay, excitement might have been expecting too much, but I thought you might at least be interested," Ned chided his friend and manager.

"It comes as no surprise, Ned. You have talked of nothing else for weeks now. The farm is under cane. Do you propose continuing with cane on that property?"

"For the time being; I believe an initial planting of cane can be cropped for years without needing to replant. I propose allowing the farm's crop to run its course before making any changes. Is that a problem?"

"Only in as much as none of us know anything about growing cane."

"How hard can it be?"

"If it is to pay well, I am told technical knowhow is required."

"Hmmm, seems as though we might have a problem."

"Well, maybe not. A solution might be soon to hand." Alf shared Mads' information regarding Rose's family friend arriving the next day.

By the end of the next week, Lachlan Dunbar was engaged as the Trevallyn Farm manager, and plans were being made for him to occupy the residence there. Existing barracks accommodation on the property would be utilised later when necessary labour was recruited to grow and harvest the crop.

The new venture and the successful construction and commissioning of the central mill kept Ned interested for a couple of years, but soon they too presented no new challenges. To keep himself interested, he invested in various new enterprises, including new mining ventures. While they created new inter-ests, they did not occupy him. Those around him sensed he was becoming restless. He dropped his bombshell on New Year's Eve 1879.

With the children doubled-up in bedrooms to free a room for Mads and Rose, the whole extended family spent the

Christmas-New Year period together at Rangelands. After the children were put to bed at their customary hour, the adults sat talking and reminiscing as they waited for midnight. That's when Ned delivered his shock.

"As you know, I have been investing in mining of late. Some of that is in small Australian ventures. I also invested in a major overseas mining company to the extent that I am now one of three partners in that company. It has successful mining operations in a couple of countries, but is now looking at potential new opportunities at a location in Mexico. It was proposed, and I have in the last few days agreed to take over direct management of operations in Mexico." A collective gasp went up from his audience. Mathilde's hands shot up to cover her mouth. Her eyes reflected nothing short of terror.

"You are planning to leave us…?" she blurted out a little too loudly. Then, lowering her voice, she continued. "You would leave us here alone while you go haring off to the other side of the world on some wild chase for riches? We are comfortable and doing well here. Why do you feel the need to abandon us?"

"My Dearest Mathilde, nothing is further from my mind. I could not be away from you and the children for more than a few days at a time. I do not propose abandoning you here. I plan to take you with me. Oh, not to Mexico perhaps, but to America. I thought to set up home in New York. You and the children would be comfortable there while I go off to Mexico regularly for a few days each time to oversee operations there. Try seeing it as a new and exciting stage in our lives."

Mathilde sat wringing her hands as Ned outlined his plans. When he finished speaking, she sprung up from her chair, spilling her drink as her glass tumbled to the floor to break and lie in a myriad of shards at her feet. "How could you …? How could you?" she shrieked at Ned, before rushing from the room with tears streaming down her cheeks.

A short uncomfortable silence cloaked the room until embarrassed guests recovered sufficiently to find their feet and leave. Only Ned and Mads remained. Mads struggled to contain his anger and keep his voice as normal as possible when he spoke.

"While it did not matter about the rest of us perhaps, that was the most insensitive way to break the news to my daughter. I had hoped you thought enough of her to discuss it with her first before announcing your plans to all and sundry; to discuss and seek her input on the matter. I misjudged you. You didn't mention your plans for this property and everything you have amassed here. No doubt, now Alf is worried sick about his future as well."

"I don't know what to say. I am shocked. I thought you all would be excited for us, maybe not as excited as I am, but excited nevertheless. Alf has nothing to worry about. I will continue to own what I have here, and Alf – unless he indicates otherwise – will manage everything here for me. We might return one day. Who knows where the future lies?"

"You are missing the point, Ned. You have not consulted Mathilde on this considerable upheaval to her life. You have not remembered how we came to be with you in the first place."

"I don't understand. You came from Sweers Island with me. That's how we all came to be here. What is there to consider?"

"Think back, Ned. Think back to how we came to be on Sweers Island."

"The shipwreck…?"

"Try imagining how terrifying it is for Mathilde to face another long ocean voyage to another country. She was frightened every time she got on the boat to travel down the coast with you. Then try imagining how worrying it is for me to send my only remaining child – and my grandchildren – off on another long ocean voyage. How do you think I feel after losing my wife and other children on such a voyage?"

Ned slapped his forehead. "How could I not think about the lasting impact the shipwreck would have on Mathilde? Is there anything I can do to undo what I have done," he asked. "Mads, we have never talked about your voyage to Australia. You haven't talked about it and neither has Mathilde. I suppose I wanted to avoid stirring up painful memories for you all. Perhaps sometime soon you might help me to better understand what prompted such a move."

"Now is as good as any time," Mads said quietly. "I told you our family farm was too small for all of us. My brother, Emil's father, as the oldest son, would inherit the farm. I became a carpenter. Later, I worked for a big international construction company. They sent me to England for some time before I returned to Denmark. In England, there was a lot of talk about Australia, the opportunities it offered and its healthy climate. A particularly severe winter greeted us when we returned to Denmark. We decided to move to Australia for a better life. Emil's father asked us to take the lad with us to give him a chance too."

"It seems to have worked out that way for you – apart from the shipwreck, of course."

"At first, we all were excited about it. Then, as it came closer to time to leave, my wife became terrified. She tried to persuade me to change my mind. It is a land too far away, she would say. We don't know what it will be like. We don't know if we will survive the voyage. It is too far; too far to risk our lives and those of our children. But I didn't listen to her. I thought she was nervous about facing something new and different. I told myself, once we were on the ship, she would relax, settle down and look forward to our new life. That's not how it was. If it is possible, she became even more terrified once we were on board, and she remained that way until that fatal night when I lost them all – all, except Mathilde and Emil."

"What an insensitive fool I have been. What should I do to fix this mess?"

"I don't know. I don't know that it can be fixed. I can only tell you how I feel about this matter: it is too far. A land too far away; many things can happen on the way… and after you arrive. Good things might await you … but so might tragedy – and heartbreak for me."

The night ended – and the new year began – on a despondent note. After Mads retired to bed Ned remained on the veranda for some time before deciding to turn in for the night. He found himself locked out of the bedroom. No amount of fuss brought Mathilde to the door. Realising nothing would change the situation, Ned gave up and spent the night in a cot on the veranda. That's where he spent the next few nights until he decided it was time for a showdown to sort out the situation between him and his wife.

Mathilde remained furious and refused to speak to him. Everything he tried was to no avail. His frustration rose by the minute. Exasperated, he demanded, "Are you and the children coming to America with me, or are you determined you all will remain here without me. You should know that I am going with or without you. I would prefer all my family came with me."

"I am your wife and must honour my husband. My obligation is to accompany you. But, if we manage to arrive there safely, you should know this, I am wife in name only. Where there is no respect, there can be no love. And, where there is no love, there can be no true marriage." With that, Mathilde flounced off leaving a stunned Ned in her wake. From the doorway, she turned and spat back at him, "You should make yourself as comfortable as possible in that cot on the veranda. It is your place from now on."

Ned retreated to town, where he spent the next week drunk most of the time, until Tom Croxley had enough and turfed him out. "You might be the boss and own this establishment, but it is time you left my quarters. If you intend staying in town and getting drunk every day, you had better book into a hotel. Of course, you could act like a man and go home to face whatever comes your way."

Next morning, Ned nursed his throbbing head as he rode out of Marathon and started up the valley towards home ... home and whatever reception might await him there.

Chapter 22 Farewells

Ned's return home after his drunken week in town met with total disregard by all the women at Rangelands. While Elizabeth and Ruby, conscious of their positions there, adopted a formal relationship with their employer, Mathilde remained unforgiving and distant. Out of concern for both his daughter and her husband, Mads made a half-hearted attempt at brokering a reconciliation between the pair. Although aware he was interfering where he shouldn't, his efforts didn't work anyway.

Mathilde, with set jaw and defiant zeal, set about sorting out their belongings in readiness for the major upheaval of their lives. The formalities dragged on. It was May 1880 before everything was in place for their relocation. In the couple of weeks after they received word everything was in readiness for their departure, tears flowed on many occasions. And then the big day arrived. The family left to board the boat for the first leg of their journey across the Pacific.

Everyone came to the homestead to see them off that morning. It was an emotional farewell. Elizabeth and Ruby wept openly. A stony-faced Mads fought to contain his emotions as he hugged his daughter and each of his grandchildren. Rose, silently weeping, followed along behind him. Emil struggled to maintain what he considered an appropriate 'manly' behaviour, but his tears escaped to roll down his cheeks as he hugged his cousin, almost bringing her undone with him.

Then they were in the wagon and heading along the track to town. Children, red-eyed and sniffling sat in the back of the wagon while their mother, like a block of granite, sat resolutely up beside her husband. After one night in a hotel and an early morning embarkation, the family stood at the railing waving farewell to Marathon as the boat sailed. Contrary to Mathilde's fears, their voyage was without incident.

Ned's contacts organised a couple of houses for him to view on their arrival in New York, so the family's stay in a hotel there lasted no more than a week before they had a home to move into. Life in their new home was somewhat primitive until the rest of their belongings arrived. Mathilde refused Ned's offer to find her appropriate domestic help.

During the third week after their arrival, Ned made his first trip to Mexico to inspect the mining company's operations there. Life settled into a steady pattern after that. In her letters home to Mads and Elizabeth, Mathilde spoke of life in New York as pleasant, with good shopping and plenty of opportunities for entertainment and recreation. The children attended school only about a block from home, and all of them were doing well according to their teachers. There was little mention of Ned other than the occasional comment about his work keeping him busy.

Over the next few years, Ned's business interests flourished, and New York society began embracing the family. Ned loved being at home and accepted every invitation that came his way. Mathilde was less comfortable with it and curtailed her involvement to those times when Ned was around. She softened her attitude a little when her eldest daughter turned sixteen. The 'society scene', as Mathilde referred to it in her letters to Rangelands, offered her daughters opportunity for a good marriage when they were of marrying age.

While unaware of the nature of Ned's correspondence with Alf Grant, or if there were any, from their earliest days in New York, Mathilde maintained regular correspondence with Mads and Rose, Emil, and Elizabeth Grant. On occasions there were letters intended for only her closest confidante, Rose. Mathilde knew any letter arriving for Rose would be shared with Mads, so she devised an alternate approach. She would write to Elizabeth and enclose with that letter a sealed envelope containing a letter to Rose, which Elizabeth would pass on the next time the two women met.

Those letters to Rose painted a different picture of Mathilde's life in New York from that described in her letters to the others. She told Rose of being lonely and bored, were critical of the attitudes of other high society matrons, and of being disappointed and fed up with Ned's absences in Mexico. Over the next five or six years, Mathilde's letters to Rose told of her mounting unhappiness with Ned's increasing lengths of time away from his family. Things deteriorated to the stage where she felt compelled to throw herself into the role of a society matron and attend various functions unaccompanied in order to ensure her daughters' continued involvement in such circles.

In one letter to Rose, she wrote: *Our marriage was never the same after the way he disregarded me in making his decision to move to New York, but things have settled between us. However, I can never forgive him for his actions and lack of concern for me and his children. While his long absences insult and frustrate me, perhaps life is easier when he is not here. I feel my resentment rising again.*

Then, at the end of 1887 when Ned returned to New York to spend Christmas with his family, he unwittingly ended their life together. After they saw in the New Year together, Mathilde asked Ned what his plans were for 1888 and, more specifically, whether he would continue to spend such long periods away from home.

"We are about to start exploration of a new area where the possibility of mineral deposits have been identified. I leave in two days' time to join the exploration party when they leave for an area near Guadalajara in the Jalisco State of Mexico. While I am there, I will be based in Guadalajara, but do not anticipate spending much time there. I will be keeping an eye on work in the field."

"How long are you likely to be away from New York this time? I only ask so I can tell our daughters when they ask when they will see their father again."

"I have no way of knowing. We allowed for the initial exploration to take six months. After that, there will be a review of how we will go forward, if at all. So, it is fair to say, this next trip will be for at least six months but, beyond that, I can't tell you more with any accuracy."

Their conversation resulted in 1888 beginning in much the same way as 1880 began … with Mathilde flouncing off to bed and Ned having to find himself other sleeping arrangements until he left for Mexico. On the morning he left, Mathilde locked herself in her bedroom and refused to come out to see him off. In spite of Ned's pleading for her to come out, Mathilde refused. "I don't care if I never see you again. You care so little for me and your daughters, perhaps it would be better if you stayed permanently in your precious Mexico, and made your life there with whatever attracts you to it."

"Not again, please Mathilde; not again. I want nothing more than for us to be together as a family, but for the present, that is where my work is. Perhaps you might visit me in Mexico sometime to see the country and what we are doing there." He received no response, and the handsome cab had arrived to take him to board the boat for Mexico. By the time he disembarked, Ned was well and truly drunk.

For the next couple of weeks, Mathilde spent most of her time in her room and had little contact with anyone. Her obligation to her daughters put an end to hiding away in her room, but she could not bring herself to leave the house. Then, one day around the end of the first month Ned was away, Mathilde surprised the household by announcing she was going into the city to take care of some business and might be gone all day. It was late afternoon when she returned home.

Another 'secret' letter was written to Rose: Today I spent hours investigating what is involved in returning to Australia. The thought of an ocean voyage terrifies me still, but to return to what I consider 'home' requires another trip on a ship. Nothing is in place yet. All I have done thus far is to find out what is involved and what I must do if we are to leave here. If my final decision is that we will return to Rangelands, on the day we leave, I will send Ned a letter explaining what I have done.

Wish me well with my deliberations on my future and that of my family.

While returning to Australia continued to dominate her thinking, she had reached no firm resolution on the matter when an event decided it for her. Around mid-morning, two police officers came to the house. Their message was short and to the point. As they said, there was no easy way to say what they came to tell Mathilde. Ned Rixon was dead. According to the information they received from the Mexican authorities, Ned suffered a heart attack while out with a prospecting party. They rushed him back to Guadalajara for medical attention, but he died within an hour of his arrival there.

Regardless of how things were between them, he was her husband and there was a time when she loved him dearly. If she was honest, she still loved him. If that were not so, why would she be so upset by his absences? A cold numbness settled over her. Her grief was compounded by her daughters' reaction to the news their father was dead. They adored him; could see no wrong in him ... and he had loved them.

The next few weeks passed in a blur of police stations and solicitors' offices. Then it was all over. There was no funeral in New York. Ned was buried in Guadalajara, surrounded at the time by company officials, work colleagues and a couple of that town's leading citizens. Mathilde had not sought to repatriate his body. It was almost too late to do so by the time she learned of his death, and her belief was that he had been happiest there.

With all the formalities dealt with, and Ned's will settled, Mathilde was a free woman once more... free but now solely responsible for her daughters' futures. After another week of sleepless nights worrying about making decisions that were 'right' for everyone, she decided. The trip into the city took up all of the next day. By the time she returned home in time for dinner, everything was in place. All that was left to do was to tell her daughters. That happened immediately after dinner, and was received with mixed emotions by the girls.

"I know we have not had time to fully realise your father will not be coming through our front door ever again. It will be difficult for us ever to accept that while we continue to live in this house. We had another life, a home and good friends and family back in Australia. For me to recover from my loss, I need to be back there amongst all that, and I believe that is the best place for you to adjust to this next phase of your lives. The arrangements are in place for our departure at the end of the month. This house is now on the market. If it sells before we are to leave New York, we will move into a hotel for as long as required. Now, I must prepare a letter to post tomorrow. I need to advise Mr Grant of our plans."

There were two lengthy letters to write, one to Alf Grant and one to Mads. Both contained much the same information. They advised when the family would arrive at Marathon, and that they would move back into the homestead. The cottage should be extended or a new house built for Alf and his family as they needed to move out of the homestead again, and that Alf should continue to manage the businesses there. As well as posting the letters next morning, Mathilde wired shorter versions of the letters to Alf and Mads to allow them time to ensure Alf and his family had suitable accommodation to move into before she arrived home.

A round of farewell functions followed as the end of the month approached. Her eldest daughter sulked for days after she learned they were leaving New York. She was quite infatuated with her new beau, the son of a prominent New York family, but that changed when she learned he had switched his attention to someone else soon after she told him she was leaving. She challenged him about it. He replied, "Well, you aren't going to be around. I had to find someone to replace you."

In their last week in New York, the house sold. They were allowed to stay in the house until the paperwork was completed and the money deposited. That necessitated just the last night in a hotel before they joined their ship. The long but uneventful voyage across the Pacific deposited them at Sydney. After two nights in that city, they joined a coastal vessel for the trip to Marathon.

The township was much changed when they returned. It had grown. More substantial buildings lined the streets and shopping had improved. There was another night in the hotel – now with much improved facilities – before Mads arrived with a carriage next morning to take them up the valley to Rangelands.

For the family, it took little time to settle back into the rhythm of life at Rangelands, but the girls were fast approaching adulthood. Mathilde's eldest daughter became smitten with a young solicitor recently arrived in town to join a major law firm. A little over a year later, her wedding was added to the growing list of such events held at Rangelands. Shortly after, the young couple moved to Sydney where her husband became a partner in his father's law firm.

Marriage was the last thing on the mind of Mathilde's second daughter. She became something of a rarity when accepted to study medicine at a major university. Becoming a doctor was her long-held ambition. Her career occupied her into old age, even after she married in her early-forties. Mathilde's other children all married local lads and settled in the district.

Following Ned's death, Mathilde resigned herself to a long widowhood spent at Rangelands. That proved not to be the case. Early in 1892, Elizabeth Grant became ill. At first, she ignored it, believing it no more than some passing affliction. In time, others noticed her deteriorating condition and urged her to seek medical attention. It was too late. The cancer consumed her over a painful three months before finally releasing her from her misery. Alf was beside himself with grief. Everyone rallied around him as best they could, but grief is a personal thing to be dealt with only by its owner.

Two years later, it came as no surprise to those closest to Mathilde when she and Alf announced their intention to marry. All of both families came home for the occasion, including Mathilde's grandchildren. Once more, for Mathilde, the world was a happy place. She and Alf were happy together. Their families were settled and getting on with their own lives. A significant piece of good news came from Mads and Rose.

Sometime after their marriage, Mads paid out the lease on the farm and Rose insisted it be transferred into both their names. Rose had two sons with Sam Tomlins. Both, when barely old enough to join up, went off to fight in the Crimea; neither returned. That's when the Tomlins decided to emigrate and start a new life in Australia. With no living offspring of her own, she insisted that, in the event of their passing, the farm go to Emil. Mads agreed.

Happiness took a long time to become a way of life for Mathilde. Twice she had travelled to lands too far from where she had been comfortable and happy, and twice she had known soul-destroying grief. But at last, she knew that whenever her end came, she had done all she could for the people she loved, and they all seemed happy in their chosen lives.

ALSO BY THE AUTHOR

Revenge is not Enough

Harbour Plaza: built on dreams

On the Way to Istanbul

An Unsuitable House

ABOUT THE AUTHOR

KAYLA DANOLI spent her early years traipsing around Australia and then Europe with her parents, and then completed her tertiary education in England before returning to Australia. There were a variety of jobs in various parts of Queensland before eventually making her way towards the coast. She now lives in a small coastal town on the Queensland coast where she works part-time on a charter vessel.

In the early days after settling in that small town, to fill in her spare time, both when at home and while on cruises, she started scribbling down her ideas for stories. These days, she writes whenever time permits. Her *Harbour Plaza* series, previously released in 2015 as monthly eBook episodes, was updated, extended and released in 2016 as the *Harbour Plaza: built on dreams compilation. Revenge is not Enough,* also released in 2016, was her first full-length novel.

A Land Too Far is Kayla's fifth full-length novel.

Discover more about Kayla and her work by visiting

www.kayladanoli.com

or contact her at

contact@kayladanoli.com